Kiss The Devil Goodnight

Love Always!

Kiss The Devil Goodnight

By

Jonathan Woods

JL Woods

Fahrenheit Press

Key West
Nov. 15, 2018

For Dahlia, always

Whoa, thought it was a nightmare, low, it's all so true?
They told me, don't go walkin' slow, the devil's on the loose
Better run through the jungle?
Better run through the jungle?
Better run through the jungle, don't look back to see
- "Run Through the Jungle" by John Fogarty

Do not be dazed by the whirl.
- To Himself by Marcus Aurelius Antoninus

Part I

The Warren Commission Report

The Report of the Warren Commission on the Assassination of President Kennedy is 726 pages long.

Edie bought a copy the other day at a yard sale for two bits.

As if she'd ever read it. Or me. Edie was always better known for her tits than her literary taste.

Anyway, it's ancient history. A bookend. Plus, everybody knows the CIA did it.

Those bastards are out of control. A secret cabal running roughshod under the radar of our democracy.

I tossed the Warren Commission Report onto the floor of the front passenger side of our navy blue, special edition Tahoe. It landed with a small shudder next to an empty Coke can. The can rolled sideways, spewing forth a swath of dark, sticky, carpet-staining elixir.

Fuck! I was sure it was empty.

I'd been back from I-rack for almost two years now, but it seemed like just an hour ago. IEDs, ex-Ba'ath Party snipers, religious zealots and raghead gangbangers armed to the teeth. And there was always the inside risk of some batshit recruit from Cedar Rapids going rogue in the Green Zone with an M16 and a sack of grenades. All the memories from over there kept hauling ass through my head and I kept diving for cover. Since I got back home to Atlanta, almost every night I dreamed of waking up to sand dunes outside my window. Nothing but fucking sand dunes as far as the eye could see. When the sand dunes dream didn't come, nothing replaced it. Those dreamless nights were like hitting a blank wall.

What I remembered most about over there were all the olive-skinned guys sitting in shaded alleys for hours drinking cups of mint tea and smoking. Sullen cocksuckers, they just stared when you walked by, as if your zipper had come open and your wee-wee was hanging out. Those guys had one thought on their minds. They wanted you dead, a cadaver covered in flies rotting in the sun.

Anyway that was all in the past. After I got out of the mental wing at the VA Medical Center hospital in Decatur, they got me a job with the city driving one of those humongous waste disposal trucks. Everything was fine until the big ass recession hit. Now it was furlough time in the Waste Processing and Recycling Department of this great Southern metropolis where Edie and I lived. Fourteen weeks, no pay.

They gotta balance the budget on somebody's back. Might as well be Bill Derringer's.

We were six weeks into the furlough period and the kids were bored. Edie was bored. I was bored.

We were all fuckin' bored out of our fuckin' gourds!

Besides that, I was pissed off as hell.

Like Peter Finch in that movie Network.

I served my country; almost got my ass blown off a bunch of times. Came home mentally compromised. Had to work through some things. Then they got me a job. I was happy as an ant in an anthill.

Now the job was on hold, along with my life. I was ready to shoot somebody. The next person who gave me the slightest bit of shit about anything.

The real issue: there was no money coming in, except from some part-time work Edie found at a local FedEx. There was nothing like being bored and strapped for cash at the same time. Now I knew why they burned down ghettos.

"Hey, Bill," said Edie. "What about that murder trial in Orlando?" In a post-coital daze we sat naked across from each other in the breakfast nook with steaming mugs of coffee. Edie's heavy boobs hung low over the tabletop. Our kids, Mary Beth and Ben, ages 14 and 11, were at separate sleepovers, so we'd just fucked like a pair of wild apes on the kitchen counter while the coffee was brewing. First time in two weeks.

"What murder trial?" I asked back.

"Woman in Orlando killed her baby and ate it. Or something like that. To get rid of the evidence. It was on CNN."

I recently started watching a bunch of those Alfred Hitchcock TV shows from the eighties. I swear one of them was about a woman eating her baby. Or was it her husband after she'd murdered him? I didn't let Edie watch that one. No point in giving her any wild-ass ideas.

"Let's go to Orlando," said Edie. "We can get free tickets for that murder trial. Maybe the kids can go to Disney World or something. My Aunt Ida will put us up."

"What about your job at FedEx?"

"Fuck FedEx."

"Sounds like a plan," I said.

After one more go at spearing the bearded clam, and after the kids got dropped home from their sleepovers, I gassed up the Tahoe while Edie and the kids packed. By eleven we were on the Interstate, headed south.

Never should have bought the damn Tahoe. Ate gas like a motherfucker.

*

I kept the speedometer at eighty through red dirt and scrub pine countryside. Being a weekday, clusters of eighteen-wheelers pounded south on 75. The only radio station that didn't fade out was WGFX Double Wide Classic Country. Which was okay by me. Merle Haggard, Johnny Cash, Hank

Williams, Tammy Wynette and Lucinda Williams. Shit, it didn't get any better than that.

I figured it would take us six hours to get to Aunt Ida's, provided we didn't pick up a nail or fall victim to some other disaster. Imagine six hours of pine trees, soybean fields and billboards for BBQ and roadside porn. How long can you look at that shit? After two hours, my teeth were on edge and a headache was worming its way into my consciousness.

We were just crossing the Georgia-Florida line, when Edie turned from staring out her window and said:

"I sure wish I'd had the chance to meet your mother."

Why was Edie bringing up my past? She knew I hated revisiting all that water over the dam.

How my father Morris Levi Derringer had siphoned off large sums from his clients' accounts to pay for his flamboyant lifestyle. When it all came out, he put a shotgun in his mouth and pulled the trigger with his big toe.

How my mom, Saving Grace, grew up dirt poor in Noplaceville, Alabama. Looking like some tobacco road hussy in crotch-nipping cutoff jeans and a Red Man chew T-shirt that had shrunk up real good in the wash. One minute she was leaning over the fender of my father's shiny, black Mercedes checking the oil, the next she was sitting in his lap toying with his dipstick.

I'm not making this shit up. I found some old Polaroids.

I was their sole offspring, a half-breed combo of city slicker and piney woods bimbo.

Three weeks after Morris Levi killed himself, Saving Grace lit out for the territory with some new age conman she met in a bar. She was never heard from again. Devastated by this double tragedy, I dropped out of Yale. Later, I became a killer for the U.S. military. These days I had zero interest in reliving those days of yesteryear.

"I barely remember my mom," I said. "Besides, she was a nutcase."

"I'm sure she was a very interesting woman," said Edie.

"Jesus Christ, Edie, give it a rest."

It was just after seven when we finally exited the Interstate near Orlando. Edie squinted at the handwritten directions she had taken down over the phone from Aunt Ida. My own sense of direction had always been shitty.

"The blind leading the blind," I said.

After a series of twists and turns on rural byways and shoulderless county roads, I sensed we were getting close.

"Turn here," said Edie. "This is it."

Aunt Ida lived in an area that was half suburban and half country. Small single-family homes on half an acre lots, a couple of duplexes mixed in with patches of undeveloped land and even some fields planted with stuff. A lot of the houses needed work, a paint job, a new roof. Here and there the owners had let the vegetation run hog wild, vines and broad-leafed plants clawing and grasping their way like green-blooded carnivores over stunted palms and rusting chain link fences. Deep within these rampant vegetable eruptions, you could see the sagging outline of a bungalow rotting away in the gloom.

"Which one is Aunt Ida's?" asked Mary Beth.

"Yeah, which one?" asked Ben, poking Mary Beth in the side.

"Don't touch me, you creep," screamed Mary Beth hugging the passenger door on her side.

"Leave your sister alone," snarled Edie. Her hand flew sideways, smashing smartly into Ben's face. In the rearview mirror Ben's pale blue orbs stared back at Edie with unmitigated hatred, as tears water-skied down his cheeks. Mary Beth had this look of utter pleasure, as if she'd just had her first orgasm.

You've gotta love families.

"We're almost there," I said.

*

When we got to Aunt Ida's house around the next curve, she was standing in the front yard holding a shotgun.

Pulling in the concrete driveway and cutting the engine, I leaned out my open window.

"What's up?"

"Moles," she said.

I could see where the little fuckers had dug their tunnels, pushing up the sod. There were some spots were the force of a shotgun blast had torn up the earth. The grass shoots stained with blood where Aunt Ida had vaporized a couple of the critters. Clearly Aunt Ida was a tough cookie.

Luckily her house was in an unincorporated rural portion of the county, so you could shoot off a firearm without any trouble with the law.

I think I met Aunt Ida only once before, at Edie's and my wedding. Which was fourteen years ago. So it had been a good while. But still…I should have remembered.

Because Aunt Ida was one fantastic piece of eye candy.

Peroxide blond hair just brushing her shoulders. A hard-edged, even cruel face that reminded me of Courtney Love, with those pouty bowtie lips and heroin-haunted eyes. Her late-30s, taking-on-ballast body was resplendent in washed-out blue jeans and a way too small tropical green T-shirt.

Lordy, Lordy, as my mother used to say.

"Yeah," I said. "Moles can wreak havoc on your lawn."

I added an ironic smile, tinged with lust, even as I felt Edie's eyes burning into my back.

Aunt Ida cocked her hip aggressively. The shotgun was even with my open window and pointed at the side rearview mirror.

"So, are you lost?" she asked. "Or just using my driveway as a parking lot?"

Edie leaned around me and gave Aunt Ida a little wave.

"It's us, Aunt Ida. You remember my husband Bill from the wedding. And these are our progeny, Mary Beth and Ben." She turned to look at the kids, sitting straight up in the back seat like a pair of wooden Indians. "Children, say hi to your Aunt Ida."

Edie loved to use five-hundred-dollar words like progeny.

8

She played cutthroat Scrabble and was always working on her vocabulary. I had to hustle my ass off to keep up and not lose every game. I kept a copy of Merriam Webster's college edition in the bathroom, resting on the shitter's water tank.

"Didn't see you sitting over there, cousin," said Aunt Ida. "Come on in. I made a big pitcher of gin fizzes to celebrate our reunion. And lemonade for the kids."

"Maybe we can bake some chocolate chip cookies," said Mary Beth.

"What's a gin fizz?" asked Ben.

*

I have only a vague, uneasy recollection of that first dying afternoon and evening at Aunt Ida's. Cookies were baked. I stoked up the charcoal grill. The gin fizzes went down easy. While the burgers sizzled and spat, Aunt Ida mowed the back yard, using an old-fashioned push mower, its blades honed to a razor's edge.

We all sat down to eat around eight. Overdone hamburgers, potato salad and steamed cauliflower drizzled with Cheez Whiz. Ben and Mary Beth were cranky from the long car ride. Edie hustled them off to bed right after supper, while Aunt Ida made a fresh pitcher of gin fizzes and I tuned in a baseball game on Aunt Ida's hurricane emergency radio. There was too much static, so I turned it off and poured a gin fizz into a tall glass. As Aunt Ida and I clinked glasses, she winked at me.

She didn't say anything. We just looked at each other. Then Edie came into the kitchen and broke it up.

It was a hot night and the three of us with the pitcher of drinks sat at Aunt Ida's picnic table under a big old live oak. The cicadas hummed like a small orchestra of violin virtuosos. Everyone was too buzzed to play Scrabble, so Edie and Aunt Ida started to arm wrestle. The loser had to remove an item of clothing. Next thing I knew, the two of them were down to bras and panties.

Everyone was laughing, though I don't remember what the joke was. Maybe it was me. Were they laughing at me?

Just for fun, I made a drunken grab for Aunt Ida. She laughed carelessly and cavorted out of my way. Lunging after her, I tripped over the push mower she'd left lying in the grass and fell forward, almost cutting my hand on one of the blades. Instead my nose hit the picnic table seat. THUNK!

"Ow! Shit! Shit! Shit!"

My nose hurt like a mother-raper.

My inebriated pass at Aunt Ida set Edie on a rampage, as she pointed at my wounded, blood-dripping proboscis. "Ha, ha. You deserved that and worse, you feckless goat fucker," she taunted.

In graphic detail she described my failures as a bedmate, my inability to pleasure her between the sheets. Pathetic at foreplay. And the moment I got stiff, bingo, I shot off, whether I was inside her snatch or not. The dread premature ejackulation. Did I spell that right?

This got me pissed off and I started slapping at Edie with both hands. Missing most of the time, because she had her hands up and was defensively slapping back at me and because I kept stopping to wipe the blood gushing from my nose.

Amid this domestic ruckus, Aunt Ida got the hose and turned it on me full blast. I sputtered and all the anger left me and I fell to the ground, where the cool water splashed over me.

Next Aunt Ida turned the hose on Edie. The circles of Edie's areolas sprang like dark, lurid mushrooms through the wet sheerness of her Kmart bra. Aunt Ida cast a sly smile at the hard-on poking against my wet shorts.

Abruptly Aunt Ida turned off the hose and walked into the house without a backward glance, leaving Edie and me to stagger after her.

The kitchen was a mess from the dinner preparations. "Fuck this," said Aunt Ida and left for her bedroom. I wasn't much interested in cleaning up either, so I poured myself a glass of straight gin over some ice cubes. Edie started putting things in the fridge.

The next thing was me waking up with a hangover. Edie was still sleeping. And still wearing her bra and panties. I noticed they didn't match and that the underwire of one of the bra cups was poking through the cloth.

Our fourteenth anniversary was coming up in two days and all of a sudden I had the idea that I would buy Edie some fancy lingerie. There had to be a Victoria's Secret around somewhere. Then I remembered we were broke.

I got up and gazed blurrily out the bedroom window onto the boring front yard of Aunt Ida's mauve cement block ranch. The grass needed cutting. A lone egret, a white stick figure from a bad dream, worked the drainage ditch along the road. At least there were no sand dunes.

The house faced east and the intense morning light made me squint. I felt sick to my stomach. A door slammed and Aunt Ida sashayed down the narrow cement walk that curved from the front door to the driveway. She looked good even in a baggy scrub top with giant smiling purple teeth and green toothpaste tubes with wings printed on it. Beneath her tight-assed, blue skirt her rump rolled from side to side like a sailor crossing a pitching and yawing deck in a squall. A tingling sensation surrounded my nads.

Did she know I was watching? No way. As far as she knew, I was still deep in some boozy dreamland. Unless she had deduced from my ravaged face and ringed eyes that I didn't sleep much.

Aunt Ida was one of those women who were always on. It was seven o'clock on Monday morning and she was headed for her day job as a dental assistant for a bunch of dentists rolling in dough.

I ground my teeth thinking about those fat cats with their perfect choppers and spit polished Porsches.

According to Aunt Ida her dentist bosses were always grab-assing her in the corridors, pressing her to participate in a swingers group that carried on in the dental lab in the idle minutes between patients. A total pain in the ass she confided. But she needed the rent money.

I wondered if an outsider in for a teeth cleaning might have an opportunity to join in the dental lab frivolities. It had been more than a year since I'd had my ivories scraped and polished.

Aunt Ida's tire-squealing departure in her high-mileage Nissan 350Z bulldozed over my train of thought. Then came Edie's sleepy voice:

"Bill, come back to bed."

As I slipped between Edie's legs, prurient thoughts of Aunt Ida sprawled across my mind like a stripper in some tenderloin bar.

A while later childish feet ran up and down the hall outside our locked door. Mary Beth started yelling.

I pulled on my skivvies, opened the door and stepped into the hall.

"Your mom's sleeping," I said in a loud, eviscerating whisper.

"Sorry, Dad," said Mary Beth. She stared at her feet as if she'd never noticed them before.

Ben smirked.

I made them breakfast. Toast, mugs of half coffee-half milk, some kind of diet cereal that Aunt Ida had. The cereal was stale.

On the counter Aunt Ida had left a handwritten note introducing me and Edie and the kids to Rev. Peebles of the Witnesses to Christ's Conundrum Church. WCCC had a three-week summer school program that was just starting. Rev. Peebles owes me big time Aunt Ida had said the night before. For services rendered? I wondered. "So haul ass, Bill, and get those two brats signed up for arts and crafts day camp," said Aunt Ida through a mouthful of potato salad.

When I got back from slipping Rev. Peebles my last twenty-dollar bill, Edie was up, sipping a cup of black coffee at the kitchen table.

"Let's go to the mall," she said.

"What about getting tickets to the dead baby murder trial?"

"They don't give out the tickets for the next day until the afternoon."

"Shouldn't you be there early?" I said. "In case there's a line?"

Edie ignored me and left the kitchen to get dressed.

*

There was nobody at the mall at ten-thirty in the morning. We walked around looking in store windows, but we didn't go in anywhere. The sales staffs hovered, impotent. No one was buying shit in the worst depression since The Big One of 1929.

When Edie went to take a piss, I stood for an eon in front of the Victoria's Secret window. Finally a cop came by and told me to move along. They were only mannequins but they still looked hot.

We ended up in the food court. I had enough for a regular tuna fish sub.

"Go wash you hands before we eat," Edie said. "God knows what you've been touching."

Touching you between the legs, I thought.

It was only eleven-thirty. The men's room was halfway across the mall, near where we came in. The guy washing his hands at one of the sinks wore a blue oxford cloth shirt and grey trousers. Nondescript summed it up. Otherwise the restroom was empty.

Just me and some guy I'd never see again.

When I hit him in the side of the head with my fist, he fell to the tile floor without a cry or moan. He didn't move. Just to be sure, I kicked him a couple of more times in the head and chest. Then dragged him into a stall. He was still breathing when I took the forty-six dollars from his wallet.

Pissant. But enough to buy the lingerie set with the climbing rose pattern I'd seen on the buxom, blonde mannequin.

Why did I beat a stranger senseless for forty-six dollars? Because I could and I wanted to buy Edie a present.

And who cared anyway? The only likely candidate for that was the dude lying unconscious on the dirty tile floor of the men's room.

I bought the lingerie. Waiting to pay, I stood in line behind three women, each one more stunningly beautiful than the other two. So many tits, so little opportunity. As I handed over the cash for the goods, Edie answered her cell.

"Meet me back at the car," I said.

"Okay," she said

"And don't dilly-dally," I said.

She hung up.

I took my change and the fancy paper sack containing Edie's new undies, and walked as fast as I could without being alarmist toward the entrance where we'd parked.

When I got to the Tahoe, Edie was already standing on the passenger side, waiting. She twisted her mouth at me, like what the fuck, Bill? Without explanation I clicked open the doors and we got in. I started the engine.

"Here."

I handed her the bag with the sexy undergarments.

"Wear them in good health," I said.

Edie opened the bag and took out the frilly tidbits.

"Bill, these were expensive. We can't afford…"

"Don't worry about it," I said. "It was found money. Happy anniversary a day early."

Edie's eyes grew wide. She knew I'd done something bad in order to buy her a present and she liked it. Without a thought she slipped out of her T-shirt and old bra right there in the car as I drove through the mall parking lot traffic. Bending forward, she coaxed and squeezed her ample boobs into the soft confines of the Victoria's Secret contraption. Turned sideways in my direction. "Well, what do you think?"

"Nice," I said. "Very nice."

Back at Aunt Ida's, Edie was all over me like hot sauce

on Mexican beans and rice. I could barely get the front door unlocked fast enough.

Later, we ate the tuna sub and I fell asleep reading an old Dave Robicheaux thriller I found stashed on a shelf in the family room.

Edie was just back from picking up the kids when Aunt Ida rolled in. I could tell she had a hair up her ass when she came in without a word of greeting, stomped down the hall to her bedroom and slammed the door behind her.

Aunt Ida for drama queen.

"I better see what's up," said Edie.

She disappeared into Aunt Ida's bedroom. I boiled some hot dogs and opened a can of Heinz BBQ beans for the kids' dinner. Afterward I let them watch TV in the family room while I went in the living room to read.

Soon enough Edie and Aunt Ida appeared in the doorway.

"Let's have a drink," I said, approaching the tray of liquor bottles resting on a low, Oriental-looking cabinet. "Whiskey all around?"

Aunt Ida took a sip of her drink. When she drew the glass away, a fey smile cut her pulp fiction lips.

"Hey, lover boy, those are some fancy little nothings you bought your gorgeous wife. Guess I'll have to wear earplugs tonight with all the wild thank-youing that'll be going on."

Edie seemed jumpy.

"Though I do recall both of you swearing on the Bible that you were as broke as sharecroppers."

"I unexpectedly came into some dough out at the mall," I said. "Anyway, it's none of your business."

"Well, well. None of my business. But just supposing you hit the lottery or rolled some suit with a fat wallet, I could use a little help with the rent now that I'm on the dole."

"Aunt Ida got laid off," said Edie.

"You mean shit-canned," spat Aunt Ida. "After I smacked Dr. Zeitgeist in the side of the head for putting his hand between my legs while I was suctioning out some patient's mouth."

Tears welled from Aunt Ida's pissed-off baby blues, coursing in ragged squiggles down her cheeks.

"Don't waste your tears," I said. "There isn't enough left over to rent a cheap motel room for the night. Even if I was in the mood to offer you solace."

I was still keen on the idea of a threesome.

Edie poked me angrily in the ribs. Aunt Ida rolled her eyes.

Leaving Aunt Ida in Edie's comforting arms, I grabbed my paperback and headed toward the bedrooms. When Edie came to bed four hours later, I was lying awake in the dark, my mind playing over and over the same homemade video about what it would be like to give Aunt Ida solace on a double bed at the nearest Motel 6.

Edie got undressed and climbed into bed. I pretended to be asleep, while adding her lush nude figure to the video.

*

The next morning, Tuesday, I sat smoking at the picnic table in the backyard, looking at nothing. I had five dollars in my wallet. Enough for another pack of cigarettes. A mockingbird kept scolding me for mooching on his territory. I considered getting Aunt Ida's shotgun and blowing Mr. Bird into next week.

Edie got the kids up, fixed them breakfast and drove them to camp two hours late. There was no sign of Aunt Ida.

When Edie returned, she saw that I was in a mood.

"Snap out of it, Bill. You could have prostate cancer or some other terrible disease."

Ignoring her, I concentrated on my game of solitaire, running through my stack of cards in groups of three. I was dead in the water, unless I decided to cheat. Throwing down the cards, I walked past Edie into the kitchen and poured myself a cup of lukewarm coffee. The quart of milk had turned, so I drank it black.

"OK, Mr. Fun Guy," said Edie. "Guess I'll go down to the courthouse and see if I can get some tickets to that murder trial. They said on the news the woman's attorney is starting her defense tomorrow."

After a long silence, she said: "You'll feel better if you eat something."

"Fine," I said.

"I need to put gas in the Tahoe," she said.

I handed her the five-dollar bill that was weighing down my wallet.

"See you later, sweetie." With a little wave Edie was gone.

As soon as Edie left, Aunt Ida started banging doors. Glancing down the hall to the bedrooms, I gazed agog at her bare ass disappearing profoundly through the entrance to the single bathroom. The door closed and the lock clicked.

Finding a can of Budweiser way in the back of the fridge, I snapped it open and went back to the picnic table.

Aunt Ida appeared in the open sliding-glass doorway from the kitchen. She wore a too big, terrycloth robe that yawned open above the tied belt, revealing an abundance of cleavage.

"Aren't you bored just sitting around here all day?" she asked. "Why don't you do something useful?"

"Like what?" I replied, setting down my paperback.

"I don't know. Something. Something you've always wanted to do, but never had the guts to."

"Hard to do something like that in this day and age without getting caught. Too many cops. Too many video cameras. Too many smart phones."

"Be creative. Think outside the box."

"Maybe you've got something specific in mind that you'd like me to do?"

"If you mean 'Do I want you to fuck me?' the answer is no."

"The way I see it, you'd be a pretty risky fuck anyway."

"I'll take that as a compliment. But the truth is I'm just a

17

lonely little girl living by herself in the burbs. All I want to do is cuddle up and watch old movies on TCM."

"What I need is another beer."

"I'll get it for you."

As she walked back into the shadowy depths of the kitchen, I watched her derriere swish and sway like the back end of an old Chevy with worn shocks going up a rutted dirt road. When she returned a few minutes later, she had another can of beer, a mug of coffee she'd run through the microwave and that day's edition of the Orlando Sentinel still in its little plastic wrapper, that she'd retrieved from the front lawn.

Sitting opposite, she handed me the beer, then unwrapped the paper and dangled the Entertainment Section in my direction. I took it. Some entertainment was definitely what we needed.

Opening the section, I paged through until I found my horoscope.

Libra (Sept. 23-Oct. 23) – Because you're always a step ahead of the crowd, you might think you can ease up on your guard, leave the 9mm pistol home in your wife's lingerie drawer. Think again. The moment you do, someone will shoot your legs out from under you.

I closed my eyes and shook my head like a dog. Was I going fucking nuts? That couldn't be what it actually said. Maybe I was having some kind of episode relating back to my time in I-rack. Or maybe the stress of having no money coming in was finally eating up my brain like acid thrown on a beautiful face. I glanced at Aunt Ida to see if she'd noticed anything funny, but she was bent over the employment opportunities section of the classifieds, her forehead rucked into a mini-washboard.

A shiver of fear ran through my body. My nerves wouldn't let me look at the horoscope again. Who knew what it would say second time around. I folded the newspaper closed and set it on the table.

Aunt Ida looked up at me. "So, big shot, what would you

18

say to an opportunity to get your hands on a serious chunk of change? Not the price of a pair of lace panties but enough do-re-me to live for a good long while down Mexico way."

Now the truth would out, I thought. Aunt Ida had big dreams. A lot bigger than getting laid after watching Jimmy Cagney flame out in White Heat on TCM. But Aunt Ida was scary as shit and I wasn't sure I wanted any part of it. I rolled my eyes.

"Don't roll your shit-brown eyes at me, Bill," Aunt Ida snarled. "This is not some bimbo pipe dream. I have a plan. It's a simple plan. But I need a little help in the execution. When Cousin Edie called to say y'all were coming down and that you were out of work, I figured it was an opportunity as blessed as the appearance of a blind albino child at a tent revival."

"Only problem is, Ida, when I got back from wasting ragheads on the banks of the Tigris, I swore an oath of nonviolence," I lied.

"Leave the violence to me," said Aunt Ida. "You'll just be backup."

Reaching into the pocket of her robe, she pulled out an old-school .32 caliber Beretta pistol and set it on the table next to my empty beer can. Then she stood up and sloughed off her robe like a boa constrictor its skin. I was consumed, devoured, drowned and overrun by her nakedness.

"This can all be yours if you play your cards right."

I was at a loss for words.

Holy mama! I thought. Aunt Ida had been walking around all morning armed and virtually naked. She was more dangerous than Simone Simon as the cat woman in the 1942 horror film Cat People. More dangerous than anything I'd come up against over there, inside or outside the Green Zone.

I picked up the handgun and weighed it in my ice-cold hand. My balls were sweating.

*

The blackhead, oozing upward from the nose pore in which it had been crouching like a pedophile on the run, revealed its white, dead-fish underbelly. My finger flicked the tiny cyst of oil and dirt away into the vastness of the bathroom. From the depths of the mirror my wasted demeanor stared back at me. Was this the face of a fornicator and a sinner? Damn straight. I intended to screw Aunt Ida six ways to Sunday.

The only question was how Edie would react. For surely she would find out, if not through her psychic powers, then by the redolent bouquet of a foreign vagina left behind on my cock no matter how hard I tried to scrub it off or drown it beneath a veneer of Brut cologne.

I hoped Edie and I could discuss the matter without resorting to emotional overload or random violence. After all, it had been her idea to stay at Aunt Ida's.

Step number one on the road to Aunt Ida's snatch was to help her rob a fucking bank.

Just as I formulated this plan, Edie walked in the front door. She had a gauze bandage taped across her left cheek and the flesh around her left eye was swollen and mottled in black and yellow.

"Jesus, Edie," I said. "What happened?"

"Some fat fuck standing in line for tickets outside the courthouse accused me of cutting in and made a rude suggestion about my privates. When I slapped him, he socked me in the eye. Then a cop came over and told me to clear out or he'd throw me in the tank on a solicitation charge."

"So I take it you didn't get the tickets?"

"Screw you, Bill, and the Tahoe you rode in on."

Edie made a beeline for the assorted bottles of booze in the living room, poured herself a shot of vodka and tossed it back.

"OK," I said. "All better."

Just then Aunt Ida walked into the living room.

"Holy Toledo, cousin! What happened to you?"

"Don't ask," said Edie.

"Let little old Aunt Ida take care of that."

"Edie's a big girl," I said. "No need to make a fuss."

Aunt Ida glared at me. "Come on." She drew Edie toward the bathroom. "Let's put some ointment on that."

Soon enough Edie was medicated up the wazoo with antibiotic cream, a fresh bandage and a double dose of hydrocodone with a vodka/soda chaser.

It was getting on toward three. Aunt Ida, topless, lay on the living room couch eating white cheddar popcorn from a sack and watching The Getaway with Ali McGraw and Steve McQueen. With the air conditioning turned off to save money, a sheen of sweat covered her body like a coating of CVS baby oil. I couldn't take my eyes off her.

Steve and Ali made it to Mexico with half a million.

Aunt Ida stretched.

Jesus!

Next Aunt Ida sat up, eased into her brassiere and came into the kitchen where Edie and I had been talking and drinking coffee, me leaning in the doorway to the living room. Putting her arm around my wife, Aunt Ida started kissing her on the lips and neck, squeezing Edie's right boob through her T-shirt.

"Hey," I protested.

Aunt Ida and Edie stopped kissing.

"Hey yourself, lover boy. Your wife and I've been lovers off and on since high school. Whenever we had the chance. You know, holiday visits, summer camp, family reunions." Her forehead wrinkled. She looked askance at Edie. "Edie's been wanting to keep the whole thing hidden under the mattress. But that just builds up a bunch of puss and rottenness that's bound to burst just when you don't want it to. Best to get all the cards on the table."

Cards? What fucking cards!?

My heart was broken.

I felt like a junkyard dog that had been kicked around the block once too often. As if some biker dyke had dropkicked me in the pecker department.

Now I was just laid low.

Had Edie been faking her orgasms all those years? A tear hung in the corner of my eye.

"But not to worry, Bill," said Aunt Ida. "Edie likes it any way she can get it."

Needless to say, I did not feel reassured.

With a goofy embarrassed grin, Edie twisted out of Aunt Ida's embrace and, stepping to the sink, filled a glass with water and drank deeply.

Conflicted emotions tossed me higgledy-piggledy like a manic-depressive riding a rubber raft down a Freudian cataract.

First came murder and mayhem. If I strangled and buried them in the back yard, what would I tell Mary Beth and Ben? How soon would the bodies be discovered? Would the moles dig them up? Did I have the cojones to grind up the bodies in Aunt Ida's food processor? What were the odds the food processor's motor would burn out partway through?

Then came lust. The idea of a ribald romp with my newly outed Sapphic spouse and her bodaciously endowed lover made me dizzy. I had to sit down in the breakfast nook. Edie handed me a glass of ice water.

"No ice," I said.

"Don't be upset, Bill. I love you. I've always loved you. But this thing for Aunt Ida goes way back. Long before you and me. I thought I was over it. Then coming down here and seeing her made me wet between the legs."

"Swell," I said.

Aunt Ida sat down across from me. She too had a glass of ice water. It was always good to hydrate, especially in hot weather.

"Now that we've worked that out," Aunt Ida said. "Let's talk about my plan."

"Worked what out?" I said. "What plan?"

Aunt Ida ignored my first question.

"For the big score," she said.

*

It was a simple plan. Simple and audacious: rip off the local guns and ammo show coming up the following weekend. So simple I decided to go along with it.

I needed time. Time to figure out how to fix things up with Edie. How to get Aunt Ida out of the picture without causing Edie heartache and emotional distress. We'd been together for fourteen years, tighter than a pair of fornicating horseshoe crabs. We were soul mates. It had been her angelic face that kept me going through two tours of duty in a desert hellhole and through all the horseshit that went down afterward. If we pulled it off, the loot from a big score would go a long way toward paving over any lingering feelings Edie might have for the missing Aunt Ida.

While I bided my time and gnawed on my options, the days of the week rolled by like little tumbleweeds of dust, pubic hair and dried cat shit.

During the daylight hours Edie and I were still together like old times. We lounged about the house drinking beer and playing Scrabble. We went to the mall and walked around holding hands, looking at stuff we would buy when we were rich.

But at night she was a prisoner of Aunt Ida's bloodsucking lust.

Each evening after the kids went to sleep, Edie disappeared into the vampire crypt of Aunt Ida's bedroom, and I lost track of time and everything else in my life. Mostly I sat in the breakfast nook working my way through a bottle of Cuervo, throwing a biker knife at the wooden pantry door. Sometimes Aunt Ida's face appeared on that wooden door like a visitation of the antichrist.

Wednesday night, Thursday night, Friday night.

Nada, nada and more nada.

Finally time rolled over to Saturday, the day of the big

score.

I awoke at first light still drunk and feeling like shit. Omens and portents abounded. A dead roach floated in the toilet bowl. When I went to retrieve the newspaper from the front yard, a mole lay eviscerated on the cement walk, a raven pecking at its eyeball. Making eggs for the kids, the first egg I cracked open contained a tiny blood spoor. I threw the egg in the trash. In the end, taking too long outside for my smoke break, I burned both the bacon and the toast. The fried eggs fused into an ovoid mass reminiscent of a mouse pad.

"How come Mom and Aunt Ida are sleeping in Aunt Ida's room?" asked Ben between spoonfuls of Cheerios.

"Well, it's sort of a girl thing," I said.

"Are Mom and Aunt Ida lesbians?" said Mary Beth.

"Not exactly."

"What do you mean, not exactly?"

"What's a lesbian?" interrupted Ben.

"It's when women kiss and have sex and stuff," said Mary Beth.

"Eew!" said Ben.

"Finish your cereal. We're late," I said.

When I got back from dropping them at Rev. Peebles', I found Edie and Aunt Ida frolicking in the bathtub.

What the hell, I thought. I shed my clothes and stood naked in the bathroom doorway.

Edie was dreamily scrubbing Aunt Ida's shoulders and breasts using a soapy washrag. Aunt Ida's eyes were closed, a libidinous smile tainting her lips as she leaned in my wife's arms.

Far from inducing an erotic quickening in my schlong, the scene before me brought on a wave of black despair. My fists clenched. The vein in my right temple began to throb.

Perhaps the sound of my teeth grinding made Aunt Ida open her eyes. When she saw me, her peepers grew hard and pig-like. "If you're thinking of joining us, think again, buster."

Aunt Ida burst from the tub, water cascading off her glistening body. She yanked open a drawer by the sink. An open straight razor flashed in her hand as she whirled toward me. She was a wild beast.

For an instant, I thought about putting my fist deep into her feral face, breaking that smartass jaw. But now was not the time. That would come later. After the big score.

I twisted backward out of the path of the blade. Then swooped in close, intercepting Aunt Ida's arm with a vice grip that made her cry out and drop the razor. Wrenching her arm up, over and behind, I forced her to her knees, her face staring into the toilet bowl like some trailer park naiad contemplating her time-plundered visage. I could have drown her in that cesspool or broken her neck or picked up the razor and slit her throat from ear to ear. That's what I had been trained to do. To kill without a moment's hesitation.

But I felt Edie's eyes on me, pleading for mercy for her lover.

As if a switch had been abruptly turned to the off position, I released Aunt Ida. She collapsed in a dripping heap of pink flesh. Scooping up the razor, I walked down the hall to where I had left my clothes.

"You'll never fuck me!" Aunt Ida screamed after me. "Never!"

It was now suddenly clear to me. An eon ago out by the picnic table, when Aunt Ida had offered herself to me as the cherry on top of the banana split, if I joined her gang, she had been lying through her teeth.

Later, the three of us sat in brooding silence in the breakfast nook, staring at a plate of cold toast and mugs of tepid coffee. I took a final bite of toast and chewed it fifteen times before swallowing. It still went down like a ball of steel wool.

"It's nine thirty-five," said Aunt Ida, breaking the silence.

We synchronized our watches and waited.

And waited.

And waited some more.

I dozed in the back yard in a plastic chair, dreaming of creative ways to snuff Aunt Ida. When Aunt Ida left to gas up the Tahoe, Edie came outside and gave me a neck massage just like old times. In short order we adjourned to the bedroom and screwed as though we'd just met at a cocktail party.

Aunt Ida returned bearing Nutty Buddy ice cream cones as some sort of a peace offering. At two o'clock, Aunt Ida, in jeans and braless under a snap-front black and grey plaid cowgirl shirt, climbed in the driver's side of the Tahoe and tucked the shotgun, wrapped in a white bath towel, under the dash. As I settled into the opposite seat, she handed me the Beretta. Edie hunched in the backseat with two empty sports duffle bags.

With a high-pitched squeal and a ka-thunk, the Tahoe dropped into gear. Aunt Ida drove with devil-may-care swagger across the St. Augustine lawn, bounced through the drainage ditch and veered onto the county road with a spray of gravel. I wondered if the transmission was going bad.

Thirty-five minutes later we arrived at the General P. G. T. Beauregard Mid-Florida Convention Center. Three stories of steel, glass and cement that some third-rate architect had foisted on the public coffers. We cruised through the visitor parking lots. They were full. It was the second day of the annual Gunslinger's Guns and Ammo Show.

We drove around back and parked facing outward in the service entrance area. Unbuttoning her cowgirl shirt to her navel, Aunt Ida walked toward the lone security guard standing on one of the loading docks.

"OK if we park there?" She nodded back toward the Tahoe. "We'll be right back. Just making a delivery."

A shit-eating grin spread like peanut butter and jelly across the guard's flambé-glazed face, as he took in the details of Aunt Ida's exposed hooters in all their pale and prurient promiscuity.

"Maybe you and me could go for a beer later," he

suggested.

"Maybe," said Aunt Ida.

Edie and I hotfooted it past Aunt Ida, up a half dozen steps to the loading docks and thru a metal door. Edie carried the two duffels and the towel-wrapped shotgun. Aunt Ida came last. The security guy's eyes never left her behind.

Inside, Aunt Ida took the lead, bounding three steps at a time up two flights of wide, vibrating metal and cement stairs, her delirious ass working in overdrive. I flailed after her, desperate to keep up. At the top of the second flight I stood, my smoker's lungs wheezing.

"You're pathetically out of shape," chided Aunt Ida.

"Bite my ass," I said.

Instead, Aunt Ida kicked in the beige door directly across the hall in front of us.

WHAM!

We burst into a large, high-ceilinged room. Holding the shotgun against her shoulder in firing position, Aunt Ida scanned the room like a cyborg killer from an old Jean-Claude Van Damme flick.

"This is a stick up! Anybody moves, I'll kill 'em!" she shouted, paraphrasing William Holden in The Wild Bunch.

Ten middle aged women of various sizes and shapes sat frozen as ice popsicles in front of two rows of folding plastic tables stacked with piles of greenbacks. Two men, who looked like bank tellers, stood at one side, mouths open, eyes blinking behind wire frame granny glasses. Aunt Ida's inside info was accurate. There was no armed security, perhaps on the theory that no one would be stupid enough to hold up a guns and ammo show.

"Everybody up against the far wall!" shouted Aunt Ida. She strode toward the two men. Next instant the butt of the shotgun took the older one in the gut. With a groan he doubled up and collapsed to the floor.

I moved toward the other side of the room, the Beretta raised high in my hand, herding the women toward the back wall.

Edie jumped into action, hustling up and down the table rows, thrusting stacks of currency into the sports duffels. When one was full, she zipped it tight and started on the other.

Except for the injured bank teller, who lay on the floor in a fetal position, moaning, the workers all stood facing the back wall, hands above their heads. I walked over to the malingering supervisor and told him to cut the histrionics if he wanted his nads to remain intact.

Then it occurred to me: Why weren't we wearing masks? At the same moment I observed two security cameras in opposite corners of the room. Even if Aunt Ida disabled them with a couple of shotgun blasts, we were already immortalized on videotape for all eternity.

What a bunch of fucking amateurs!

After that all I could think about was how I would never get my job back with the Waste Processing Department. And that Aunt Ida and Edie would end up sharing a cell at some Florida women's prison chock full of dykes and hard-as-nails babes you'd surely regret meeting in a dark alley.

All I wanted to do was get the hell out of there.

Edie had filled both duffel bags but one table was still half covered in stacks of cash. She looked at me questioningly.

"Leave it," I said.

"No fucking way," said Aunt Ida, tossing Edie a cardboard box from under one of the tables. Edie filled the box with the remaining money and the cell phones Aunt Ida had confiscated from the hoi polloi.

"We're going now," said Aunt Ida. "Except my friend here is going to wait for awhile just outside the door and if anyone comes out. Bang!" She surveyed the line of hostages. Then cold-cocked the other bank teller with the butt of the shotgun. "So don't anybody leave this room for twenty minutes. Got it? Any questions?"

One of the women half turned her head away from the wall. "I need to pee real bad," she said.

"Hold it, honey," was Aunt Ida's pithy advice.

I was sure Aunt Ida had been the cruelest kid on the playground.

Then we were out through the door, leapfrogging and ricocheting down the stairwell.

At the bottom I pushed the exit door open a crack and looked out. A flock of pigeons burst into the sky like a shotgun blast. The security guard stood at the end of the loading dock, staring into the heat haze.

I took him down the same way I'd nailed the guy at the mall. He lay there like a dead fish, blood seeping from one ear.

Aunt Ida came up behind me and spat in the guard's face, then laid into his privates with the toe of her cowboy boot. I didn't bother to tell her she'd just left a bunch of DNA evidence.

"Edie," barked Aunt Ida, as we reached the Tahoe. "You drive."

As I hefted the second duffel of cash into the back seat, I felt the cruel steel of the shotgun barrel kiss the skin just behind my right ear. The stifling heat of late afternoon transformed into arctic night.

Fool!

In the pell-mell rush of our getaway, I had lost track of my plan to rid the world of Aunt Ida. Now the tables were turned and I was a dead man. I waited for Aunt Ida to pull the trigger.

"Give me the Beretta. Then get in the front. We need to amscray."

I complied in all respects. Edie hit the gas and we tore out of the convention center like a hearse running late for a state funeral. The barrel of the Beretta replaced the shotgun at the back of my head. I stared bleakly out the front window of the Tahoe, as Edie merged onto the cross-town expressway.

For some unknown reason Aunt Ida wasn't ready just yet to put an end to my picayune existence. To stay alive I needed to convince her that I still added value to the operation.

"We should have been wearing ski masks," I said. "They'll know who we are in a couple of hours. So I hope you've got a damn good getaway plan."

Silence hung over us like an elephant suspended on a bungee cord.

"Shit," said Aunt Ida.

In the rearview mirror I saw her brow knit with worry, as if she might actually be thinking. You could almost see the little black clouds of a cold front of doom forming in front of Aunt Ida's vision.

Suddenly, out of left field Edie blurted: "Oh, my god. We've got to pick up the children at five."

Yikes! We'd forgotten all about the kids! I looked at my watch. It was a quarter to five. What were we going to do with the kids?

I was totally deranged. Or soon would be. The proverbial shit was hitting the fan faster than I could shovel. TILT!

"Maybe we should stop somewhere and get a beer," I said. "Discuss what we're going to do next."

Edie swerved the SUV off the cross-town expressway onto a wide boulevard heading east. We passed a Publix, a Chinese buffet restaurant and a low-slung, cement block bunker with a red neon sign that read: Johnny's

A couple of old pickups were parked in front.

"How 'bout that last place," I said.

"We don't have time for a fucking beer," snapped Aunt Ida.

The barrel of the Beretta rasped against my skin. I inched forward, away from the threat of oblivion. At some point I would have one chance, and one chance only.

In mute disarray we zoomed onward, soon passing the last gas station, the final strip-mall. Then we were in the country, a single lane in each direction. A black water swamp festered on one side. To our right a cantaloupe field stretched as far as the eye could see. Well, not really. But it was big.

"Slow down," said Aunt Ida. "We don't want to get pulled over by a cop."

Edie eased up on the gas. The speedometer dropped to thirty. I edged sideways so I was half leaning against the passenger door. My eyes met Aunt Ida's in a sudden squall.

She pointed the Beretta at my heart.

Intoxicated with fear, my mind raced like a steroid-pumped cyclist on day six of the Tour de France.

"Hey," I said. "I did everything you asked. Edie is yours. End of story. I don't even want any of the money. And take the Tahoe. They'll be looking for your Jeep from the get-go. It'll take them longer to identify Edie and me because we're from out of state."

"Good thinking, Bill. But you're still toast."

Aunt Ida leaned threateningly toward me. I moved away as far as I could go, lost my balance and tumbled part way into the passenger side footwell in a twisted knot of arms and legs. Was this the end of the road? What a pathetic way to die.

"Here, take my Rolex," I said, holding out my arm. The watch was a fake I'd acquired from a sallow-skinned stranger in a Baghdad back street.

"Bill, we've got to pick up the kids," said Edie, her voice fraught with urgency.

"We talked about this," said Aunt Ida, looking at Edie, who remained facing forward, eyes on the road, both hands on the steering wheel. "We said we'd kill Bill and leave the children. You know that's our only chance for happiness."

"I can't leave the children," said Edie.

Her right hand swept sideways and back, grabbing for Aunt Ida's gun.

I squirmed this way and that in the footwell. Under the passenger seat my hand felt something hard and angular. I pulled it free. It was a book. The one Edie had bought weeks ago at a yard sale. The Report of the Warren Commission on the Assassination of President Kennedy.

My other hand found the car door handle. I yanked on it and the door swung open behind me.

Edie screamed as Aunt Ida slammed the barrel of the Beretta into her cheek. The pistol swerved back, once more aimed at my heart. Without a second thought Aunt Ida pulled the trigger. I lurched backwards as the bullet came to a screeching halt 7/8th of the way through the 726 pages of The Warren Commission Report. In the next instant, curled into a ball I tumbled backwards through the open passenger door, hit the gravel road edge and rolled onto the grassy margin.

I lay there for a moment, my ticker pumping as fast as the heart of a winning greyhound coming around the far turn. My body was scraped and bruised but I had suffered no serious injuries.

Then I was on my feet and splashing through the drainage ditch, scrambling up the other side and sprinting hell bent for leather across the cantaloupe field.

Glancing back, I saw the Tahoe swerve wildly. Somehow Aunt Ida had clambered into the front seat and the two women were locked in a melee.

I just kept going, my cigarette-destroyed lungs seared with pain.

When I looked back again, the Tahoe was moving away into the distance. With a wink of light off the windshield, it disappeared around a curve.

*

I was charged with armed robbery, felony assault and a string of related crimes. The State of Florida took custody of Ben and Mary Beth. Based on my military service and only one prior for beating the crap out of some drunken suit who'd suggested Edie was the illegitimate spawn of an ewe and a sheep fucker, my court-appointed lawyer worked out a plea. Ten years, reducible to five and a half if I was a model prisoner.

While I languished in a county jail cell awaiting sentencing, a picture postcard came in the mail. It was sent in care of my attorney and showed the façade of a restaurant with two sexy couples standing in front, smiling. The back of the card identified the restaurant as Emilio's Casa de Schnitzel in Mexico City.

The message space was blank except for a primitive smiley face. The address was printed in Aunt Ida's childlike hand. I could see, as if it hung in the air in front of me, the smirk on Aunt Ida's face as she dropped the postcard in the mailbox.

One of these days I would catch up to her and Edie. It was as inevitable as my own demise.

Personally I didn't think her little joke was very funny. But then that was Aunt Ida's problem: she didn't know when to quit. Neither did I.

Part II

Five and a Half Years Later

1

In the brutal glinting light of a summer dawn, Oopawalla
State Prison, a maze of dank cement and steel cellblocks and
razor wired exercise yards, squatted like a poisonous bufo
toad on the flat south Florida landscape. On all sides
sawgrass prairie stretched to the horizon, offering neither
cover nor solace to the orange jumpsuit-attired escaped con
running for his life. Occasional sluggish canals and creeks
and impenetrable hammocks of palmetto, scrub oak, palm
and gumbo-limbo interrupted the monotony. Sweat stung
the con's fear-glazed eyes. The sawgrass clutched and cut at
his exhausted legs that propelled him Frankenstein-like
across the endless plain that had once been the bottom of a
vast shallow sea. The raucous baying of bloodhounds and
the thwap-thwap-thwap of helicopter blades rose to a
deafening, hopeless crescendo.

What the fuck!

As I swam out of the dream, my eyes blinked open and I
stared at Robbie Dee's wide, archless feet and hairy calves
dangling over the edge of the upper bunk. With the squeal of
protesting bedsprings, Robbie launched his hulking body
from bed to floor. Drawing a paw through thinning hair, he
turned and looked at me, his face cut by a broad grin.

"Time to get up, buddy," he said.

The deafening squawk of the PA system announced the
morning cell inspection that preceded the breakfast hour of
artificial OJ, watery scrambled eggs, limp toast and pretend

coffee, a forgettable repast consumed under the sullen gazes of our fellow diners and the beady, crow-eyed guards. Ahead stretched a grueling day of stamping out Florida car and truck plates and assembling citrus packing crates.

Except today was different.

Today was the day of my early release after five and a half years of exemplary behavior, unmarred by brawls, stabbings or freak-outs.

This was the day I'd dreamed about every day, day in and day out, since the grey convict transport bus delivered me and a dozen other losers into the fetid bowels of Oopawalla Prison.

This, and another dream sustained me. A dream of revenge most sweet, and as cold and deep as the iceberg that took down the Titanic. For plotting my demise, for taking the money and leaving me to pay the piper and for every horror and indecency I had suffered in Oopawalla's dank, rat-infested dungeons, my lost love Edie and her demonic lover Aunt Ida would pay dearly. However long it took, I would track them down and, when I found them, meter out a thrashing such as they had never dreamed of.

Today I was free at last! Soon the rich honey of retribution would be mine!

"Hey," said Robbie. "You're all sweaty lookin'. You okay?"

"Some kind of nightmare."

Sitting up, I shook my head from side to side, as if I could cast off the ill luck that had affixed itself like a leech to my shit-from-Shinola soul from the moment my wife Edie suggested we visit her Aunt Ida down in Orlando.

"Gee, Bill, today's no day to have a nightmare. You're getting outa here."

"Must have been the horsemeat we had for dinner."

"Cheer up, Willy boy." said Robbie. "You got the whole rest of your life in front of you. Only way I'll be leaving this dump is in the back of a hearse."

William Derringer, the name I traveled under, was one of

those names that sneaks up behind you and shoots you in the back. That threat and three tours of duty in I-rack to back it up had kept me out of trouble during my stay in Oopawalla. Rooming with Robbie Dee had been a big plus too.

Almost nobody messed with six-three, 240-pound, smiling, good-humored Robbie Dee.

He was a lifer, having strangled his wife, the beloved Tina, and her lover with his bare hands. He'd done them both in less than sixty seconds. Then he sat on the bed where he'd caught them fornicating, dialed the police and waited.

On day two of my incarceration, I'd taken down a demented doofus of the Arian Brotherhood persuasion who intended using a shiv to remove the smile from Robbie's face. A single blow to the windpipe. It happened so fast, none of the guards saw anything. As a result Robbie and I were pals for life, whether I wanted a pal or not.

"I don't deserve to be getting out of here," I said to Robbie.

"Life is a great mystery. You have to accept your fate as being unknowable. Take the good and bad as it comes. Some day an angel will come for me."

"I don't believe in miracles or visitations," I said. "What I know is I'm going to track down the two cunts who put me in here and meter out some serious payback."

"Revenge will choke up your soul with negative energy."

"I guess I'll just have to live with that."

At that moment two warders entered our cell. One of them started to pat me down. When he touched my dick, I almost went off on him, which would have been the end of my parole. Instead I swallowed my anger, which left my stomach burning.

My last lousy meal at Oopawalla Prison came and went. At 10 o'clock I was relieved of duty at the license plate press and escorted to my exit interview with Warden Draper. It was conducted in the prison library to avoid sullying Warden

Draper's office with lice and bedbugs.

Did I mention that Warden Draper was one of the weirdest SOBs I'd ever met? He had this wide head like a pumpkin that had grown sideways instead of up. He wore his hair buzz-cut short, as if he were one of the inmates, and favored black country-preacher suits that always looked slept in.

When I entered the library, the thing I noticed first was Warden Draper's hands. Resting on the table, folded together, fingers entwined, they were encased in white Latex gloves, the kind your doctor wears when he grabs your balls and asks you to cough. Cooks in restaurants also wore them. On occasion I had wondered whose balls they were squeezing.

Beneath those clasped hands lay a file folder with a red flag at one corner.

"Sit down," said Warden Draper, his mouth a dark wound in his orange-ish face.

I pulled out the gray metal straight-back chair with the gray vinyl seat and sat.

Warden Draper contemplated me in silence. His eyes were full of righteousness and fervor. Then ever so slightly, he opened the cover of the folder and eyeballed some notation on the first page.

"You're leaving us today, William. Do you think you're ready for this?"

"Yes, sir."

"You have a very high opinion of yourself. But don't be too quick to brag on your chances of survival out there in the war zone."

"No, sir."

Warden Draper's eyes became as mean as a bad drunk.

"Don't patronize me. I don't think you're rehabilitated one bit. The Parole Board made a big mistake letting you out early. You're a very bad boy. Your parole runs for 24 months. If you step an inch out of line, I'm going to nail your ass. Do you read me loud and clear?"

"No, sir…err, I mean, yes, sir."

I had zoned out. I was blowing it.

"Sit up straight."

I did.

"Do you smoke?"

"Sometimes."

"It's not good for you."

Warden Draper took a deep breath and blew it out from between puffed out cheeks. He raised one hand, palm up, above his shoulder. One of the guards handed him a black book with gold edging on the pages and a gold cross imprinted on the fake leather cover. Warden Draper set the Bible on the table and opened it to a page marked with a black ribbon.

"Get down on your knees."

I did what he said. What I wanted to do was smash a tire iron into the soft pumpkin flesh of his head.

He began to read:

"We are all infected and impure with sin. When we display our righteous deeds, they are nothing but filthy rags. Like autumn leaves, we wither and fall, and our sins sweep us away like the wind. Isaiah 64:6.

Remember those words, Mr. Derringer, when you're crawling on your belly in the slime out there. Now, get the fuck out of here."

A travesty of a smile broke Warden Draper's lips.

"You'll be back," he said. "Back before you can say Jack Robinson."

Who the heck was Jack Robinson? And who the fuck cared? There was no way I was ever coming back to Oopawalla State Prison.

The interview was over. I was dismissed.

I struggled to my feet, bowing and scraping like some hat-in-hand Jim Crow nigger. Except I didn't have a hat.

The guards hustled me out.

*

The warder in charge of intake and release emptied the contents of a manila envelop onto the counter top: my fake Rolex watch, its face corroded with green mold, a worn leather wallet containing an expired Georgia driver's license and a picture of a young, braless Edie in a wet T-shirt, two dimes, three quarters, a 1943 steel penny I always carried for luck, the postcard Aunt Ida sent from Mexico City, bent in half and yellowing at the edges, and the dried iridescent-green carcass of a small beetle.

I shoved everything but the beetle into my left front pants pocket.

The warder counted out $279 in cash. My meager prison wages. The warder's fingernails were bitten to the quick.

"Don't spend it all in one place," he said. "And keep away from floozies and booze. They're the surest road to perdition."

Everyone was full of advice today. All of it bad.

The money went in the other front pocket.

Besides the clothes on my back: blue jeans, a blue oxford cloth shirt and black wing tip brogues as ugly as cement blocks, my only other possessions were what the warder had just given back to me and a letter from Mary Beth, my daughter. Her letter had arrived out of the blue a few weeks ago. She was fourteen when I'd last seen her on the morning of the big score.

Now Mary Beth was just turning twenty.

The letter, written in blue pen on a single sheet of lined school paper, was short. The handwriting large and determined. The words brought tears to my eyes.

Dear Dad,

For a long time I hated you and mom for what you did to me and Ben. But my therapist helped me get beyond that. She says hate can fuck up your life (!) and that revenge is never sweet. I'm finally getting my life together and I guess I wanted you to know that. My therapist helped me find out where I could write to you. I hope you're doing OK.

Actually, I don't give a shit. Just stay the fuck away. We're done.

Mary Beth

The light pink envelope bore a Miami postmark but no return address. Before Mary Beth's letter, my plan, that I'd nursed from a tiny seed into a gnarled and blasted tree of obsession and revenge, was to blow off my parole and head down to Mexico City to Emilio's House of Schnitzel. If I sniffed around long enough and hard enough, sooner or later I would pick up the scent of Aunt Ida's vagina. Sooner or later I would nail her worthless pelt to the wall.

But now the tide of blood that binds generation to generation had pulled me off course. I had decided to report to the halfway house in Miami to which I'd been assigned. I was desperate to find Mary Beth. To tell her I was sorry. For what good that would do.

Maybe I would stumble on the trail of young Ben as well. He would be sixteen now.He had always been closer to Edie than to me, and I had received no word from him since my incarceration.

"Sign these." The warder's who-gives-a-shit voice interrupted my reverie. He slapped a stack of lawyer papers and a pen stolen from a Sheraton Gardens Inn on the counter. He knew he was a lifer at Oopawalla. Had taken the job right out of high school. Now he was 41. Same age as me. What other kind of work could he do? Drive a waste disposal truck? Hold up a guns and ammo show? I, on the other hand, was getting out.

Among other things, I pledged on my good name to lead the life of a model citizen, eschew association with felons, dope fiends and other scumbags. And on behalf of me, my heirs and assigns, I released Oopawalla Prison of and from any and all claims, real or pretended, I might have, now or in the future.

The guards escorted me out of the property room and through two barred checkpoints before we exited the cellblock. Across the packed earth of an open yard area, the front gate loomed like a gas station in the middle of nowhere. Double wire fences with a gravel no-man's land in between surrounded the prison on all sides. Razor wire swirled along the fence tops like poisonous steel vines from some heavy metal jungle.

When I stepped through the gate into freedom, the air outside was just the same as before in the yard, blistering and thick with humidity. The imagined image of a woman I'd never met named Margaret Menendez hung in my vision. Tall, dark and ripely bodacious with flashing Cuban eyes. She'd started writing to me about a year ago. It was a pen pal kind of thing sponsored by some do-gooder organization out to save my soul. Marge had promised to pick me up on the day of my release.

At the end of the short entry road to the prison, a narrow two-lane blacktop highway sped emptily north and south like twin black tongues. Water-filled ditches paralleled the road on either side. Low-slung sawgrass and other unnamable vegetation stretched to the horizon. No car was waiting for me. What the fuck!

There was no shade.

Story of my life.

I turned right and started walking.

2

I had walked maybe two miles in the blistering south Florida heat. My shirt was drenched with sweat, my undies twisted into a soggy knot that chafed against my nads. My eyes were slits in the glare. My brain on autopilot. I felt like a ham and cheese panini in a sandwich press.

On the right side of the road, the drainage ditch had merged into a sullen, slow-moving creek maybe ten feet across, its black surface like polished onyx. On the far bank clumps of vegetation snarled.

The growl of a high-performance automobile coming up fast behind me intruded. I stopped, half-turned and haphazardly stuck out my thumb to hook a ride.

A white Mustang convertible was at hand, its outline wavering in and out of focus in my heat-fried brain. As it slowed, then stopped, the engine's growl diminished to a low rumble of indigestion. The snazzy sports car featured three snazzy young scumbags, modeling fancy sports shirts and expensive-looking shades. They were drinking beer.

The blonde one in the front passenger seat held out his beer toward me.

"Hey, man, you look hot. How about a cool brewski?"

"He's totally wasted by the heat," laughed the back seat rider, a dark-haired lout with an attack of acne crawling like red spiders up his neck and chin. "What're you doing way out here in the middle of nowhere, daddy-o?"

"You an escaped con?" asked the driver. "A stone cold

murderer, a rapist of innocent young women?" His wiry red hair and square jaw had the air of Irish trailer trash that had by chance come up in the world. He wouldn't have known an innocent young woman if he'd stumbled over her at a drunken frat party. "No, you don't look like you escaped from anywhere. Because if you had, you'd be sweating bullets in an orange jump suit and there'd be a pack of dogs about ready to chomp your ass. No, I'd guess they let you out cause somebody figured you paid you debt to society. You're just a chump looking for trouble."

My fingers felt the metallic edge of the fake Rolex in my pocket. Placed just right and with enough force, it could do some damage, take out an eye, crush a trachea. But the wild card was whether or not they had guns.

"What badass thing did you do to end up in Oopawalla?" shouted the monkey in the back seat. "Speak up, old man, or we'll beat it out of you."

I said nothing.

The frat boy who'd offered me the beer turned the can upside down, letting the remaining suds splatter on the pavement. He retrieved another brew from a cooler behind the front seat and popped it open, took a long drink.

"I hate fucking warm beer," he said.

I looked only at the driver, who was putting on a pair of latex gloves. This was how they did it now. Leaving no trace. No DNA. Was that why Warden Draper wore throwaway gloves? It was a big day for latex.

"Okay, pops, it's time for us to teach you a lesson. Set you straight in your new life as an ex-con."

Scumbag the Driver opened his door and stepped out. Beer Boy followed suit. Back Seat Lout vaulted over the side of the Mustang. I edged backward, my brogues scrunching on the gravel verge. Behind me ran a narrow strip of sedge grass, then the steep bank of the creek. I had nowhere to go.

Coming around the front of the Mustang into full view, Scumbag the Driver weighed a tire iron in one latex-clad hand. A snarl of loathing disfigured his freckled face. A loud click announced the open switchblade that appeared in Beer Boy's grip. His eyes were black holes sucking in all light. Back Seat Lout, a leer of sadistic joy on his snoutish mug, drew a small shiny pistol from his back pocket. It looked like a .25 caliber, a pansy's pick, but still plenty deadly against an unarmed man. Barely an hour as a free man and I'd taken one hell of a wrong turn somewhere, stumbled onto the set of a cheap remake of Clockwork Orange.

Another step back and I felt the earth gave way. I tilted backwards at a crazy angle, arms flailing, before tumbling ass under nads into the tropical tarn. A tumult of water exploded around me. As I sank beneath the surface, piss-warm liquid rushed into every orifice, mouth, nose, ears, you name it. I burst to the surface, sputtering and coughing. Regaining a standing position, I struggled toward the opposite bank, my feet sinking deep into slime. To ascend the steep opposite slope was impossible. I slid back faster than I could climb up. The thick, primordial mud of the creek bottom sucked at my wing tips.

"He's getting away!" shouted Beer Boy, charging into the water. Scumbag the Driver came at me from the other side, sliding recklessly down the slope on his blue-jeaned buttocks. Together they lunged toward me through the waist deep water.

Next moment Beer Boy screamed. A scream so wrought with terror I imagined one of the Devil's henchmen had split open his chest and grabbed his soul. I gaped in disbelief as a gigantic V-shaped set of jaws lined with yellow, razor-sharp ivories slammed closed with a distinct crunching sound around Beer Boy's torso. A single, shimmering, greenish, unblinking eye above the gator's grasping maw gazed at me with hypnotic malevolence. I froze. It was the Devil himself!

The gigantic, primeval alligator thrashed its human catch from side to side to finish the job its teeth had begun. The stagnant water boiled with the creature's fury. Rivulets of blood streamed from Beer Boy's crushed body, tarnishing the silvery explosion of H_2O.

From the bank Back Seat Lout gaped, his mouth open wide enough to ingest a plague of flies. Getting a grip, he pumped seven shots into the beast to no effect, threw the pistol to the ground and ran toward the Mustang. Scumbag the Driver, having fled the stream in a frenzy, leaped behind the wheel. With Back Seat Lout aboard, the engine revved wildly, before Scumbag released the clutch and the Mustang fled down the highway until its low-slung shape merged with the flat horizon line. A slowly dissipating cloud of acrid blue smoke was the sole proof it ever existed.

Beer Boy was done.

Kaput.

The gator dragged him under, leaving behind one final ripple made by Beer Boy's disappearing hand across the black mirror surface of the sluggish stream.

Somehow in the chaos I had become reanimated and scrambled out of the creek on the highway side, my shoes lost in the mud. Covered in muck and streamers of plant tendrils, my brain raging in an adrenalin rush, I leaped up and down like some demented primate, screaming after the disappearing Mustang.

"You got yours, you dirty swine! You cock sucking mother-rapers!"

After a while I stopped jumping up and down and collapsed in the exhaustion of shock and awe. Tears coursed down my cheeks, cutting streams through the grime covering my face. Hunched at the side of the road, arms around my knees, I rocked back and forth between despair and ecstasy. Saved from extinction by happenstance no wider than a cunt hair!

Slowly I came back into the real world, the world of survival of the fittest, where you trudged onward day after day after day, taking it in the ass, until finally your number came up and it was your turn to be eaten.

In some ways Beer Boy was the lucky one. He was out of the game. Free of this torturous existence.

Yet, I was joyful in my aliveness!

With an idiot smile on my face, I lay back and looked up at the wide, endless sky. A swallow dove and swooped like a dream of light. An ant crawled aimlessly over my mud caked toes.

I still had lots of things I needed to do. Like finding Mary Beth and Ben. And catching up to Edie and Aunt Ida and taking them for a thrashing in the woodshed.

To my relief I discovered that my few possessions, Aunt Ida's postcard, Mary Beth's letter, were damp but not seriously damaged. Beer Boy's gun glinted in the sedge where he had thrown it. I ejected the magazine. It was empty. The firing chamber too.

I was sure that even holding the gun for five seconds was a parole violation. Like I gave a fuck.

When I wiped the road dust off of it, I held a beautiful, intimate, small caliber Colt automatic. A weapon designed for shooting your lover up close and personal. Perhaps as part of a murder/suicide after catching the party of the first part in frenzied fornication with the FedEx delivery guy.

Beyond that, it was a failure as a killing machine. Though for sure it would look stylish as shit when some broad pulled it out her designer bag and threatened to blow your pecker off.

Its shiny nickel barrel and trigger mechanism were intricately engraved in exotic swirls and curlicues. The handle appeared to be genuine ivory, the remains of a hapless pachyderm slaughtered under the African sun by some deranged neo-Mau Mau poacher.

I slipped the gun into my back pocket.

Just then a doorless, olive drab, rust-pitted Jeep Wrangler sporting a bikini top pulled to a stop next to where I was sitting, weeping.

The femme fatale behind the wheel I guessed to be a few hard years past fifty. But she was the first dance-card-carrying dame I'd set eyes on in the flesh in five and a half years. So, saggy stomach, flaccid tits, sea green eyes and all, I thought she was one fine representative of womankind.

She leaned toward me, squinting.

"Your name Bill Derringer?"

I nodded, sniffing.

"What the fuck happened to you?"

"It's a long and pretty unbelievable story."

"Remind me to ask you about it some day when I don't have anything else going."

"By any chance are you Marge Menendez?"

"It's Margaret to you. Get in."

*

"Well," I said, licking my lips. At that moment my skinny pen pal Marge Menendez, in jean shorts and cropped Joey Ramone T-shirt, looked like nothing short of a lusty Vargas nude. Looking back, my sex-starved eyes and brain were pretty unreliable in their analysis of Marge's finer points.

She kept her eyes on the road.

"So, what do you want to do first?" she asked.

"I don't know."

"Look in the glove box."

I did. The spliff and the matte-black Taurus .380 semi-automatic lay side by side, like an exotic dancer and a coiled cottonmouth.

I took the spliff and left the gun. Another parole violation. Or two.

Firing up the jay, I inhaled deeply and passed it to Marge. My eyes bugging out as I held the smoke deep in my lungs, I studied the details of my driver's face.

I catalogued the squint lines of her eyes, the droopy, brackish skin beneath those eyes, the raw streaks of violet eye shadow drawn rashly across her lids. Her lashes were weighted down with enough mascara to drown a horse. Her nose was long and imperial with one mogul-like bump midway down where she had most likely run into a doorknob. Her jet hair was lusterless and had been amateurishly hacked off at shoulder length. Maybe not quite a Vargas original after all. More like a pin-up whose time had come and gone. But then, who was I to complain?

Sucking greedily on the jay, her lips were fat and happy, hinting at the prospect of astonishing erotic possibilities. She was in no hurry to hand the doobie back to yours truly.

Finally, in a coughing fit, she relinquished it.

"What do you think?" she said.

"Yeah, " I said, taking a second hit.

In the middle of nowhere, we came to an intersection with a red traffic light. Cane fields stretched to the horizon. On three of the four corners sat, respectively, a combo Shell station and liquor store, a Cuban rotisserie chicken joint and a 7-Eleven. The fourth corner was a weedy empty lot.

As inscrutable cosmic thoughts looped through my THC-zonked brain, the light turned green. Marge chugged through the intersection and into the Shell station/liquor store parking area. Stopping next to a gas pump, she cut the engine.

"Gotta pee," she said.

"Me too," I said with a wide stoner grin. It was really good shit!

"You should clean up a little while you're in there," she said, handing me a wine-red hand towel from the back seat.

Once I was in the men's room, I became lost. Splashing water on my mud-smeared face, I thought I was back in the ditch with the alligator and had to sit down on the broken toilet seat while fear sweated off me and my legs shook.

Finally Marge stuck her head in the door.

"What's up, Bill?"

After reassuring me that I wasn't playing hide and seek with a 700-lb carnivore with a taste for human flesh, she helped me stand, unzipped my fly and held my dick while I pissed. By the time she shook off the last drop, I was sporting an erection muy grande. With a smile Marge awkwardly tucked my engorged schlong back into my pants. Closing my fly, a tuft of pubic hair caught in the zipper teeth.

"Ow! Ow! Ow!"

"Sorry."

When I calmed down, Marge made me bend over the sink, so she could wash the caked mud off my face and neck.

"I've got some clean clothes at the apartment that you can have. They belong to my ex but he'll never miss them. I think they'll fit you," she said.

Back at the Wrangler, we gorged on junk food from the Shell station's convenience mart. Marge bought Twinkies, extra spicy Doritos, a couple of those tube packets of stale peanuts and a jumbo can of Arizona green iced tea.

"Wow," I said. "That was amazing."

"I've got a splitting headache from the Twinkies," said Marge. "You drive."

"Maybe you should take some Aleve," I said.

"Just drive."

"I don't have a license. What if some cop pulls us over?"

"Fuck it."

Back on the empty highway, she produced a pint of Jim Beam from under the seat and proceeded to pour it into the half-empty can of iced tea.

She took a long pull of the booze-infused tea. Then, as casual as tying a pair of shoelaces, she leaned over, unzipped my fly and encircled my limp, dual-purpose hose with her red lips.

I appreciated the gesture. An act of charity that put Marge at the pinnacle of good works intended to integrate me back into society. The Mother Teresa of blowjobs. Alas, despite Marge's best effects, I couldn't get there. Driving, I didn't dare close my eyes and drift off into some Larry Flynt-inspired sex fantasy. With a sigh I said:

"Give it a rest."

Marge sat up, wiping spittle from her lips.

"Maybe later," she suggested.

"Yeah," I said.

After that, we shared the rest of the whiskey and tea combo and got a little buzzed.

*

As the afternoon wore down, the spires of Miami-Dade County at last rose in the distance, a hallucinatory skyline of ghostly condominium towers, geriatric hospitals and Indian casinos amid teaming thunderheads. Marge was driving again.

"Tell me one more time the address of your halfway house," she said.

It was in a Miami suburb called Hialeah Gardens. When I told her, she said:

"Habla español?"

"No. Solamente ingles. What's the deal?"

"Hialeah Gardens is where I live."

"So."

"I'm Latina."

I shrugged my shoulders.

"If you don't speak Spanish, it'll be hard to blend in," she said.

"Who wants to blend in? I just want to get laid. Then find my two kids, whom I haven't seen for a half dozen years."

"Oh."

Marge whipped the Jeep onto the exit ramp we had just driven past. The driver of an eighteen-wheeler across whose bow Marge cut to make the exit threatened to have Marge spayed at a later date if and when he caught up with her.

Ten minutes later Marge pulled into a parking space in front of a jaundice-colored, two-story, stucco apartment building with window air conditioners.

"Home sweet home," she said.

She raised her arms over her head and stretched, her breasts beneath her T-shirt doing some irresistible things.

I didn't have a watch and the clock in the dashboard of the Jeep was broken. But the sun was still hot as a motherfucker. I had plenty of time before I had to report in at the halfway house.

Marge's apartment was a one bedroom on the second floor.

Cheesy knick-knacks consumed every flat surface. Herds of cute colored-glass animals, marble ashtrays adorned with bronze nude dancers, Snow White and the Seven Dwarfs, Mickey, Minnie and Goofy, phalanxes of Japanese lucky cats and smiling Buddhas, a cacophony of porcelain shepherds and bare-breasted nymphs, a black marble bust of a busty African wench with a bone through her nose.

Marge gave me a towel, a fresh bar of Ivory soap and a spare toothbrush and urged me into the bathroom. I took a long, hot shower, free from the sidelong glances of homeboys and boyz n the hood checking out my privates, comparing mine to theirs, contemplating yet other possibilities.

When I stepped out of the shower, my skin still stank of the raw, rancid, testosterone sweat of five and a half years of incarceration with psychopaths and degenerates of every shade and flavor. It would take weeks, months, maybe years, to rid my flesh of that noxious reminder.

As I toweled off, I realized my ruined clothes were gone, but no replacements had been provided.

What was I to wear?

After the blown blowjob in the Wrangler, was Marge expecting me this time around to waltz into the living room with an outsize hard-on?

Well, why not.

I brushed my teeth vigorously, my head filled with images of naked women behaving badly.

Blasé as hell, I strolled into the living room with my semi-stiff schlong pressing against the pink bath towel I'd wrapped around my waist.

Marge, in a paisley print cotton robe, lay tilted back in the eggplant-colored leatherette La-Z-Boy, staring at the popcorn ceiling. Her rabbity teeth gnawed a fingernail. Dark clouds hooded her eyes.

"Que pasa, Marge?" I'd picked up a little Spanish in Oopawalla.

"Goddamn it, I told you before, it's Margaret to you. You're here because I decided to help you get your bearings on your first day out of the slammer. As a Christian woman, it's the least I could do. But don't start overstepping your boundaries."

"What about the attempted blowjob in the Jeep?" I stammered. "Was that just the Christian thing to do?

She turned her face to the wall.

Things were not looking good. Marge had worked herself into a tizzy. Not knowing her from Eve, I had no idea what kind of baggage she was lugging around.

At the same time my stomach was churning. I hadn't had a decent meal all day. I was hungry as a wild dog.

"Okay, sorry," I said. "I was out of line. How about I fix us a drink? Then you hustle up those clothes from your ex. We'll head out and get a steak sandwich with peppers and onions and melted cheese, some fries, maybe a piece of Key lime pie."

Still feeling a tingle of lust, I stepped closer. Her feet rested side by side atop the recliner's footrest. They were attractive feet, long and slim with blue veins running under the olive skin and carefully manicured nails painted phosphorescent pink. I ran my fingers along the arch of the nearest one. The foot twitched away from my touch.

"Please don't," she said.

"Come on, Margaret. A quick and dirty romp. For old times' sake. Just to see if I remember how to do it." I paused, wondering if I'd gone too far. "Afterward we can still go out. Get that steak sandwich. Or lobster thermidor. Whatever you want. Then you can drop me at the halfway house and we'll never see each other again."

Suddenly I was nervous as hell. Was fucking more like riding a bicycle, something you never forgot? Or was it more like a complicated puzzle that, if you hadn't done it in a long while, would be impossible to solve?

Marge was crying.

Suddenly, she ejected herself from the La-Z-Boy. The robe fell away.

"Look at me," she sniffled. "I've lost forty pounds in the last two months. My breasts are dried husks. I'm nothing but a pile of old bones in a shapeless skin bag. I can't bear to look at myself in a mirror."

Marge was indeed very thin. Too thin. Her flaccid skin mottled in harsh reds and purples. Her bedraggled nipples hung floorward. How had I not noticed her emaciated condition before?

"What is it, Margaret? What's wrong with you."

"It's the fucking big C. Lung cancer. It's everywhere and inoperable. You're talking to a corpse. And the funny thing is, I never smoked. Not even when I was a teenager."

This confession seemed to exhaust her. She withered to the floor, her fingers clutching at the robe, drawing it over herself like a thin blanket. Her shoulders quaked.

Jesus.

I wondered if I could bear the weight of Marge's darkness on top of my own. Or would I stumble and pitch us both into the abyss?

Dropping to my knees, I put my arms around Marge's paper-thin body as it shook with spasms. Gently I picked her up like an old paper sack of odds and ends bound for the Salvation Army and carried her into the bedroom. I pulled back the quilt and laid her on the pure white sheet. Then I lay next to her.

"You are the most beautiful woman I've ever seen," I said. I began to kiss her and explore her ravaged body. My pepperminty teeth encircled the raspberry-textured flesh of a nipple. My tongue crept into the deep hollows between her thighs. In no time at all, we were fucking to beat the band.

Because she was dying, I was intoxicated by her odor. Rooting and snuffling at the gates of her vagina, in some dark abyss of my mind I caught a whiff of smoke rising from the ovens at Auschwitz-Birkenau.

When we finished, I lay there exhausted, letting the cool air cast by the ceiling fan dry away the sweat and moisture of lust.

Marge had fallen asleep.

After a little while, I too nodded off and dreamed of alligators up the wazoo.

Compass House, the halfway house to which I had been billeted, was run by Captain Ahab and his Asian mail order bride. Suki Wa was her name. The Captain had served a prison term for manslaughter, the details of which were lost in the mists of time. Later he had studied psychology and received some sort of certificate. Framed, it hung behind the desk in his office. The print of the certificate was too minute to be readable by anyone standing in front of the desk. Sitting was not allowed, and no chair was provided.

For the record, The Captain's left leg had been severed at mid-thigh in a boating accident in the Keys during the celebration of his forty-ninth birthday.

The Captain was now pushing sixty but his libido still functioned in fine fettle. After a few beers of an evening, the diminutive and much younger Suki Wa was wont to refer to The Captain's cock as the great white whale.

Built in the 1930s as the upscale home of a rising hardware entrepreneur, Compass House consisted of two stories of dilapidated stucco, plus the mildewed basement apartment occupied by Suki and The Captain. Of a bilious yellow on the outside, inside the place was a rundown shithole, despite liberal funding from the Feds, the fine folks in Tallahassee and the county.

Five wide steps ascended to a broad, shaded veranda. Three rotting wood pillars and a segment of four-by-four where the fourth pillar should have been supported the veranda's tin roof through which patches of sky leaked. On the first floor were a lounge, two bedrooms and a bug-infested, enclosed back porch for a kitchen. Upstairs were four more sleeping rooms and the only bath, outfitted with an ancient, rust-stained claw foot tub and no shower. Each room was crammed with chipped and mismatched furniture from some bygone era of bad taste. Lying on the thin mattress, you could feel the springs nipping at your ass.

Like I said, a shithole.

At this juncture in time, four transient ex-cons, including yours truly, lived at Compass House.

All this I learned in due course.

On the evening of my arrival, vague portents loomed. A squashed iguana lay in the street, a Day-Glo green stain. A madwoman dressed in motley wheeled an empty shopping cart through an intersection against the light.

Marge, mostly mute after our fatalistic frolic, dropped me at the curb in front. I was tricked out in a black, orange and green tropical shirt that reminded me of a recurring nightmare that had plagued me in Oopawalla. Light grey rayon slacks with razor-sharp pleats and a pair of black canvas All Stars sneakers completed the new me. All courtesy of Marge's ex.

"Thanks for everything," I said. "I'll see you around."

"I doubt it," Marge said.

She hit the gas and was gone.

I was alone, bereft of my one personal connection. As if I'd been stripped naked and dumped on a street corner in an unknown city where I couldn't speak or understand the language. Those few desperate letters Marge and I had written to each other had linked me to someone in the real world, the world outside Oopawalla. Now, the umbilical cord severed, I was scared shitless.

I looked up from contemplating the gum stains on the sidewalk. A woman with blond hair streaked with magenta sat on the top front step. Beneath her short black skirt, a swath of white cotton panties covering her pussy dazzled between partially spread, suntanned legs. A man's ribbed, tank-style, white undershirt was stretched over her upper body. So there could be no doubt, as she studied me in silence, her legs opened a tad wider.

Having no suitcase to lean down to and pick up, I gave her a cheap, jaded smile. I rested one All Stars-clad foot on the bottom step.

The lady in question had a thin, deeply tanned face, except for the rounded tip of her nose, which was pink and peeling. I figured mid-forties by the cross hatching around the eyes and a sag to the cheeks, but still attractive. I seemed to be developing quite the fetish for older woman. But there was something to be said for a mature outlook, where a fuck was just a fuck and not the stuff that pipedreams were made of.

Her brown eyes stared at me with the detachment of dirt.

"Did you get to see what you wanted to see?" she asked.

"What are you talking about?"

"I don't know. What are you talking about?"

"This is Compass House, right?"

"Was that your girlfriend?"

"Who?"

"The lady in the Jeep. She looked a little old for you."

I shrugged.

"Though sometimes older women can be very comforting. Like sleeping with your mom."

"It's been great talking with you," I said. "But I really need to check in with the management. I don't want to be late on my first day."

"The management around here sucks."

She spat a wad of saliva into a ratty-looking azalea bush to one side of the steps.

"I'm Jane. Jane Ryder. Originally from Ottawa, Canada."

She wiped her right hand on her skirt and held it out in my direction. I stepped up one step and took it. It was limp and perspiry.

"Bill," I said. "Bill Derringer."

"Small but deadly," she said. She laughed. "Check in with Captain Ahab. Around to the side and down three steps. Tell him I said to give you the room with the pool view."

"Ahab?"

"That's the name of the loony-bird who runs this sinking barge." She snuffled, then wiped her nose with her hand. "To his face it's best to just call him The Captain. And 'Hey you, asshole,' won't win you any points."

"Thanks for the advice," I said.

As I followed her directions to the office, she called after me:

"The cook starts drinking seriously around eight. Personally I never touch anything stronger than iced tea."

I heard her tinkly laughter again, like loose coins being stirred in a pocket.

*

As I knocked and entered the low-ceilinged basement room, the man sitting at the wide olive-drab metal desk looked up. His tarnished penny eyes sliced and diced my persona: swaggering ex-Special Forces killer trying to hide the scars from five and a half years of being beaten down in Oopawalla. I had no secrets from The Captain.

Other than the military style desk with its gooseneck lamp casting a glare upon a sheaf of outspread newspaper pages and two olive-drab filing cabinets to one side, the room was empty of furniture. On the wall behind the desk hung a photo of the current governor of the great State of Florida, a Hollywood publicity still of Gregory Peck as Captain Ahab and an indecipherable certificate.

Folding the newspaper closed and heaving himself to a jittery standing position, The Captain hobbled on his peg leg to one of the filing cabinets, from which he removed a thin file. Attired in starched and pressed khaki shirt and trousers with a strong military air and one lace-up camouflage boot on his one foot, his face lurid in the light and shadow cast by the gooseneck lamp, The Captain could have passed for a sadistic chain gang guard out of Cool Hand Luke.

He resumed his seat and studied the single piece of paper in the file.

Since there was no chair, I stood in front of the desk like an out of work cigar store Indian.

"You're late," he said.

How can that be?" I said.

The Captain pointed to an institutional clock on the wall behind me. The hands showed twenty-three minutes after seven.

"My watch is broken," I said. "And that woman, Jane something. I met her on the steps upstairs. She tied me up with her endless chatter."

"Bullshit! There are no excuses around here, mister. Either you're with the program or you're against it. If you keep fucking up, I'll send you back where you came from so fast you'll have whiplash. If you're on board with the program, I'll treat you fairly."

The Captain pulled a piece of dry skin from his lower lip, eyeballed it, then flicked it away.

"You'll work five days a week from eight to four-thirty at the job we've found for you, to give you a sense of confidence in your new life. Saturday is cleaning day up until one p.m. and free time after that until five. Sunday is the Lord's Day. Deacon Dobbs conducts services in the lounge beginning at nine, with plenty of hymn singing. Sunday afternoon there's bible study. Mr. Dobbs is bound and determined to save your fucking souls. Each evening you and the other residents will take turns assisting my beloved wife Suki Wa in preparing the evening repast."

"Sounds like a plan," I said.

The Captain jerked back at these words. One finger tapped menacingly. "I don't like smartasses," he said.

Like I gave a shit.

I shifted my weight from one foot to the other. Bring it on.

Suddenly The Captain relaxed, folding his hands on the desktop. The tension in the room went flat. But his relentless eyes, like those of a hungry spider, pinioned me like a fly against the back wall.

"I'm counting on you, Bill. That you'll get serious about your life." He grimaced. "And those clothes. My God!"

For a moment I thought he was going to order me to strip them off and go naked into the night.

But he continued tartly:

"After your first paycheck I don't want to see them again. Now get upstairs to the kitchen and introduce yourself to Suki. She'll requisition you sheets and a towel and check your cock for VD. She might even fix you a sandwich, since you've missed dinner."

In my excitement to get the fuck out of there, I fumbled the door handle. I wondered when we would begin harpoon practice.

*

Mini Suki Wa stood a mere four feet, seven inches tall. Her hands were childlike. Her eyes a pair of sideways almonds pressed in a cherubic, silly putty face.

"Beew Deewenger. Bery nice to meet, yes? You caw me Suki."

She thrust out one of her miniature hands. I shook it. It was like taking the paw of a dog. Or a small monkey.

"Take seat," she commanded.

I sat at one end of a white oblong metal table surrounded by fold-open chairs for eight.

Bustling about, Suki set in front of me a murky cup of coffee and a tuna salad sandwich on a chipped plate covered in Cellophane.

I realized I was starving. Marge and I had never gotten around to going out for the steak sandwich or the lobster thermidor.

As I sank my teeth into the soft white bread and pasty

fish spread, a tall, sandy-haired gent in a pink polo shirt strode into the kitchen, grabbed a chair, swung it around and straddled it backwards.

"I'd be careful about eating that sandwich, if I were you," he warned. "Suki Wa is probably the worst cook this side of Angkor Wat. I never eat here."

I set the sandwich, teeth marks and all, back on the plate.

"Graydon Pennington. Choate Academy, New Haven, Harvard Business School. And most recently Winona Correctional Institution. Welcome to Philip K. Dick land."

A silver ring bearing a fiendishly grinning skull and crossbones adorned the fourth finger of Graydon's outthrust right hand. It was a fascinating ring. I wanted to cut off the finger and steal it.

Instead, I ignored the hand, picked up the tuna fish sandwich and took an enormous bite.

Suki, who had taken a seat at the far end of the table, tipped up a Red Stripe for a deep, gurgling swallow.

"Nushing wong my cooking," she said defensively.

Graydon eyeballed me and said: "Except it'll kill you for sure. Guaranteed." He winked. Or maybe it was just a tic.

Next instant the amber Red Stripe bottle hurtled through the air, whizzed past Graydon's head by a sliver, and exploded against the wall.

"You shitbag gook!" roared Graydon. "You almost hit me."

In a flash he was up and lunging down the table, chair spinning away behind him. Then he stopped dead in his tracks. Suki too had leaped to her feet, brandishing a meat cleaver like a ninja dragon sword. The blade whistled through the air as she whipped it back and forth.

"Frucking write boy! Stay brack or I quew you."

Jane Ryder stepped into the room.

"What's going on in here?" she said. "With all the hullabaloo, I can't concentrate on my puzzle book."

"No need to get all worked up," I said. "Y'all are giving me indigestion. Let's all just sit back down and take it easy."

"You first, write boy."

Ever so slowly Graydon righted his chair and sat back down. His face was as pale as the bum of a vampire stripper at the Cypress Lounge back in Atlanta.

"Jesus Christ," I said. "That sandwich made me thirsty."

"Haff Led Stripe," suggested Suki. She too was sitting again, the meat cleaver out of sight.

"Drinks all around," I said.

Jane Ryder found a dustpan and brush and, down on her knees, was sweeping up the shattered glass, her snow white undies on full display from the opposite direction. I retrieved three cold Red Stripes from the fridge. There was also a pitcher of iced tea. I poured a glass for Jane.

"Breer extra," said Suki with a toothy, chink grin. One front tooth had been broken off at an angle and had turned brown like a triangular fragment of a fortune cookie.

"Deduct from praycheck."

Whatever.

*

The next morning, suffering from a modest Red Stripe hangover, I managed to ride two city buses from Hialeah Gardens to downtown Miami, the location of my new job as stock handler for Rothman's Department Store. I arrived an hour late but nobody seemed to mind.

They didn't much care for my tropical shirt any more than Captain Ahab had. So before I could make a customer appearance, they rounded up an olive drab work shirt with Rothman's embroidered over one pocket and Ramon over the other. It was a little tight in the shoulders and across my gut.

Had Ramon been a Compass House resident? A predecessor who had graduated to a fuller life as a warehouseman or dishwasher? Or had he been sent back as irredeemable? In this life most would disappear without a trace. In Ramon's case at least there existed a shirt with his name on it.

Rothman's was situated in an older retail zone of cheesy, open-air storefronts catering to Cubans and other Latinos. Occasional chicken, beans and rice joints and dead-end bars had been thrown in for local color. Atop the building, the "R" in the Rothman's sign was partially unmoored and hung at a precarious angle. The bronze front doors were no longer polished. The store felt neglected, like a child left at home while one parent drove to Key West to fuck a stranger for the weekend and the other flew to Puerto Vallarta for a similar purpose.

Ms. Blanche Garcia, my overseer in the Housewares Department on the third floor, wore low-cut print halter dresses that someone her age with a double D cup bosom should never wear.

Whenever someone bought a microwave or a Fiesta dinnerware set for twelve or a Formica dinette set in the cheerful sunflower pattern, it was my job to root around in the stock room for the item in a boxed version and wheel it out for the customer on my hand truck.

I quickly fell into a dull routine. Work: Monday, Tuesday, Wednesday, Thursday, Friday. Each night on the way home, I picked up a six-pack of PBR or whatever else was on sale. Drinking with Suki and Graydon after dinner. Jane kept pretty much to herself, reading or doing crossword puzzles in the lounge. Sunday I spent on my knees with Deacon Dobbs.

During my free time on my first Saturday on the outside, I went to the public library and tried to get a line on Mary Beth. When I googled her name, only one Mary Beth Derringer came up, a 39 year old housewife in Tulsa, Oklahoma, who worked as a receptionist in a sex clinic. She achieved her fifteen minutes of fame in a lurid online article describing her batshit attack on her next-door neighbor with a grill fork when he suggested she had the sexual predilections of a she-goat. Convicted of attempted assault, Mary Beth, the Okie, got a fortnight in jail and 36 months probation.

Not my Mary Beth.

But reading the story in the Tulsa World sent fissures of dread crackling through me. My mind blistered with speculation as to Mary Beth's absence from the Internet. That she had been swept up in a CIA dragnet of jihadist lunatics. That a bandit queen oddly resembling Aunt Ida was holding her prisoner in a basement cell until she succumbed to her captor's lusts.

Or maybe she had just changed her name.

By the time the transit bus dropped me a block from Compass House, I was so hopped up it felt as though my jaw would shatter from the tension.

Jane Ryder, thrust into myth-creating pink shorts and a white T, sat in her usual place on the top front step.

"You look like crap," she said. "I'll get you a glass of water."

She leaped up, her free-range boobs flip-flopping with libido-arousing political incorrectness.

"It's okay," I said. "I'm just worried about my kids."

The other evening, Friday, after a dinner of meatloaf and Brussels sprouts prepared by Suki, I'd confessed to Jane over a few cans of PBR my hopes and agonies about finding Mary Beth and Ben. I even showed her Mary Beth's letter.

"Sounds like she's gotten over you," said Jane. "Just like I got over my last serious boyfriend. An artist of some renown. Claimed he was descended from Russian aristocracy. Crock of shit. He's dead now. Drown in the lake behind the apartment complex where we were staying with his second cousin, whom he was screwing off and on. She was quite the little number." She took another sip of iced tea. "For months the fucking D.A. tried to pin that one on me. It's stupid to get sentimental over a dead man."

A huge black rhino of death thundered through my head. "Oh, God!" I wailed. "What if Mary Beth is dead. Then I'm totally fucked, with no chance for redemption." I broke down in tears.

Pathetic.

Jane coaxed me up the stairs, past the closed door of Ray Deets, the fourth denizen of Compass House, whom I'd never met, and into my room. She undressed me and rolled me under the shabby sheet. Then she got naked too and climbed in next to me. But nothing happened. I was still sobbing and hiccupping. She held me until I fell into a sleep as dreamless as my future.

Now after my futile Internet search, I had worked myself up into a frenzy again. I sat next to Jane on the front steps and hung my head, one hand covering my eyes.

"I couldn't find any trace of her. I'm worried sick."

"Jeez, honey, I'm sure it's the heat that's gotten you all buggie. And this humidity. Just thinking about having sex, imagining all that activity, makes me sweat like a Cuban window washer working a high-rise without a net. Come and lie down in the lounge. I'll get a wet towel for your forehead. Or maybe you've got low blood sugar. Maybe we should walk down to Jorge's Hispani-Mart and get you a Cuban mix and a cherry Slurpee."

Jane began stroking my thigh. Her motherly instincts were in full bloom. Or she just wanted to get laid.

Finally, I consented to a neck message. But on the front porch, so it wouldn't degenerate into hardcore hanky-panky.

As I sat there, Jane kneeling behind me, her slim fingers kneading the taut flesh of my neck and shoulders, Margaret Menendez's Wrangler pulled to the curb.

I looked at Marge. She looked at me; flipped me a decorous fuck you with her raised eyebrow.

Vroommmm-vroommm.

Her hand flexed and unflexed around the throbbing knob of the gearshift. At any moment about to slam it into first and leave me in the dust. She wore a white cotton dress that was mostly hiked up to her crotch. Her olive skin went perfectly with the dress.

"Don't go!" I shouted. Broke free of Jane's fingers. Bounded down the steps. "What are you doing here?" I asked.

"I was in the neighborhood. But I see you're otherwise engaged."

"It's not what you think. I've been really tense lately, strung out. Living on the raw edge. Jane lives here. She's studying to be a massage therapist."

"Yeah, right."

I shrugged.

Why was Marge so angry? Why were women so angry? I remembered Aunt Ida screaming: "You'll never fuck me."

"Let's get a cup of coffee," I said.

"Oh. Now it's coffee. The road to my vagina paved with buchis and con leches."

"For old time sake."

I climbed into the passenger seat. She slammed the Jeep into gear and tore into the traffic. Cars scattered out of our way.

I reached my hand between her legs. She was already wet.

"How've you been, Marge?"

"Shitty."

She didn't bother to chew me out for not calling her Margaret.

"Me, too," I said.

She actually gave me a sort of smile.

"Well, at least you're not fucking dying."

"We're all fucking dying," I said. "Just some of us sooner than others."

"You sure know how to cheer a girl up."

Marge drove to a little Cuban joint. We ordered large café con leches and cream cheese and guava pastries.

We talked intermittently. Marge's chemo was making her sick. She could hardly keep any food down. She'd lost a bunch more weight.

Without warning her hand flew sideways, sending her half-full Styrofoam cup cascading across the room.

"Let's get the fuck out of here."

The counter staff gaped at her fleeing derriere. I dropped

an extra five on the table for the mess.

Soon enough we were screwing on Marge's living room rug, giving all the little glass animals and lucky Chinese cats a wildass show.

Afterward, Marge shrugged into her paisley cotton robe and we sat on the couch smiling at each other and sipping dark añejo rum over ice.

Finally I said: "I've got to get back to the monkey house before I'm declared AWOL. But this has been pretty swell."

Dressed and ready to go, Marge handed me a wad of bills. When I unfolded and ruffled through them, I counted a hundred dollars.

"What's this?" I said.

"No one in their right mind would sleep with me unless I paid them."

I stuffed the money in my front pocket, along with a scrap of paper with her phone number. I knew Marge would get upset if I argued with her. And as Rothman's paid minimum wage, I was always in need of extra cash.

*

Next Saturday, after swabbing down the hallways, kitchen and bathroom floor and scouring out the tub, sink and toilet, I dialed Marge on the landline in the lounge.

The phone at Marge's end rang and rang and rang. I let an hour pass and called again, with the same result.

These days I was a knot of nerves anyway, having given up almost all hope of finding Mary Beth. When not gnashing my teeth over that subject, I brooded impatiently to be on the trail of the evil duo, Edie and Aunt Ida. A trail getting colder by the minute.

All week Jane, pissed at me for fucking Marge over her, glared demon cat like at me, hissing and spitting behind my back. On Thursday at breakfast, The Captain accused me of leading his beloved Suki down the garden path to alcoholism. The night before Suki had gotten shitfaced and danced naked on the kitchen table. It was none of my doing. Graydon recorded the event and posted it on Vimeo, where The Captain saw it. At work Blanche chewed me out for some minor fuckup.

So when Marge didn't answer the phone the second time, I went nutsoid. Little black bugs crawled over my skin, between my toes, inside my navy blue, low-rise nylon Jockey's. I scratched like crazy. Rolled around on the lounge floor. Luckily there were no witnesses. My mouth went dry. Finally I went upstairs and into the bathroom and masturbated with the door closed. But it didn't help.

Why wasn't Marge answering her phone? She'd promised we'd get together today. Something bad had happened.

Terrorized, I hopped a cab.

"There! There!" I shouted, pointing wildly, as the cab driver barreled down Marge's street. He screeched to a halt. Then threw it in reverse.

I leaped from the taxi, throwing a twenty at the driver's outstretched hand. Across the curb lawn and sidewalk I sprinted onto the blacktop parking area, heading for the gray metal door to the stairs leading up to Marge's apartment. The door pushed open and a man in a coal black suit came forth. In one hand he held a leather medical bag. His face was turned away, hidden in the shadow of a black fedora.

Then he turned to look at me.

My eyes gaped in horror.

The face was a skull of bleached bone, from which fragments of skin peeled away. Empty sockets plummeted into blackness as deep as bottomless wells. Rotting yellow teeth cast in the demon doppelganger of a Cheshire cat grin.

"Dr. Death, I presume," were the whispered words on my lips.

We'd met before over in I-rack.

He made a slight theatrical bow before breaking into an antic dance step that took him skittering across the parking lot and up the street, disappearing into the descending dusk.

I found Marge in the leatherette La-Z-Boy, ice cold,

sleeping the sleep of the dead.

4

I mumbled a few remembered lines from Ginsberg's Kaddish, written on the occasion of his mother Naomi's death.

Strange now to think of you, gone without corsets & eyes, while I walk on
the sunny pavement of Greenwich Village.
downtown Manhattan, clear winter noon, and I've been up all night, talking,
talking, reading the Kaddish aloud, listening to Ray Charles blues
shout blind on the phonograph
the rhythm the rhythm—and your memory in my head...

I'd read the poem back in Oopawalla, when I had nothing else going. When my memory faltered, I drew a sheet over Marge's arctic cadaver. We'd shared an odd simpatico during our short involvement. And with a little luck one of these days we might hook up again on the other side. If there was one.

Finding Marge's purse on the coffee table, I ruffled through it. A brush entangled with strands of hair, a jar of green eye shadow and a nub of reddish-brown lipstick, several sticks of gum, tissues used and unused, hairpins, and a tarnished silver locket containing a man's dark hued face and a dried rose petal. Nothing of value, unless you counted the sentiment of the dude and the flower petal.

The eighty-three dollars in her wallet I folded and thrust into my pocket. She would have wanted me to have it.

To ransack the apartment for other items of value seemed in poor taste. Plus, the longer I hung around, the more likely I would be drawn into the matter. As the minutes marched by with the obviousness of a ticking time bomb, I ran an ever-increasing risk of being discovered lurking on the premises, with the consequence of somehow being found complicit in Marge's demise. As a man with a past, I needed to avoid the dead and dying like the plague.

As I wiped down the apartment's various door handles with one of Marge's cutesy embroidered hankies, I noticed her car keys on the kitchen counter. Grabbing them up, I checked the stairwell. No one was about. Outside, I found Marge's old Wrangler parked under the flame-fringed canopy of a Royal Poinciana. The .38 caliber Taurus, with a full magazine, was still in the glove box, but without an accompanying spliff. I wondered where Marge kept her stash of dope.

But it was too late to look for that.

I thrust the Taurus into a brown paper bag I'd taken from under the kitchen sink. Dropping the keys under the seat, I rolled up the paper bag and, tucking the package under my arm, headed up the street in the same direction as Dr. Death.

Adios, Marge. I'll catch up with you one of these days in the Elysian Fields and we'll screw till the cows come home to roost.

It was a perfect September evening. Maybe eighty-five degrees out. A slight breeze. People strolling up and down, picking up a pizza at the local Domino's, a twist of crack from a tatted dealer.

Just passing time at the corner bodega, waiting for the next drive-by shooting.

I walked back to Compass House. It was only a couple of miles.

Jane was in her usual spot on the top front step. The smell of pot wafted on the night air. The sky was the deep blue black of a well into which I was afraid I might fall and never get out. As I trundled up the steps, Jane spoke:

"What's in the bag, Bill?"

"Nothing."

"That's the way it is around here. A whole lot of nothing."

"You're not depressed, are you?"

"Fuck, no." She offered me her weed pipe. "Sail away with me, Bill."

"I need to do something in my room."

"You mean stash the gun you've got in that bag?"

I laughed, perhaps a little too shrilly.

"What would I be doing with a gun?" I said.

"Planning to kill somebody?"

"Right."

"Can I see it?"

"It's not a gun. It's a sandwich."

"Then can I have a bite?"

"No."

"Well, can I at least look at your sandwich?"

"What are you talking about?"

"Let's go in the kitchen. You can get a beer, sit at the table and eat. I'll just watch. And you can tell me all about your day."

"I've got to go," I said.

Upstairs in my room, I closed the door and hefted the chest of drawers in front of it. None of the doors had locks and I didn't want Jane or anyone else popping in unannounced.

I lay down on the bed with the Taurus resting beside me, my hand touching it. I was exhausted but my eyes wouldn't close. I tried to call up a holographic image of Marge and her ironic, postcoital, I-can't-believe-that-just-happened smile. But the image faltered, then morphed into the leering face of Dr. Death.

I wondered what things would have been like if Marge hadn't been terminally sick, hadn't chosen this moment to die.

But there was no point to this speculation. She was a goner. And I was alive and at another dead end. I needed to figure out what I was going to do next.

Maybe I should shitcan the idea of finding Mary Beth. In all likelihood my twenty-year-old daughter wanted nothing to do with her ex-con, crapola dad, whom she'd finally gotten past with the help of some gimcrack therapist. That's why there had been no return address on her letter. Besides, nothing had changed. I'd just stolen a pistol and eighty-three dollars from a dead woman.

My one true dream was to track down Aunt Ida and train the sights of the Taurus on her sneering mug until the sweat of fear burst out on her face and she fell to her knees begging for her life.

And then there was Edie. Beautiful, corrupt, malleable Edie. What was it I wanted to do to her? Murder her too, with the same zeal I planned for Aunt Ida? Or was there a chance that I could drag her back from the lesbian abyss? Bring back the olden golden days?

It was a tossup.

In any case, if I packed my bag tonight and flew to Mexico City in the morning, there was no way I could take the Taurus with me. Without it I would be naked in a hostile country where everyone spoke Spanish except me.

I'd taken the handgun on a whim. It gave me a misguided sense of security. Possessing it only increased the chances that I would do something stupid. But it was a thing of beauty. I ratcheted a bullet into the firing chamber. It felt good to hold its cocked hardness in my hand. I wasn't ready to leave it behind.

Besides, as a member of the ex-con underclass, I couldn't afford to buy a plane ticket to anywhere.

I slipped the Taurus under my pillow.

*

A few days later on a dull Wednesday evening, I was in the lounge playing strip poker with Jane.

The Captain had gone to Tallahassee to raise money for a new porch roof. Suki was despondent. Started drinking before dinner. Got into the cooking sherry in a big way. We ended up ordering in. I can't remember what.

Unexpectedly, Suki ralphed up her meal and the cooking sherry in 3D right there at the dinner table.

"Yuck!" said Graydon, throwing down his linen dinner napkin.

"Double yuck," said Jane.

Suki burst into tears and ran out of the room and up the stairs.

The second floor was where Graydon and I and Ray Deets, the resident I'd never met, lived. Deets worked the graveyard shift at a toilet seat factory. Whenever anyone passed by, his door was always closed. He never came to meals or hung out. Half the time I figured Deets was a figment of our collective imagination.

Though I'd felt and half seen his ghostly presence passing to or from the bathroom, or entering or departing Compass House at some ungodly late or early morning hour, a freakish, misshapen shadow of a man.

Had Suki run upstairs to ride the porcelain bus? Or had we in fact heard the special squeak of Deets' door opening and closing? Rumor had it Deets' equipment rivaled The Captain's. But that he was loath to share it with others.

After Suki's throw-up, dinner was definitively over.

I helped Jane clean up the barf, while Graydon washed the plates and silverware. Task finished, Jane got her weed pipe and we smoked some on the front porch and one thing led to another.

Jane was a pretty good poker player and in short order I was down to my black socks with dark blue clocks on them.

"Your deal," she said, eying my partially stiff centerpiece

with blasé indifference.

I drew to an inside straight against her two pair. Maybe my luck was turning. Jane leaned forward and, reaching behind her back, unhooked her bra. Her terrific boobs tumbled forth, big and foxy and in your face. A man could lose himself. Veer crazily off course. Run aground in deep shit.

Movement flashed in my peripheral vision. It was Graydon lurking in the hall, pretending disingenuous apathy to Jane's wanton display of skin.

"Let's go to your place," I said.

As my words trailed off, a blood-curdling scream ripped open the night.

Even as Jane, in terror, leaped up and hugged me from behind, her body one with mine, my cock went as limp as an old athletic sock. I could feel her heart beating like a retarded monkey on a drum.

The high-pitched scream belonged to a woman. There could be no doubt of that, unless a eunuch had somehow snuck into the house. As it came from upstairs, it had to be Suki. She and Jane were it, as far as females went in Compass House. Female visitors were strictly prohibited in the bedrooms. House rules.

And Jane was in the lounge with me and clearly hadn't screamed. Yet.

Extricating myself from Jane, I leaped into my camouflage cargo shorts, and rushed into the front hall. Graydon, pretending to have just arrived from the kitchen, stared up the lugubrious, shadow-strewn stairway.

"Turn on the goddamn light," I yelled. I flipped the toggle switch. A bare bulb high above us flickered on.

Another banshee scream, suddenly stifled, echoed off the ancient plasterwork ceiling and tumbled down the stairs up which we gaped in horror. This was followed by some thrashing noises.

"It's Deets," I said. "The motherfucker is murdering Suki."

"What should we do?" said Graydon, wringing his hands.

"What do you mean 'What should we do?'? We've got to rescue her. But Deets is probably armed to the teeth. We need to find some weapons."

"Maybe we should call 911," said Jane, who had retrenched into her bra and come up behind me to stare up the stairs. But I was already making a mad dash down the long hallway into the kitchen.

Jane and Graydon nipped at my heels.

Weapons. What kind of weapons could there be in Compass House?

I went for the knife drawer, yanking it all the way out so that razor sharp cutlery cascaded helter-skelter onto the yellowing linoleum. Amid the spectrum of blades, I spied Suki's meat cleaver and grabbed it.

Graydon emerged from the pantry closet hefting a broom. Jesus, what a dingbat!

"That's no good," I said. "Get something short, that you can maneuver in a tight space. And find some rope. We'll need to tie Deets up after we beat the crap out of him."

Jane, looking scrumptious and unflappable in bra and short shorts, stood with her hands on her hips, chest thrust forward.

"What about the gun you snuck in the other night?" she said.

"Why do you insist on making shit up?" I said.

"Because it's true."

"Even if it were true...and I'm not admitting to that...it would be in my room, which is further down the hall from Deets', past the bathroom, so it would be pretty risky to try to get it."

"You could climb up on the back porch roof and in through your window."

"My windows are nailed shut from the last hurricane. Besides, we're running out of time. God knows what Deets is doing to Suki, while we're jerking off down here. Come on, let's go."

I glanced over at Graydon. The best he had been able to come up with was a plastic Wiffle bat left behind by some previous Compass House inmate. We'd never played the game, because we couldn't find any balls. In his other hand he held a clump of laundry line.

Moments later, we huddled in a pack at the bottom of the stairs, listening. It was as silent as fucking Christmas Eve. Not a creature was stirring, not even a rodent.

Cautiously I began to climb the stairs, which creaked like a broken down old geezer trying to climb out of a recliner to answer the phone on the other side of the room. Stealth was not in the cards.

Throwing caution to the wind, I bounded up the remaining steps and threw myself at Deets' door, twisting the knob. The unlocked door flew wide. Cleaver in one hand, with the other I caught myself on the doorframe, my eyes scanning the scene of carnage.

Suki, sumptuously naked, lay spread-eagled across the bed, arms and legs strapped by torn segments of cloth to the four corner posts. Her quim was hairless. A sheen of sweat coated her flesh. A swath of torn sheet was wrapped and tied across her mouth, which was stuffed to overflowing with a pair of pink lace undies, probably hers. Though, in this day and age, there was always a chance they were Deets'. Life was full of surprises.

Cloth-drowned, nil-of-meaning words burbled around the edges of the gag. Terror twitched and floundered in the depths of Suki's eyes.

On the night table: a wine bottle, two half full glasses of red, a jar of Planter's dry roasted peanuts fallen on its side, peanuts spilled higgledy-piggledy, and Suki's eyeglasses, neatly folded.

Lolling back in a chair on the opposite side of the bed, Deets, insane, pointed at me the .25 caliber Colt I'd liberated from Back Seat Lout back in the Everglades. He must have stolen it from my underwear drawer. I'd never gotten bullets for it. Had Deets? Or was he bluffing?

His eyes lunged at me.

In their depths mad mullahs and demented dervishes leaped and plummeted and foamed at the mouth, calling up my worst nightmares in I-rack. Eyes that wanted to cut you into little pieces and eat you.

"How's it going, man," I said.

"None of your fucking business."

"Let's go have a drink. Talk things through."

"What would we talk about?"

Jane pushed past me into Deets' room. She held the Taurus semi-automatic two-handed, extended in front of her.

"Your funeral arrangements," she said, firing away. I became instantly deaf. Deets became instantly dead.

Driven by the force of Jane's close in shot, Deets' chair, riding on two legs, flew backwards, carrying him crashing against the wall, where he slumped, head fallen forward.

Despite his instantaneous passage to the netherworld, Deets' trigger finger spasmodically popped off three shots from the Colt, all into the ceiling above the bed, causing a downpour of plaster dust.

The room became pregnant with silence, except for the air whistling from a large entry wound in the center of Deets' chest.

I stepped around the bed to where he lay.

"It's still early," I said, looking down at him. "It still might work out for you…" He didn't look up.

"No, I take that back. Absolutely nothing is going to work out for you," I said, stomping his head with the heel of my sneaker. In protest Deets slipped sideways, his head hitting the floor with a thud. He didn't move again.

Then I remembered Suki.

Jane was struggling to untie the knot holding the gag. Graydon stared down at Suki as if he'd never seen a naked woman before. Her stately, plump, buck naked, buxom bod would, under other circumstances, have been ripe for the taking.

"Sot i wuz gonging to die," Suki said.

Soon she was free, sitting on the edge of the bed, messaging her wrists.

"Can you walk?" asked Jane.

I grabbed Jane's arm and pulled her aside. "You went in my room!" I yelled in a loud whisper.

I felt violated. Someone had entered my private space without my permission. As if some quack doctor checking out a precancerous mole on my butt had stuck his finger up my ass. To you it may sound like no big deal. But after years in the slammer where every aspect of my life was on candid camera, where you were strip searched on a whim, Jane entering my crappy little room without a formal invitation was a BIG FUCKING DEAL!

"Calm down," said Jane. "Of course I went in your room. Where else would I have gotten your fucking gun? It was a matter of life and death. I didn't touch anything else. I took the gun from under your pillow where I figured you'd put it for instant access in your current paranoid frame of mind." Then as an afterthought: "The safety was off."

"I'm not paranoid," I said. "But don't ever go in my room again unless you clear it with me first."

As best she could, Suki brushed off the plaster dust from her clammy skin, slipped her dress on over her head and zipped up the back. I couldn't put her nakedness out of my mind. Jane had big boobs but the rest of her was skin and bones. Suki was a vat of creamy vanilla pudding.

Since Deets wasn't going anywhere, we helped Suki down to the lounge. Graydon went to the kitchen for some cold brews, while Suki called Ahab on the landline and told him what had happened.

He asked to talk to me.

"Well, fuckin'-A," he said. "You need to put Deets on ice in the bathtub. Some people I know will pick him up tomorrow. I'll catch the earliest flight back that I can. Don't be worried."

"Who's worried," I said.

In fact I was bat guano crazy the cops would show up at any moment and I'd be back in Oopawalla on a murder rap before you could say Jack Robinson. I hoped and prayed The Captain had his shit together when it came to disposing of dead psychopaths.

Suki had to pee but she didn't want to go back upstairs. So she peed on one of the azalea bushes by the front porch. Graydon went out to watch. That left me with Jane.

"Where'd you learn to shoot like that?"

"Same place I learned to play poker. My father was Canadian military. He wanted a boy, but got me."

"I owe you one," I said. "Any time you need someone to go down on you, I'm your man."

"Your place or mine?"

In the end she and Suki slept together in her room because Suki was too frightened to sleep by herself in the basement apartment. I kept thinking about Edie and Aunt Ida bunking up together.

Graydon and I threw Deets in the claw foot tub and walked down to Jorge's Hispani-Mart for a half dozen bags of ice.

"Having a party?" asked Jorge.

"Yeah," I said. "A party. But you're not invited."

"Fuck you," said Jorge.

5

The next morning, Thursday, I had to be at work. No special treatment for last night's life and death tussle with our resident sex-crazed psychopath. Deets' decomposing corpse still occupied the claw foot tub, so I couldn't take a bath, though I badly needed one. Tepid water splashed on my face, a quick shave and a vigorous brushing of the old choppers would have to do. Deets' dead eyes kept following me around the bathroom, so I draped a towel over his head. I slathered on extra deodorant.

Deets' remains gave me the heebie-jeebies. I wouldn't be safe until his flesh and bones were dumped in a landfill or disintegrated in a vat of acid or chopped up for chum.

Just as I was going down the front steps to retrieve the early edition of the Miami Herald that the paperboy always tossed on the bottom step, a sinister looking van pulled up in front.

The color of dirty snow that had been pissed on, blank metal doors in the back, windowless, unreadable signage eating through a recent and shitty paint job on either side panel, front windshield cracked in the oval shape of a human head, bald hubcapless tires. The kind of van used by serial killers and white slavers.

A huge black man in overalls and a scrawny white guy, looking ready to succumb to heat prostration in grey corduroys and a flannel shirt, disembarked.

"This 1801 Garden Terrace?" asked the black man. His

English sounded over polished, foreign. A dinge gook of some sort.

I nodded.

"We're here for the package," he said.

"Package?"

"Guy named Deets. No longer with us," snorted the older white guy. He looked like he suffered from a wide swath of ailments, any one of which would shortly bring him to his knees. His arm muscles were twisted saltwater taffy. His face, cadaverous.

"Oh, right. He's in the bathtub," I said. "On the second floor."

"Thanks, bud," said the old guy.

Opening the back of the van, the black man heaved a rolled up carpet onto his shoulder. The old guy grabbed a mop, galvanized pail and a squeeze bottle of liquid detergent.

They started up the steps.

In the kitchen I made coffee. Then got out the iron and ironing board and pressed my shirt for work. The one that had belonged to Ramon. Everyone else in the house was still sleeping.

As I sipped my black coffee and munched on a Pop Tart, a loud crash sounded from the front hall. I sprinted to investigate.

At the bottom of the stairs, Deets' putrefying body, the unfurled rug and the old guy lay in a jumble. The black man, part way down the stairs, cursed a blue streak.

The old dude, leading the way, must have lost his balance, with the resulting crackup. Despite the ice Graydon and I had packed around him the night before, Deets looked seriously the worse for wear. Mouth agape like a black wormhole straight to hell, eyes ghastly gelatinous orbs, cheeks sagging like melted plastic. The south Florida heat and humidity were doing their usual number on the living and the dead.

The old fart picked himself up and began tugging at Deets' dead weight, pitched sideways across the bottom stairs.

"Shitbag!" cursed the black man. "Let me do that."

Together they arranged the rug flat on the floor in the front hall. Laying the stiff on one side of the rug, its end curled over him, they rolled Deets up inside until he and the rug looked like a giant stuffed manicotti, the old guy moaning and groaning about his injured back, the black cat swearing to high heaven.

Across the hall the door to Jane's room opened and Jane's face appeared around the edge, her brow knit into a scowl.

"What the fuck!" she said.

"It's okay," I said. "It's the cleanup crew The Captain arranged for."

"Well, for Christ's sake, keep it down to a dull roar."

Jane's head retreated back into her room and the door slammed.

I gave her the finger.

When they finally got Deets re-rolled and tied up at both ends so his head and feet were hidden from view by casual passers-by on the street, the dynamic duo made their labored way out the front door and down to the van. They heaved the trussed up carcass into the back and slammed the doors. The old number came back in and upstairs to retrieve his pail and mop.

Cleanup gear in hand, he exited without a word of farewell or a backward glance. The van, driven by the black guy, leaped dangerously into the midst of early morning traffic and squealed around the corner.

I expelled a deep breath of relief at the departure of Deets' rotting corpse. When I went back up to my room for my wallet and bus pass, I glanced into what had been Deets' abode. Through its east-facing window, the morning heat was already lumbering into the room like a nine-hundred-pound iguana. The same shitty furniture decorating my four-walled cage down the hall crammed the high-ceilinged space. There was nothing personal in the room. Nothing except the rust brown stain on the wall, where Deets had bled out.

*

That evening, instead of going home after work, I caught a bus out to South Beach. I'd saved Suki's life at great personal risk. I couldn't take another of our mandatory group therapy dinners. These sessions were to help us reintegrate into polite society. Sometimes The Captain even brought in guest facilitators. It was a fucking waste of time. But I wasn't in charge.

Tonight I desperately needed a break from Compass House and its deranged inmates. The Captain would just have to cut me some slack.

Besides, by the single shot that had taken down Deets, Jane had shown herself to be a tad too dangerous for my taste, recalling that other moment in time when Aunt Ida pointed a .32 caliber Beretta at my heart and, without the slightest qualm, pulled the trigger.

What I yearned for was a good old fashioned hump session between the no nonsense thighs of a *nymphe du pave noir*, as we called the pretend Parisian whores I'd boffed in another life in Baghdad's fake French quarter.

*

South Beach, famous for its douchebag club scene pulsing amid the art deco hotels along Ocean Drive, where Sonny Crockett and Tubbs got their rocks off, called to me. Having no better idea, I decided to check it out.

The moment I stepped off the bus, I realized I was hungry enough to eat grilled cat on a skewer. The aroma of rancid grease from the exhaust fan of a flyblown Middle Eastern joint wafted up my nose. I went in and ordered a Gyros sandwich and a Coke.

The smarmy counterman, of some raghead extraction, leaned over the counter holding my Gyros in a square of wax paper.

"You want tahini sauce?" he asked.

"Radical," I said.

He took that as a yes.

Back outside, munching on my Gyros, I moseyed up Ocean Drive, hustled and bustled by the milling throng of cool cats and kitties.

In the crush of guys and dolls, suddenly I felt lonely, desolate. Adrift. It wasn't Jane Ryder I missed. But that other long-time-ago time, before the dead baby trial, when I'd held beautiful Edie in my arms and she'd laughed without a care and we'd smooched and groped each other like movie matinee lovers.

Or was I kidding myself that a different, happier time had once existed in my life. Time had a way of dulling the harsh details of living, just as the endless tumbling surf smoothed the razor edges of broken glass.

The tahini sauce was messy and turned the Greek bread to mush. I threw most of the sandwich in a trash bin and walked on, licking my fingers. I should have gone for a strip steak, bloody.

Though it was only Thursday night, everyone in Miami Beach was already in a weekend frame of mind, jamming the narrow sidewalks and the front porch hotel bars. The mostly amber skinned ladies were mostly naked in expensive ways. Multi-pleated Italian pants and two-hundred-dollar designer shirts did it for the guys. Gangbangers in Chargers and other throwback cars equipped with neon underlights and cranked up sound systems cruised the boulevard, talking shit to any woman who even remotely glanced in their direction.

Needing to take a leak and wash the tahini sauce off my hands, I finally went into a club called Oh Calcutta. It was done up in mirrors and black Naugahyde with antique photographs of sahibs shooting tigers and putting the moves on bare breasted native girls. Besides the usual white and Latino clubsters, there was a large contingent of dark complexioned revelers from the subcontinent itself. The throbbing beat of the DJ'ed dance music made my teeth hurt. No one seemed to be having much fun.

As I stood in the bar area, irresolute as to whether or not this was my scene, a waitress in tight leather jodhpurs and a shimmery Mylar micro halter top passed close at hand. The jodhpurs looked like they were binding her ass. When I reached out and touched her on the arm, she arched back as if I'd made a grab for her boobs.

"Which way to the men's room?" I shouted.

She eyeballed me like a sushi chef considering the purchase of an overpriced blue fin tuna that might have turned. I was still wearing my Rothman's work shirt.

"The restrooms are only for customers," she said.

"What? I don't look like a customer?"

"You don't have a drink," she said.

I couldn't argue with that.

"If I buy a drink, will you show me where the men's room is?"

"What do you want?"

I considered telling her I wanted to get fucked by a *nymphe du pave noir*, but figured she probably didn't speak French, so what was the point? Instead I said:

"What kind of imported beer do you have?"

"Amstel Light, Dos Equis and Budweiser." That was the first time I realized Budweiser was imported.

"Give me a Bud," I said. "In a bottle."

Poof! And she was gone, just like Tinker Bell.

A stool opened up at the bar and I went for it.

Indians to the right of me, Latinos to the left, I sat sidesaddle, one arm resting on the bar, my head turned outward scanning the crowd for Tinker Bell's return.

From behind me a male voice said:

"What's your poison?"

I glanced around.

The barman looked like a Xerox copy of John Waters.

"I just ordered a beer from one of the waitresses," I said.

"Good luck with that. They only work the tables. If

you're sitting at the bar, you have to order from me."

"OK," I said. "I'll have a Budweiser."

"Twelve dollars."

"You're shitting me."

His sad brown eyes said he wasn't.

Setting a haze-covered bottle of ice-cold beer on the bar, he waited, bottle opener poised, as I scrounged in my pocket for some dough. Twelve bucks was a lot on my meager Rothman's wages. When I finally forked over the cash, the barman flicked off the bottle cap, releasing a tendril of moist air like gun smoke.

I had just taken my first sip when Tinker Bell appeared next to me. Sweat glistened on her glitter-spangled breasts. As I watched, a huge droplet did a forward roll into the deep crevasse of her cleavage.

"Here's your beer, hon. That'll be twelve dollars."

Fuck!

She grabbed the greenbacks out of my hand and was gone before I could ask again for directions to the pissoir.

By now I really, really, really needed to pee. But if I abandoned my stool, even for a minute, I'd lose it. So I held on, sipping my beer and surveying the room.

A couple of chicks with nice bods but not so great looking mugs checked me out. One, with a ragged scar disfiguring her cheek, even came up close and personal.

"Hi," she said as she waved her arm past my nose and called out for a shot of Maker's Mark. I could see the five o'clock shadow in her arm crotch, smell the sharp lemony tang of armpit sweat. As she tossed back the drink and smacked her lips, her breasts quivered. Fondling them could have been richly rewarding.

But all I could think about was how badly I needed to go. My dick was drawn up tighter than the twisted rubber band on a toy airplane propeller. My bladder ached and pulsed to the beat of the sound system. When I grimaced in response to her fake smile, she tossed her head and disappeared into the mob.

My nostalgic mood returned. None of the babes jostling for position in the crowded bar held a candle to Edie's bodacious charms, even with her late 30s pooch. If I ever caught up with her and Aunt Ida, maybe I would give her a second chance. But only after I'd slapped her around a bit for all the trouble and heartache she'd caused me.

On that note, halfway through the second beer I made a desperate dash for a dark passageway where I'd seen various revelers disappear and later reappear.

The rest rooms!

Inside the door bearing a sign reading Sahibs, a bank of urinals, like old-time phone booths, all fully occupied, stretched along one wall. Each urinator stood, bum side out, cock-filled hands hidden from view, silently reading the weird sex graffiti offerings on the tiled wall, as relief washed upward from their emptying bladders. I and several other pissers-in-waiting stood idly by, trying to look nonchalant, avoiding eye contact.

The lavatory sinks were primarily taken up with coke snorting. At the far end by the stalls, an amoebicly entwined same sex couple engaged in amatory prelims.

When a slot opened up, I pissed, zipped up and slipped out without washing my hands.

Twenty-four dollars, two imported Budweisers and a wicked piss later, South Beach was starting to drag me down. Exiting the club, I let the street crowd carry me along. At the next corner I turned into a darker side venue.

*

A tattoo parlor, cops in a white cruiser idling at the curb, three black dudes prancing and joking with a pair of white chicks so pale they might have been albinos.

Once upon a time I met an albino woman in Paris. The real Paris. She told me if I went back to I-rack, I would die. That's when I went AWOL.

Paris isn't a bad place to go AWOL. French women really

know how to screw. At least the ones I met. Eventually the military police caught up with me. But I didn't die on the sandblasted streets of Baghdad!

Just past the black and white party, someone had thrown up on the sidewalk. I stepped into the street to avoid the splatter. At the corner, light cascaded through the open door of a convenience store where a pair of Bangladeshi maidens with gold nose rings jabbered at each other in Bangladeshi gibberish.

The plain one, in native costume, stood behind the counter, next to the cash register. She probably had a sawed off shotgun stashed on the shelf beneath. The looker lounged in front, her elbows resting behind her on the countertop, her chest thrust forward. Beneath the edge of her cropped T-shirt, a rhinestone pin impaled her belly button. It shimmered like fool's gold in the florescent light. Her small, pointy breasts sang a siren's song, but I took a pass.

In America they should speak English. Just my opinion.

Across the street a sign announced OPEN in iridescent blue neon. I crossed over. Hand lettered in gold on the plate glass window it read: Antiques, Curios and Curiosa. A magenta velvet curtain drawn across the window on the inside blocked out any view of the interior.

Having nothing better to do, I entered.

Just inside, a couple stood gazing into a glass display case.

"Sheee-it! No way!" The guy pointed at something in the display. "How'd they ever prove that? Probably a souvenir some guy brought back from Afghanistan."

The girlfriend glanced over his shoulder as the bell suspended above the door announced my arrival. Obviously she didn't like what she saw, because she turned back quickly and tugged at her boyfriend's arm. "This place is creepy. Let's get out of here," I heard her whisper. They turned and filed past me out the door.

I surveyed the room, which had glass cabinets down one side and shelves of books and bric-a-brac along the other.

The center area was taken up with oddments of heavy antique sideboards, uncomfortable looking Victorian settees and love seats and ornate marble topped tables of various shapes and sizes. At the very back of the store, an oldster sat at a desk, examining a trinket through a jeweler's loupe.

He set down the loupe and looked at me. Longish white hair in need of a trim, goatee (also white), thin, sly lips. Heavy black-framed glasses hung on an Eastern European nose suggested an unsuccessful writer of pulp fiction. The spice and week-old, dead-squirrel tang of expensive cigars overhung the room.

"Just looking," I said.

He shrugged. "Look, look. It doesn't cost anything." He turned back to the bauble.

I glanced into the glass cabinet that had intrigued the couple.

A human finger, ravaged by time, rested in an open tin box lined in stained white satin. The skin of the finger had the texture of brittle, yellowed wax paper, as if it had been smoke-cured. The nail was long and black. Tiny hairs protruded from the finger joints. The end where it had been severed from the hand was sewn closed with dark, waxy thread. A typed index card read:

Poncho Villa's right middle finger.
Removed at the time of his assassination
on July 20, 1923, and preserved as a
keepsake by his illegitimate son,
Octavio Villa Coss, until his death in 1960.

What a crock.

Still, it was a pretty interesting scam. It probably even came with an affidavit, sworn to under the pains and penalties of perjury, confirming with names and dates a chain of custody from 1923 to now. I wondered whose finger it really was.

Losing it must have hurt like a son of a bitch.

I threaded my way through the clutter of furniture to the bookcase along the far wall. Most of the volumes were bound in crumbling leather. Selecting one at random, I opened it to the title page.

The Moral Dilemmas of a Courtesan of the Court of Louis XVI.

The etching opposite showed a bosomy woman in a voluminous dress lying across an ancient four-poster bed. The lower half of the dress was pushed up to facilitate a huge, hugely-hung mastiff intent upon mounting her.

Also interesting, though not my cup of tea.

The book looked old as shit. But I wondered if it was as fake as the finger.

I eased it back into its space and meandered along the bookcase, bending down to read the titles on the spines:

Possums and Pudenda: a Tale of the Deep South.
Confessions of an Ordinary Woman on Her Way to the Bottom.

Maybe I should buy a book for Jane, a little gift for saving my life. A piece of oddball erotica would appeal to her sense of humor, not to mention her horniness.

Perversions Galore sounded like it might fit the bill.

"How much are the books?" I asked the owner, who, as I approached him down the line of bookcases, was now studying a glossy catalogue.

He leaned back in his chair, took up a fat, stumpy cigar and, removing the cellophane wrapper, ran the dildo shaped object back and forth beneath his nose, sniffing deeply.

"They're all first editions," he said. "Hard to find. One of kind."

He licked the end of the cigar, fitting it between his lips. Then held the cigar aloft between two fingers. His gestures were so formulaic of the cigar aficionado preparing for the lighting ceremony, I had an urge to dig in my pockets for a pack of matches, though I knew I didn't have any.

"Which one were you interested in?"

At that moment the bell above the entrance jangled wildly. We both turned in that direction.

Two biker punks burst through the door. The tall, lanky one who came in first wore a stars and stripes pirate head rag and a sleeveless leather vest showcasing a menagerie of tats that spiraled up and down each arm and across his bare chest. The other, blue jean clad, rolled in behind, dark, squat and menacing. The hobnails of his storm trooper boots sent sparks flying from the tile floor. Greasy shoulder-length hair and scraggly beards recalled escaped mental patients.

They moved quickly to one of the glass cases near the door. The squat, Neanderthal raised a two-foot section of steel rebar above his head and brought it crashing down on the glass display. The countertop disintegrated in an explosion of noise and shimmering glass insects.

Quick as a wink the drug-gaunt half of the pair reached forward and scooped up a shiny, oblong object from within the shattered case. At the same instant a yowl of pain burst from his lips. He staggered, grasping at his wrist. A glass shard still lodged in the cabinet frame had enacted sweet revenge on the thief's withdrawing arm.

Adrenalin flashed like black powder under my skin and along my nerve endings. Just like in the old days back in I-rack when some Al-Qaeda wannabes hiding in a pile of rubble opened up on my patrol, I was instantly geared up to go. In those days I would chase the motherfucking ragheads all the way to the banks of the Euphrates to mete out a death sentence. Tonight I was ready to do the same.

"Don't fucking move!" I shouted.

But the smash and grab artists weren't listening. They had already about faced and fled.

I took off after them like a bat after a couple of lowlife insects. Passing the destroyed display cabinet, my shoes skittered over broken glass. I slammed through the exit into the night street. Thick humid air ripe with the rot of tropical vegetation, dog poop and the salt of the sea smacked me in the face. In the sudden absence of light, for several seconds I couldn't see.

As my vision cleared, I looked left, then right.

The pair had split up, one heading south, his fat legs pumping, his boots ringing out a steel tattoo on the cement sidewalk. The tall, wasted mother-raper hotfooted it in the opposite direction.

Which one?

I picked the stunted, roly-poly as my target, figuring he couldn't run as fast, and took off after him at full sprint. My pace devoured the distance between us.

At some point he heard me coming and glanced over his shoulder, terror and malevolence vying for dominance in his bulging eyes. He knew if he didn't do something drastic, in another few seconds I would bring him down, slam his face into the cement until it turned to beef carpaccio.

Desperate, oblivious to all risks, the fat biker veered sideways into the street, crossed two lanes of traffic, bounded over the median planted with dwarf palmettos and burst into the oncoming northbound lanes.

At that exact moment, a northbound city bus, empty, its destination display bearing the words Out of Service, came out of nowhere, moving at an excessive rate of speed under the bleary-eyed control of a driver who'd had enough for one day.

SLAM!

The overweight desperado sailed twenty feet through the air into a recycling bin, cans and plastic bottles exploding in all directions. Reaching the crumpled figure, I held two fingers to his neck.

D.O.A.

Seconds ticked by as I squatted, watching the broken body, waiting for some evidence that there was something more besides the flesh that dies. But no soul, no incorporeal essence, only the stink of excrement, rose from the dead.

I frisked him down but found nothing resembling the stolen curio, whatever the fuck it was. A comb, eight dollars and a pawn ticket in a wallet chained to a belt loop, a ratty rabbit's foot that clearly had not lived up to its promise and an evil clasp knife, suitable for gutting large, upright animals.

As a crowd gathered, I turned away and loped northward. There was still a chance the other thief might have stopped running, figuring he was in the clear at the expense of his partner.

When I passed the antiques, collectibles, curiosa and retro-porn store, there were no cop cars parked in front, no officers taking notes, no technicians photographing the crime scene. I figured the owner wanted to keep a low profile without a bunch of coppers sniffing around.

Maybe some of his merchandise was hot. Maybe he sold snuff films. Whatever.

Still bent upon finding the second perp, I hustled on up the street, glancing into every bar, tattoo parlor, sub shop, pool hall or other late night haunt. Now that I was trying to go straight in my own life, I was outraged at the depravity of two scumbags preying on a hardworking small businessman.

Just as I concluded I was shit out of luck in finding the other quarry, there he sat, perched on a stool in a Cuban sandwich shop, chatting up a plump waitress with the mint-green dyed hair and matching lip gloss of an urban zombie. The thief didn't notice me standing outside, so I put my face up close to the floor-to-ceiling window panel and tapped on the glass. I pressed my nose and lips against the glass and made a face. The face of doom.

The waitress' eyes did a double take. The thug twisted sideways, his brow scrunched.

"Smile, asshole," I mouthed. "It's your turn to die."

Shock and awe vied with panic in the grifter's eyes. Next instant he catapulted over the counter and disappeared through the doorway leading to the kitchen. In a flash I followed. In the kitchen a Hispanic youth, languidly working on a pile of dirty dishes, pointed to the still vibrating metal door that opened onto an alley.

"Gracias," I said.

"De nada."

I blundered into the reeking alley, stopped, listened. To the right footfalls echoed in the narrow space between two rows of buildings. Turning in that direction, I began to jog. With each passing second my pace increased, passing trash bins and dumpsters with the speed of a juggernaut. Blitzkrieg.

The alley emptied into a side street. To the right I caught a fleeting image of my quarry, just as his turned the corner back onto the main drag. I followed, redoubling my pace, my lungs starting to burn.

Once more on the well-lit main artery, Mr. Shitbag was less then a block ahead. His head jerked sideways, assessing my position, doing the math that said I would soon close the distance and take him down.

Next instant, he vanished.

The point of his disembodiment was the entrance to a multilevel parking garage. He had gone to ground, hoping somehow he could hide in the deep shadows until I gave up or passed him by.

I moved up the incline of the garage, searching around and beneath each parked car for out of synch shadows. With each switchback, the number of cars grew fewer and fewer. On the third floor there were less than a dozen vehicles scattered here and there like abandoned chess pieces.

Had I missed him on the way up?

Down on the street the roar of a motorcycle splintered the night. Then faded away, until once again the dark city was filled with the illusion of silence.

A leather sole scraped on cement! A door sighed open and closed.

The stairwell!

I was there in an instant, listening to the echo of his steps. He had gone up, not down.

What a dumbass.

The next floor was the top. Only one car. A very expensive Mercedes parked across three spaces in the center of the lot.

Where had my bad guy gotten to?

Bending down, I looked under the Mercedes. All clear. Quiet as a cat burglar in my All Stars, I circled the perimeter of the parking deck, occasionally easing myself up onto the barrier wall to look over the edge. It was a long way down.

On the third side of the quad, I found him, clinging to a narrow outside ledge, head bent in supplication.

"Hey," I said, smiling down at him.

He startled. Lost his balance. Flailed. At the last moment I leaned over and grabbed the top of his leather vest, pulling him back from the abyss. His hands clawed at the vertical cement surface, searching for a grip.

"Give it back to me if you want to live," I said.

It was an offer he couldn't refuse.

"It's in my backpack."

Straddling the low wall, I let go of his vest, grabbed the backpack's straps hung over one shoulder, pulled it free and held it up and away. He looked at me with the maimed eyes of an addict, awash with faint hope and horror.

I swung my foot back, then hard forward, catching him in the side of his head.

Uuuuh!

The force of my kick pitched him sideways. His fingernails rasped on raw cement. Unmoored, airborne, he plummeted head first to the earth four floors below, first in slow motion and then at the speed of light. THUD. Permanent brain damage.

From above I observed him for a while, but he didn't move. Nor, as best as I could tell, did his soul take wing.

*

When I reentered the high-priced junk and curiosa shop, the owner was sitting at the desk again, reading a retro skin mag.

Someone had swept up the broken glass and taped box cardboard, savagely cut with a mat knife, over the shattered display, using blue duct tape. I walked up to the proprietor's desk

"We're closed," said the owner, licking an index finger before employing it to flick over the next page of the nudie magazine.

I pulled the oblong golden ingot from the backpack.

"Here's your gold bullion," I said.

"It's fake," he said.

Why wasn't I surprised? I set the fake gold bar on the edge of the desk.

The owner closed the magazine and affixed me with a pondering gaze, as if I were an enigma beyond his wildest imagination.

"You wouldn't perchance be interested in some part-time employment?" he said. His European accent was obvious now. English as a second language.

Then I thought, MONEY. The money I needed to head down to Mexico. The money to hunt down Aunt Ida in her vampire lair and drive a stake through her heart. The money to sniff out the spoor droppings of sweet Edie to see if we had a chance in hell of starting over.

"How much does it pay?" I said.

6

While The Captain was still high on me for rescuing his beloved, not believing for one instant that the sweetly perverted stoner Jane Ryder could have fired the shot that saved Suki from the horrors of Deets' psychopathic dick, I got him to agree I could reduce my days at Rothman's to Mondays, Tuesdays and Wednesdays. We made these revisions as I ironed my shirt for the daily grind and The Captain, back from Tallahassee, sipped a café mocha.

This was the first time I'd seen him in weeks. He was almost never around. I figured he had something going on the side. That's why Suki drank so much.

Thursday, Friday and Saturday evenings I took a job as head of security at Lee's Antiques, Curios and Curiosa. In fact, I was the security.

There was me and there was Lee Kiev, the owner. Lee was very specific about the job:

"No guns, no knives, no blackjacks, no brass knuckles. No crossbows, samurai swords or tire irons. If you need to get rough with some...some dickwad, as you say in America, take him outside and trash him in the alley. One look at you should scare the bejesus out of most would be ganiffs. But there will always be a few shlimazels who just don't get it the first time." He was referring to my square jaw line, iron gray eyes and skulking, fuck-with-me-at-your-own-risk demeanor.

"You must be kidding?" I said. "Unarmed I could

get myself killed. Read the papers. Listen to the late night news. The psychos today are a new breed; willing to take out an entire shopping mall just to get back at one person. Willing to put you and me out of our misery for a twenty-five cent knick-knack. I've got a beauty of a Taurus .38 caliber semi-automatic. Can't be traced to me. Perfect for security work."

"I'm not interested in listening to your k'vetshing. The offer stands as I described it. Your compensation is a hundred and fifty dollars a night, performance review after three months. The hours are six to midnight Thursday, Friday and Saturday. There will be no weapons on the premises and no in-store violence. Your title is Director of Security. Take it or discard it."

"You mean, Take it or leave it."

"Whatever I said."

"Fine," I said. "I'll take it."

"Mazel tov!" said Lee, clapping me on the shoulder.

He poured two shot glasses of Slivovitz and we tossed them back. I figured in six months I'd have enough cash to blow off Compass House and Lee Kiev, and head down to Mexico to dish out some payback to that fuck Aunt Ida. Maybe take up with Edie again. Or not.

The bonus of working the night shift, it kept me away from Jane Ryder and her kinky carnal impulses.

No more strip poker in the lounge. No more semi-nude relay races up and down the stairs, the back hall and around the kitchen table, with Suki and Graydon as the opposing team, if Suki was rip-roaring drunk enough to throw caution to the wind. No more streaking on a dare down to Jorge's for beef jerky and lime and chili-flavored pork rinds on Friday nights after we'd smoked a bowl or two.

Sundays, of course, we had Jesus and Sodom & Gomorrah with Deacon Dobbs.

With my new work schedule, for the most part Jane was shit out of luck.

*

"Jeez, Bill, you're no fun any more," said Jane, standing tall and full-bodied and starkly naked in the doorway of my room. Her thistly blond bush confronted me at eye level, as I lay sprawled on my bed reading The Rough Guide to Mexico. It was the Sunday night following my first tour of duty at Lee Kiev's.

Jane had just come out of the bath. Water droplets cascaded down her pinkish flesh, forming a puddle on the hardwood floor, dripped from the pointy tips of her maroon nipples and the bottom of her narrow, childish chin. She dragged a towel between her legs with ardor, bent to wipe the moisture from her thighs and calves, her ample breasts diving forward like a pair of hairless, bungee-jumping, albino rabbits.

It was too much. My dick rose up like a cobra responding to the seductive notes wafting from the flute of an East Indian snake charmer.

Jane rolled her eyes.

"I'm on the rag," she said, ruffling the towel through her hair.

"Doesn't bother me."

"Well, it bothers me. I'm the one that's bleeding. And I get awful cramps. Besides, tomorrow's a workday. I have to be at the soup kitchen by seven a.m."

"And here you are," I said, "loitering shamelessly in my doorway, making a wanton spectacle of yourself. You could just as easily be lollygagging over here in my bed."

"I'll admit this set up is making me just the teensy-weensy-est bit horny. But if I give in to my base desires after you blew me off for the last three nights in favor of your new, hotshot security job, I'd totally lose face around here. Next thing, Graydon what's his name will be knocking at my knickers. Besides, if I fucked you now, I'd end up hot and sweaty all over again."

"Afterward I'll let you play with my Taurus," I offered.

A lean and hungry look suffused Jane's puss.

"That would be an offer a girl can't refuse."

She made a bounding leap for my bed. At the last possible moment I reached up and flicked the toggle switch extinguishing the overhead light, plunging us into a yowling darkness of flesh and filigree, as wan moonlight trickled through the lace curtains Suki had hung in my window.

*

Thus, another week passed by. And another after that. Life had a way of just rolling on like some big, fat, greasy, chocolate milk-colored river flowing to the sea. If you didn't watch out, you might fall in and drown.

One day a lawyer's letter came addressed to The Captain. Margaret Menendez had remembered us in her will. Her Jeep Wrangler now belonged to Compass House. No one was allowed to use it except for official Compass House business approved by Suki. But now we could go to the mall or Home Depot for stuff we needed around the place without taking two different buses. It was all good in the hood. Thanks Marge.

Nothing much happened at the curio shop. I'd arrive around sixish to find a new stack of wooden crates and DHL international express packages in the back by Lee's desk. During the first hour of my shift, I helped Lee unwrap the newly arrived merchandise.

Soon enough, customers began drifting in. Gents of various builds and hues in expensive suits, pastel shirts and Fendi shades. Lanky blondes in leather. Oil sheiks rigged out in flowing white robes and elaborate keffiyah headgear. Aging movie stars in Hollywood Babylon dresses and wide-brimmed hats, their sad eyes hidden by gossamer veils. Even an occasional Italian mobster in gaudy pinstripes and a white tie or a singing cowboy sporting illegal rhino-hide boots and a fringed buckskin jacket.

Some stepped singly through the front door, announced

by the clanging bell, where they stood surveying the room before being glad-handed by Lee. Others arrived in spit-polished black limos or armor-plated Mercedes, surrounded by their entourages of hip-hop thugs, courtesans, court jesters, dwarves and assorted camp followers.

Since the night of the smash & grab of the fake gold bullion, there had been little trouble. A woman Lee met on Match.com wrote him a bad check for a bad copy of a poster for a 1923 all-nude Parisian review. I caught another gal in the restroom getting off on one of Lee's volumes of erotica: *The Golden Chains of Lust by Rasputin*. She was having too much fun. And making too much noise.

She was just hitting the high C notes when I kicked open the door. Her dreamy eyes looked up at me as though I might have been part of her fantasy. Casually as hell she pulled up her thong, wrestling it into place, then her wide, white pantaloons. Tucking her breasts back into her bra, she strode past me to the front door and out into the evening streets washed clean by a recent tropical downpour.

Lee deducted the cost of a new bathroom door lock from my pay.

Those were the high points. Mostly I leaned against the wall next to a bust of Sappho, cleaning my nails with a metal nail file and trying not to nod off.

Lee was doing a land office business. The gold bar I retrieved from the incompetent smash & grab artists may have been fake, but Lee had plenty of real ones stashed in a safe in the back for those neo-con throwbacks who wanted to return to the gold standard. But most of Lee's clients were collectors of the curious, the odd and the outright bizarre.

A pair of lacey maroon undies worn by Madonna at a private concert-cum-orgy held in a flat overlooking the rue Mouffetard in the 5th arrondissement, an ivory strap-on dildo used by Martha Gellhorn for mutual gratification with the "great writer," Teddy Roosevelt's Masonic pinky ring, a clipping from Allen Ginsberg's beard purported to have been snipped by Yoko Ono while giving the legendary poet a handjob in an East Village stairwell, and on and on and on. Each item came with impeccable provenance. And an outrageous price tag.

Meanwhile, I was racking up my own wad of C-notes, hiding them under a loose floorboard in my room.

Working Friday and Saturday nights meant I cut back on my drinking too. Which saved even more dough. Not to mention extending the useful life of my liver.

My plans to head down to sombrero land were really starting to gel.

*

It was Tuesday at Rothman's and my supervisor slash overseer Blanche Garcia was celebrating her birthday. Turning fifty for the eighth time.

"We're going out for a few drinks after work," she said. "You should come."

Her tight French sailor's top (navy and white stripes) accentuated her female proclivities (tits), as did the sleek, tropical-green-leather skirt (ass). She had painted her mouth fire hydrant red and looked surprisingly like an able bodied seaman in drag.

I was jumpy as shit. It's weird when your boss is hitting on you, especially when you're an ex-con on parole and the slightest screw-up can ratchet you back in the slammer. During the workday whenever we passed by each other in the chiaroscuro of the stockroom, either Blanche's metallic glitter nail extensions pinched my butt cheek or her moveable crotch purred against my leg like a randy kitty cat. These predatory advances weren't something you made up for your own amusement or self-esteem.

I hoped I wasn't doing that—making this shit up.

When I called her on it, a who? me? smile flitted across her red lips amid a flash of gold-capped teeth.

Blanche was the hottest supervisor I'd ever had. But she was fifty-eight.

"Who else is going?" I said.

"Oh, you know, Larry from shoes and my friend Laura who works at CVS."

Laura, to whom Blanche introduced me at lunch one day, had earned a black belt in Tae Kwan Do. I hadn't asked her out.

"Hey, Bill. Don't be a dried up old pussy. You've gotta come out for a few pops on my B-day. Besides, Laura promised me she'd blow you under the table."

Now Blanche was making shit up.

"OK," I said. "I'll come. But just for one or two drinks."

"Fabulous!"

I noticed Blanche's nipples were erect. Perhaps now was the very moment to test the waters of her desire.

"It's time for my break," I said, rolling my eyes in the direction of the shadowy stockroom.

Blanche didn't take the bait, instead adjusting her D-cup brassiere and striding toward a customer examining the display of Cuisinart appliances. Cock tease.

I took the elevator down to the first floor and exited through the bronze doors to the street. The four o'clock sun beat down between the buildings like the truncheon of a Nazi death camp guard. On the shady side of the avenue, I stopped at a little Cuban place, where I often went on break to sip an iced coffee on the street and watch the long legs and short skirts of lust saunter by.

Back at work the final two hours were as endless as waves lapping against a pier. My last customer of the day insisted upon taking her new Oreck vacuum out of its box to make sure it wasn't defective. Now I was trying to cram it back into the same fucking box. For some reason it wouldn't fit.

Blanche and Larry (from shoes) hovered. Blanche tapped her wristwatch. Larry pretended he was jerking off, his hand ratcheting back and forth in front of his fly. The customer looked up from reading the Oreck handbook and frowned.

I tossed aside a piece of molded Styrofoam I couldn't

seem to fit anywhere, slammed the vacuum into its box and taped it shut. The plastic shipping tape screeched from its dispenser like a frog in the act of having its throat cut.

"Enjoy your new vacuum cleaner, Mrs. Gomez. The store is closed now. If you have any further questions, I'll be happy to answer them in the morning."

*

The first place we hit was the Yellow Monkey. A cousin of Blanche's worked there and was sure to give us a free round of Jägermeister shots.

Turned out he was home with two broken legs, the result of a past due debt. We ordered a round of Miller High Life and left soon after.

Next up was Wild About Hairy, a notorious dyke bar where none of the barmaids shaved under their arms, and a few sported facial hair. The clientele affected similar hairy pits. It was a weird turn-on. As if they each had three crotches.

More than I could handle, except on a really good day.

Larry and I were the odd men out. But after a couple of vodka rocks, I didn't really give a shit. Some of the lezzies hanging around in skimpy outfits and playing pool were very hot tamales. Aunt Ida came to mind.

Laura was telling me about what a drag it was working at CVS because one of her managers kept groping her in the candy aisle. I nodded in sympathy. Though I'd never worked at CVS or Walgreens, there'd been plenty of homeboys and perverted country preachers at Oopawalla who wanted a piece of my ass. After I broke a few heads, they kept their distance.

Across the table Blanche and Larry were deep into a discussion of women's designer shoes.

The cute lesbian barmaid Ariadne stood before me, hands folded atop her platinum buzz cut, each exposed armpit a snarl of black steel wool. The lemon and garlic scent wafting from those hairy regions was enough to knock your socks off, if I'd been wearing any. A wave of desire swept over me to bury my nose in one of those raunchy underarms, asphyxiate in the depths of that hairy apex.

I felt suddenly faint, about to capsize. It must have been the booze on an empty stomach. My eyes rolled upward, the scene grew fuzzy, out of focus. When I got a grip and my eyes refocused, I found myself staring at Ariadne's pale, perversely pert breasts barely held in check by a linen camisole. A tatted bouquet of blue and pink cornflowers spilled across her chest. The image of a hummingbird fluttered above one nipple like an exotic birthmark.

It was funny how it all worked. Chromosomes and hormones, pulsing nerve endings and tactile sensations, holes and things that went into holes.

"Don't get any ideas," said Ariadne with a fetching smile. She glanced down at my empty glass. "You want another?"

"Are we going another round?" I asked Blanche, tapping her on the arm. Blanche and Laura were deep in conversation, Blanche whispering romantic nonsense in her ear.

"Nah, this place blows," said Larry rather too loudly. "Let's go over to Club Risqué."

A couple of dark-eyed dykes at the bar shot him the finger.

Now Blanche and Laura were kissing. It was Aunt Ida and Edie déjà vu. I could deal with anything but that. I was ready to bail and said so.

"I'm really tired. Think I'll catch the bus back to Compass House and get some rest."

Larry put his arm around my shoulder. "Come on, Bill. You've got to check out Club Risqué. A dancer there can smoke a menthol cigarette with her pussy. Most amazing thing I've ever seen."

Obviously Larry wasn't much of a world traveler.

Blanche and Laura chimed in. "Don't be a party pooper. It's not even ten o'clock," said Laura. "Just come for an hour," said Blanche "Then we'll go for Chinese steamed buns, fried wontons and egg foo young."

I relented.

Who could forgo steamy female buns jiggling in your face followed by steamed buns stuffed with barbecue-flavored cha siu pork?

*

Club Risqué was hopping with pervs, lawyers, pussy hounds, stockbrokers, frat boys and gangsters, to name but a few. After Blanche slipped her a twenty, a topless hostess with rouged nipples showed us to a table to the left of the stage. On stage a pair of silicone-stacked redheads jumped and jived to Howlin Wolf's "Back Door Man." The music segued into a Stones tune.

The club was a low-ceilinged, grotto-like space whose fake stone walls were reminiscent of early Flintstones. A tracery of tiny projected lights darted and swirled like swarming insects across a metallic ceiling, changing color from green to orange to purple, then red, blue, yellow and back to green again.

Rows of tables rose in tiers away from the stage. Amid them topless waitresses, tricked out in faux leopard skin miniskirts and pillbox hats, wended their way with bored indifference. A bar with high stools fronted the stage for those pussy aficionados who wanted a close-up view of the club's offering of female privates.

Above tonight's smattering of aficionados, the two redheads now pranced about entirely nude. One of them squatted provocatively, her thighs as thick as those of a clay earth goddess from a bronze-age tomb. All this and more seemed strangely tedious, infusing the night with melancholy. I wondered why I had agreed to come to this palace of twisted pleasures. As usual I was just along for the ride.

Blanche had ordered champagne. It arrived in a flurry of

activity, along with several dishes of premium nuts and the double Stoli I'd insisted upon. The ice-cold vodka anesthetized my tongue, leaving behind a sharp, medicinal aftertaste that brought to mind hospital corridors late at night.

A comedian dressed as a clown and sporting a huge codpiece stuffed with fake dick took center stage, walked back and forth telling ribald one-liners. The crowd guffawed and hooted. After a few minutes a giant hook appeared from the side of the stage and the clown pretended to be yanked off into the wings. More laughter.

Tired, bored, tipsy, I was more than ready to split the scene. I gazed anywhere but at the stage; watched with disinterest the rouge-nippled hostess seat a group of raucous businessmen at the next table. Tried to count the number of leopard-print attired waitresses working the crowd. Felt Larry's sharp elbow jam into my side. Heard Elton John's "Rocket Man" soar from the sound system.

"Check out these ones," Larry said, grabbing my arm.

If comedy was a smiling dwarf decked out in pointed slippers and a funny hat with bells, tragedy was that same dwarf held upside down by his feet and plunged head first into a toilet bowl until he stopped breathing.

When, compelled by Larry's lusty enthusiasm, I looked up at the stage, I became that second dwarf, the dwarf of nightmare. My lungs burned like hellfire, as if someone had jerked open my mouth and fired a blowtorch down my throat. A street thug's jackboot buried itself in my gut. Drool dripped from my slack lips.

On stage two beautiful young women went from slow motion commotion to wild abandon, their firm breasts and lithe figures moving like stripper angels. One blonde. One brunette. One a total stranger. The other answering to the name Mary Beth.

As "Rocket Man" rose to a crescendo before fading into the endless distance of outer space, the two dancers threw off the last bits of their shimmery interstellar costumes, embraced, kissed, swept away, turned and plunged to their knees to slide stark naked to the edge of the stage. Wild applause.

I ripped my eyes away, but I had looked down the Devil's maw and seen beautiful darkness. Bent double, I dashed for the exit, brushing past the jaded hostess, the tepid waitresses, the rebar-hard Latino bouncers, to hit the pavement as every ounce of booze and whatever else I had drunk or chewed and swallowed in the last several hours exploded into the gutter. But the one thing I could never rid myself of was the image of Mary Beth on that stage shamelessly and utterly naked.

How could this be? How had Edie's and my daughter metamorphosed from sweet youth into a sex trade worker?

I had screwed up big time! Abandoning my daughter in her innocent teenage years to the laws of the jungle. As a parent I was rotten to the core, a total fuckup, a washout.

Or maybe it was a genetic thing. Twisted chromosomes handed down like dirty photographs from my backwoods hooker mom and my embezzler dad combined with Edie's perverted sexual urges inherited from who knew where.

No! If blame was to be affixed to anyone for Mary Beth's downfall, it belonged to Aunt Ida! It was she who had lured Mary Beth's mother and I into a get rich quick scheme that had gone sour. Following which, she had skipped town, her promiscuous hand thrust down Edie's undies. Aunt Ida's promise to Edie of hot sex in the torrid zone had set a disastrous example for Mary Beth at the moment of her abandonment.

Clutching these and other recriminations to my chest, I fled into the night.

The next day I called in sick to Rothman's.

I couldn't get out of bed.

Around 3 o'clock Jane, wearing not much of anything, looked in on me. She sniffed. "It stinks in here," she said. "And you look like warmed over shit."

I took another slug from the half empty bottle of Stoli.

"I could care less what you think," I said.

"Sweet talk will get you nowhere. I only fuck men who abuse me."

"Come over here so I can bite your ass."

"I beg your pardon?"

"OK, then how about an Indian burn?"

"You need to find yourself another girlfriend," Jane said. "One who revels in pain and humiliation."

What I really wanted to do was bury my face in Jane's cleavage and let the hot tears of my deep despair flow down her wayward flesh. But there was no way I could tell her that. Our relationship was still majorly in flux. Sometimes it felt like nothing more substantial then dandelion seeds cast on the wind.

"Drink?" I held out the bottle.

"Gee whiz, Bill. Do you have any ice?"

"Do I look like I've got ice?"

Jane held up two hands, making the sign of the cross with her index fingers. "I'm outa here," she said. "I'm getting my hair washed and blow dried. Suki's doing it."

I returned to my Stoli.

"Have fun slitting your wrists," said Jane.

Her bloated face, due to some kind of salt retention issue, disappeared from view. I listened to the thumping and squeaking as she bounded down the old wooden stairs.

At a little before midnight I borrowed Marge Menendez's olive drab Wrangler, drove into Miami and I parked just up the block from Club Risqué.

We weren't supposed to use the Jeep at night. Just for running errands and shit during daylight hours. The nights were a time for personal prayer and meditation, nude romps and the like. Not for getting into trouble with roving Hispanic gangs in hot cars looking to kick some gringo butt.

But tonight everyone knew my fan had hit some serious shit.

Sitting parked across the street, watching the putas and other night detritus slither and slide up and down the sidewalk in front of Club Risqué, my mind was a void. I had no plan. No idea what I was going to do. But that was Mary Beth, my daughter, up there on the stage shedding her clothes, shaking her tits, spreading her legs for all the world to see.

I had to do something.

It was midweek, so the street action was slow. A few limos came and went dropping off or picking up various thugs and business types and their arm candy. A clutch of shit-faced, strung-out bikers quarreled like wild dogs over a pointless broad. One ended up with his head cleft open by a swung chain. The rest split in a roar of Harleys before the cops and an ambulance arrived. One of the bouncers slipped the lead cop some dough to skip writing up a police report.

At three a.m. the marquee went dark and the last of the clientele spewed forth.

I hung deep in the shadows of the alley that ran down one side of the building housing Club Risqué and watched Mary Beth emerge from the employee entrance and slide into the front seat of a big, smooth, cream-colored BMW with midnight tinted windows and custom aluminum wheels. At least a hundred grand's worth of sleek, Nazi roadster.

Jesus! Not only had my only daughter taken up stripping as a profession but it appeared she had become the chattel and sex slave of a pimp drug dealer. Or a drug dealer pimp.

After the passenger door closed behind Mary Beth with a resonant heavy-metal thud, the Bavarian Motor Works extravaganza idled in place with the satisfied purr of an overfed house cat.

Perhaps Mary Beth was prattling on to her pimp boyfriend about all the excitement of her shift at Club Risqué. Of maybe the bastard was mounting her to take his pleasure before hitting the road for some after hours club! Anger exploded inside me. My fist slammed against the exposed brick of the alley wall. Blood oozed from savaged knuckles.

But whatever the delay, it gave me the chance to scurry

back to the Jeep. When the BMW emerged like a stealth predator from the alley and turned up the street, I followed.

We crossed the causeway into Miami Beach and turned north along the Intracoastal, overlooked by blank-faced apartment towers. Only a few obviously sinister cars cruised the streets at that hour, so I held back as far as I could without losing the taillights of the BMW.

The geography changed to individual homes, some of them vast looming piles in the darkness. Ahead the BMW's lights flickered, then disappeared. I hit the gas hard.

At the point marked by a phallic palm against a charcoal sky where I estimated my quarry had slipped away, a side road went off to the right, hugging a canal. I took the road's curves too fast, my tires screeching in pain.

Suddenly ahead the Beamer's taillights flashed brightly. Seconds later I passed a modern two-story white cubical structure. In front of it the BMW was parked behind a slatted metal gate that cast shadows like prison bars. Dread burrowed through my brain like a flesh-eating insect.

A few hundred yards beyond, I parked in a shadowy cul-de-sac and walked back to the house belonging to Mary Beth's mobster pimp. On the opposite side of the street, an insomniac walked his ever-patient dog at four in the fucking morning. We avoided eye contact.

Observing no signs of an alarm system linked to the metal fence separating the house from the street, as soon as the dog walker faded into the night, I hoisted myself up and over. The first floor of the house was a blank wall of stucco, except for the orange rectangle of the front door. In the flat surface of the door, a peephole squinted. Above, a pair of second story windows stared fixedly into the outer darkness like the white orbs of a corpse.

I imagined Mary Beth looking out through the peephole and seeing me standing there, my face in shadow. Her breath catching with fear. Then a wave of contradictory emotions flooding her mind and body, as she recognized my profile.

An impenetrable stand of bamboo blocked access to the

narrow space between the house and a stuccoed cinderblock wall running down the left side of the property. An identical wall enclosed the property on the other side. Along the tops of both, razor wire glinted in starlight. Walls, a metal fence and gate, high windows. A mini-Oopawalla. Suddenly afraid, I shook from head to toe, gripped by a flashback of malarial auge. I recalled I had first contracted the disease while vacationing on the Red Sea with three Bedouin whores. Or was that a fake memory?

On the right a black rectangle between the wall and the side of the house marked a passageway to the back. I hurried down the path, gravel crunching underfoot. In the pitch blackness thorny vines caught at my flesh. Blood dripped from my eyebrow to the corner of my mouth. My tongue licked it hungrily; tasted salt and sweetness. I was definitely out for blood tonight.

The side pathway opened onto a cement deck area and the undulating surface of a pool made visible by light pouring from the house. Beyond was the canal and the silhouette of a motor launch. On the far side of the waterway, an apartment block loomed.

The adrenalin sprinting through my arteries flipped me back in time and place to a perilous night raid on a jihadist safe house in some remote I-rackie village.

Moving now as slowly as a tree sloth, I crept among the shadows cast by several palms and other plantings along the side of the deck and pool until I could see into the two-story, plate-glass-fronted living area that took up the rear of the house. The usual white leather furniture, a large abstract painting in reds, blues and yellows against a white wall. An interior balcony with a light wood railing overlooked the high-ceilinged room. Light streamed from a heavy, oddly out of place, Spanish-style chandelier.

Amid this expensive southern living, my eyes riveted on the man standing in the middle of the room less than a half-dozen feet away, fiddling with his stupid smart-phone. Expensively finished Euro-style slacks and shirt looked custom-made for his six-foot, wiry frame. Heavy beard stubble past its prime, a thin, off center nose and slicked back, obviously-dyed black hair gave the appearance of a GQ model who had gone over to the dark side of thuggery and bad acts.

Dialing a number, he walked through an open sliding glass door onto the deck area, cell phone held to his ear, eyes downcast.

In a fury I bounded toward him, fist raised to strike him down with a blow to the temple. At the sound of my sneakers spitting a trail of gravel, he pivoted.

It was that animalistic reaction to an unnatural sound that saved him. My fist missed him entirely. I stumbled, compensating wildly for the empty air my sucker punch had found instead of flesh and bone, but my shoulder caught his right side, sending the cell phone flying through the air, drawing forth a grunt of pain from my adversary. As my momentum carried me past him, he swung around and leaped on me from behind, a fist pounding repeatedly into my gut. But it was a fist weakened by the damage wrought by our collision.

Bending in half, I reached up and behind, locking both arms around his neck. With a great heave, I flipped him over me onto the ground. Somehow he managed to break free enough to hit the cement in a forward roll rather than cracking his head, as I had hoped.

In a flash I was on him. We thrashed from side to side, punching wildly. My teeth found his ear. When I bit down, he screamed.

Then something hard as metal struck the side of my head and I plummeted down an exploding tube of light into a place as black as a pool of Maracaibo heavy crude.

When consciousness returned, I gazed blearily into an unblinking Cyclopean eye of death. A large-caliber handgun was pointed immodestly at my face. My hands and arms were trussed behind my back.

"What the fuck are you doing here, Dad?"

The words were like a brutal slap to the face.

As my vision cleared, beyond the black hole of the gun barrel, the image of a fallen angel appeared. Mary Beth's guileless, peach-complexioned face, twisted now with anger, disbelief and a little sadness, stared at me with ironic menace.

"You're supposed to be in prison."

"They paroled me a couple of months ago."

"But how did you get here? How the fuck did you find me?"

She shook her head back and forth, as if trying to clear away a haze of disbelief at the sudden turn of the night's events.

We were inside the house, in the trendy living space with its buku-bucks accoutrements, where I lay flat on my back on a two-inch thick white carpet. The curtains had been drawn, cutting off the view of the patio and pool area. Through the second story of glass, the dirty dishwater gray of early morning had washed away the night sky. My head pounded like a pile driver on fast forward.

"I'm sorry," I said.

"It's too late," she said. "I'm over you and Mom and what you did to Ben and me. You can't come back now. I won't have it!" She stamped her foot.

"I'll make it up to you," I said. "I promise. Whatever it takes."

"You can't do that. You're a fuckup. You'll always be a fuckup. I've got a life now. I make a good living. I'm even happy sometimes."

"As a stripper?" Despite my best efforts, I spat the words out like ejecting a poison.

"Yes," she said. "As a stripper. I'm good at it. Men fall down and grovel in the dust at my feet."

"You don't have to live like this," I said. "You don't have to waste your life supporting some fancy man's coke habit."

Mary Beth laughed. "You mean my stockbroker husband whom you nearly beat the shit out of? The one who buys me diamonds and rooms at the Ritz?"

Somehow I didn't believe he was a stockbroker or her husband.

Behind her eyes danger flashed like heat lightning.

"I should shoot you in the back of the head and dump you in the canal. No one would even notice. Just another dead ex-con. And at least I would know you were out of my life for good."

Suddenly I was afraid. As if I was locked in a room with no exit. A pump was rapidly and inexorably sucking the air out of the room until soon I would be unable to breathe. I began to hyperventilate like some asthmatic clown.

Mary Beth leaned down and slapped me hard across the face.

"Stop it!" she commanded.

I stopped wheezing.

"I'm going to give you one more chance, Dad. I want you to go. Leave town right away. Go far, far away and never come back. Do you understand?"

I blinked in disbelief. This wasn't how it was supposed to be. I was here to rescue my only daughter from her life in hell. Instead I had found my own hell.

I glanced frantically this way and that, hoping that some magician or shaman would appear and with a wave of his hand make the nightmare disappear like morning fog burned away by the sun. It was then that I saw Ben standing on the balcony overlooking the living room. Last time I had seen him, he was a little boy of eleven. Now he was sixteen, almost a man. I had no doubt that he had heard and seen everything that had passed between Mary Beth and me. I wanted to wave to him, offer a salutation. But he turned away and disappeared down a darkened passageway to the interior of the house.

When I looked again at Mary Beth, her eyes were as cold as those of a murderer. Her lips moved but I could barely hear her.

"Do you understand?" she repeated.

I nodded.

"If you do come back," she said, "I'll kill you."

7

Was it possible to be emotionally devastated and scared shitless at the same time? The answer was yes! I was there.

I don't remember leaving Mary Beth's or how I got back to Compass House. I was a zombie on autopilot. A physical and psychological wreck ready to be compacted into a square of crushed metal and shipped to the recycling plant.

In my room I couldn't stop shaking. I took a swig of vodka and it tore up my insides as if I'd swallowed battery acid. Rushing into the bathroom, I emptied my stomach and the rest of the bottle of liquor down the sink.

My one and only daughter, Mary Beth, had cast me out. Had told me to take a flying fuck.

Okay, it was true that Edie and I had left her and Ben in the lurch back when we fell under Aunt Ida's spell. I acknowledged that. But the past was the past.

I had followed Mary Beth home from Club Risqué with the best intentions of rescuing her from a life of sex slavery and degradation. But, like much in life, best intentions didn't amount to a hill of beans. Mary Beth had declared a fatwa banishing me to wander in the desert like the Hebrews of old, a death sentence on my head if I ever showed my face again in Miami.

After I dumped the vodka, I found a little weed that Jane had hidden in my sock drawer. I rolled a doobie and smoked it with rapidity, jogged down an empty beach of dreams into oblivion and slept until noon.

When I awoke, I knew I had to get out fast. The idea of languishing in Miami feeling sorry for myself and thereby pissing off Mary Beth made me as nervous as a coyote in suburbia. She probably knew guys who would do a hit dirt cheap.

Over the next several days I bought a one-way ticket to Mexico City, counted my cash (which didn't add up to as much as I'd hoped) and made some necessary purchases for the trip.

At Compass House I rebuffed every attempt by Jane to draw me into the sack.

"I've got a killer headache," I said.

"I'm not in the mood."

"I'm utterly exhausted."

"I'm burned out on fucking."

"I think I might be impotent."

"I'm a little high strung at the moment."

"I just can't get it up any more."

"I think I might be gay."

"Indications are I've caught a dose of the syph."

"Fuck you, Bill," said Jane. "You didn't get it from me."

She stomped out of my room. A half hour later when I headed out to work at Lee Kiev's, I heard Jane in the kitchen still complaining bitterly to Suki. I didn't have the heart to tell her straight out that I was dumping her.

Saturday night, my last night at Lee's, was dead. Maybe two customers meandered in, poked around perfunctorily and left. At ten o'clock Lee locked the door, fired up a fresh Cohiba and broke out the bottle of Slivovitz. We clinked glasses.

"L'chaim."

"L'chaim."

We drank.

"I'm resigning," I said. "This is my last day."

"Thanks for letting me know."

"Don't mention it."

"Ah, well. Nothing lasts forever." Lee paused

120

fatalistically. "Maybe I can get my nephew to fill in temporarily. His grandfather worked for Meyer Lansky." Lee raised his Cohiba-free hand ceilingward as part of a deep shrug. "So…you got a better offer somewhere else?"

He took a long puff on the cigar, leaned back and blew a chain of smoke rings toward the ceiling, one eye cocked inquiringly in my direction.

"Not exactly," I said. "I'm heading down to Mexico City to take care of some unfinished business that's been chafing my ass."

"Mexico, eh?"

His index finger tapped his Cohiba above a crystal ashtray around whose circumference bronze satyrs and nymphs cavorted in various obscene tableaus. An inch of white ash separated from the end of the cigar and, in slow motion, tumbled to the surface of the ashtray, where it shattered into moon dust. Leaning forward Lee poured another round of Slivovitz.

"You wouldn't perchance be interested, while you're down there, in picking something up for me."

"Why don't you just have it shipped?"

"It's a very delicate situation. The owner is an eccentric recluse. I have an agent in Mexico pursuing the matter. But I'm worried that he might blow it. He's not the most subtle businessman."

I wasn't sure I qualified as subtle myself. Or that I was much of a businessman.

"What is it?" I asked.

"What is what?

"The thing you want me to bring back."

"A suitcase."

"A suitcase? Okay, that's cool. And what's in the f-ing suitcase that requires this special handling?"

"I'm not sure."

"This is totally weird, Lee. You're asking me to find some recluse, somewhere in Mexico, talk him into handing over a suitcase full of something or other, you're not sure what, and bring it back to you.

"And what about the fine folks at U.S. Customs? What if they want a little peek inside and there are chopped up human remains or some other crazy shit I can't even begin to imagine?"

"Okay, okay. It was just a thought. I figured maybe you could use a little extra cash while you're down there taking care of that ass-vexing problem. But forget about it. I don't want to add to your stress."

"How much were you thinking of?" I said way too quickly.

"Oh. Maybe a five-thousand-dollar cash advance." Lee looked at the fingernails of his cigarless hand. Polished them against the front of his shirt. He knew he had me. "And another ten upon delivery."

Lee had just set the barbed hook in the corner of my mouth. And unlike most fish, I knew there was nowhere to run.

"Come on, Lee, at least give me some background on the provenance of this mysterious suitcase," I said.

"It belonged to William Burroughs. He left it behind as collateral for payment of a debt. He lived in Mexico City from 1949 to 1952 but left shortly after shooting his common law wife."

"He shot his wife…"

"The story goes they were playing some kind of William Tell game. You remember, the guy who shot an apple off his son's head using a crossbow. In Burroughs' case it was a highball glass on his wife's head and he was using a .38 revolver. Burroughs missed the glass. The only problem was the bullet pierced his wife's brain instead."

"Jesus."

"Some lawyer finagled a deal for Burroughs. Death by inadvertence. Something like that. He had to leave Mexico ASAP. But he had incurred certain debts while there. The suitcase was his guarantee of repayment."

"You must have some idea what's in the suitcase."

"I told you," said Lee vehemently. "I have no idea whatsoever. But since it was accepted as collateral, there must be something of value."

"Or maybe señor Burroughs was a good bullshitter," I said. I flashed Lee a toothy grin. "And, of course, you've got a client on pins and needles."

"Yes, a client who collects Beat memorabilia."

"I'm sure he comes in his shorts every time he thinks about opening that suitcase."

"I wouldn't put it exactly that way."

"But he will pay through the nose."

"In a manner of speaking."

I sighed deeply.

"So where do I pick up this suitcase?"

"A little village in the middle of the Yucatan called Boca del Diablo. By car it's a couple of hours south of Mérida, the state capital. There are a half-dozen flights a day from Ciudad de Mexico to Mérida. When you're finished with your Mexico City business, just hop down to the Yucatan, pick up the suitcase and catch a direct flight back to Miami from Cancun. For you, I'll even throw in the price of the plane tickets."

"It's an interesting offer. But..."

"But? What do you mean 'But?' There aren't any better ones waiting in the wings, my friend."

"It's like this: I'm trying to catch up with my wife. She disappeared into Mexico five years ago with her lover. The trail's ice cold. If you knew somebody that could help me out."

"That's it?" Lee reached over with one hand and squeezed my shoulder. "No problemo. My agent has more connections than the head trader at a Cayman Islands' hedge fund. I'll just give him a heads up. By the time your plane touches down in Ciudad de Mexico, he'll have your spouse and her current lover on high-resolution videotape, as well as a list of what they had for breakfast, lunch and dinner. Just bring me the fucking suitcase."

This was the second time Lee Kiev made me an offer I couldn't refuse.

*

Sailor, though the lightning flashes
Though thy sails be rent and torn
Peace shall come on Hope's bright pinions,
And deliverance with the morn.

Sailor, though the darkness gathers,
Though the cold waves surge and moan,
Trust thy bark to God's great mercy
Falter not; sail on, sail on.

The off-key jumble of voices in the lounge trailed off like the sound from an old timey record player that had been unplugged by a drunk stumbling over the electric cord. Deacon Dobbs, resplendent in a starched white shirt bright enough to blind a beggar, surveyed with a jaundiced eye the ragtag band of masturbators and miscreants before him. Standing behind a lectern at the entrance to the Compass House lounge, he blocked any attempt by the congregants to slip away, even for a smoke or a piss.

Tomorrow I would be gone. No more lost Sundays with Deacon Dobbs.

I coughed into my hand. Suddenly feeling a sentimental twinge of lust, I reached over and squeezed Jane Ryder's thigh through the watery rayon of her slinky dress. My fingers tiptoed beneath the fabric, found her quim and toyed with it. My fingertips grew wet as her breathing thickened. Desperately she slapped my hand away.

Deacon Dobbs cleared his throat with a deep rasping sound just short of the hawk and spit of a two-pack-a-day smoker. His saurian gaze circled the room, counting the heads, checking to see if anyone had passed out or fallen asleep.

Besides Jane and Graydon and me, another eight souls were vanned in every Sunday from another halfway house. Lucky bastards.

"Sinners!" boomed Deacon Dobbs. "We are all sailors on a vast and hostile sea. The sea of life. But if we kiss the ass of our Lord Jesus, we will come safely to the shores of Paradise where lusty maidens will feed us figs and honey."

Heads perked up at the mention of lusty maidens. As usual Deacon Dobbs was a little off-kilter in his approach to Jesus. I wondered what Jane thought about the prospect of being fed figs and honey by lusty maidens. Whether she would prefer well-hung lads.

There was a restlessness in the room. We were into the third and final hour of the Sunday service before lunch was served.

This week it was spaghetti and meatballs. The tang of the tomato sauce for our Pentecostal repast drifted in from the kitchen.

"Let me tell you a story," said Deacon Dobbs. "A true story."

He paused for effect.

We waited, bored, hungry, horny.

"Several years ago here in Miami, a black man named Count Ezekiel killed another of his kind in a bar fight. Beat him to death with his bare hands. The victim had made suggestive remarks to Ezekiel's teenage daughter. And she ratted on him."

Again heads perked up. Everyone had a vision in their mind's eye of that heavy-breasted, dark-chocolate-skinned, sultry, underage beauty.

"A family man, Ezekiel had no criminal record. He easily made bail. His church congregation took up a collection for the bondsman's fee. God fearing, everyone figured he was a low flight risk.

"But the fear of imprisonment wormed its way into Ezekiel's soul, my friends, just as evil burrows into the souls of each of you!" Deacon Dobbs was becoming wrought up.

His eyes shimmied. His bottom lip shook "Brothers and sisters, I can smell the evil in this room. It stinks to high heaven." His raised hands motioned upward. "Rise up!"

We stood.

"Sing halleluiah to your Lord Jesus Christ," urged Dobbs. "His name is like the sting of birch switches that will drive out the evil in you, drive it out with fury. Sing hallelujah!"

"Hallelujah," we said.

"I can't hear you."

"Hallelujah," we said louder.

"Better. Now sit down and take heed, God damn it, while I finish the story.

"Driven wild by his fear, Ezekiel jumped bail and headed for Texas and the Mexican border. At that time I worked under contract for Manny's Bail Bonds. They were on the hook if Ezekiel didn't show for trial. My instructions were to bring him back dead or alive.

"When I got word he had been seen eating deep-fried grouper in a Port Aransas seafood joint, I flew into Harlingen to get ahead of him. Ezekiel's favorite niece lived in a pissant border town called Spanish Crossing. I figured Ezekiel was heading there, before disappearing into Mexico's Sierra back country.

"Spanish Crossing had one main street. Along its reach were a pair of fleabag hotels, a cut-rate whorehouse, five titty bars and three regular ones, and the usual complement of souvenir shops and pawn emporiums.

"Taking a room at the Paradise Hotel, I walked the length of Spanish Crossing's main drag handing out photographs of Ezekiel with twenty-dollar bills. It was August. The thermometer was pushing a hundred and ten in the shade.

"Back at the Paradise, I sat at a card table in the lobby, dealt out a hand of patience and waited. Jesus urges us to have patience. I felt Him sitting close at hand in one of the sagging lobby chairs, reading a newspaper and smoking, as if He had all the time in the world."

A congregant in the back of the lounge started to saw

wood. "Bullshit," someone said in a loud whisper. A raspberry-sounding explosion of flatulence echoed around the room. Deacon Dobbs looked perturbed. After a moment, he continued.

"On the third day word came to me that Ezekiel had taken a room at the Brazos, Spanish Crossing's other hotel. The addict minding the Brazos' front desk told me he was in room 213. When I kicked in the door, Ezekiel, naked as the day he was born, leaped from the bed. A ceiling fan barely disturbed the stifling air.

"'Get down on your knees, brother,' I said, pointing my Colt .45 in his face. Shaking, Ezekiel fell to his knees. 'Don't kill me, mister,' he begged. 'Who is Lord?' I demanded. 'Sweet Jesus is Lord,' said Ezekiel, sweat pouring down his face. 'And are you sorry for killing that man?' 'Yes, I am sorry,' wailed Ezekiel. 'Then there will be a place for you in heaven,' I said and shot him dead. There was no point in taking the chance Ezekiel might turn me around on the way back to Miami."

The room hung in a dead hush. Deacon Dobbs raised his hands above us in an ecumenical gesture.

"Brothers and sisters, now you know that even murderers, if they acknowledge Jesus, may enter the kingdom of heaven. So too may your sorry-assed souls be saved if you accept Him in your hearts. Amen."

A smattering of "Amens" arose from the motley crew, followed by a cacophony of scraping chairs and a rustling rising up of bodies, as everyone thrust toward the lounge exit and the waiting spaghetti and meatballs.

I stayed seated, deeply shaken by the vision of Ezekiel lying dead in a pool of blood in that cheap hotel room, the side of his head blown off. My stomach lurched like a tramp freighter in a typhoon. A chill ran up my spine. I imaged some coked-up pistolero, for a few hundred pesos, shooting me stone dead on some dusty, generic Mexican street, cutting off my ear as proof of my demise.

And what of Deacon Dobbs? Who knew he was a

bounty hunter? A killer for Jesus? It was possible, even likely, that Dobbsie himself would come after me in Mexico, hunt me down like a dog and murder me while I lay snoring in some Mexican flophouse, dreaming of wanton women. I had been under his tutelage and rehabilitation, and my flight represented utter failure on his part.

With Mary Beth on one hand and Deacon Dobbs on the other, I was between a rock and a hard place.

"Are you okay?" It was Jane. Leaning close, her red-nailed hand made a grab for my crotch, giving it a convivial squeeze. Preoccupied with doubt and indecision, I behaved as if nothing had happened.

"Don't tell me," she said. "Captain winky's on the fritz."

"More than you know," I mumbled.

"Let's go to your place and you can tell sister Jane all about it."

Stepping into the front hall, we found the last of Dobbs' flock waiting impatiently in line to dive into Suki's meatballs and garlic toast.

Ignoring the food line, Jane bounded up the stairs to the second floor. She stopped halfway and, with a saturnalian twinkle in her eye, unzipped and let her dress fall around her ankles. Her snow white buns, like twin moons rising in the twilight of some alien world in a galaxy far, far away, cast their blinding reflection on my concupiscent soul. With a squeal of impending delight, Jane shot up the remaining steps.

Ensconced in my room with the dresser dragged in front of the door, we faced each other across my unmade bed. The room sizzled, redolent with the molecules of lust. I dropped trou. My prong, hard as the Hope diamond, quivered with pent-up yearning.

Jane held up a hand in remonstrance.

"Before we proceed, I have a question."

I was in no mood for obstructionism.

"Not now," I said.

"Yes, now!" said Jane, holding up an oblong object the

size and thickness of a business envelope. "I want to know what the fuck's going on here!"

It was, of course, my one-way Aeromexico ticket to Mexico City. The departure date was tomorrow at the crack of dawn.

I considered throwing another fit about Jane's wanton breach of my privacy, rummaging around in my room while I was absent, but decided it wouldn't play well under the circumstances.

"I was going to tell you later today."

"Fuck you, Bill. You were planning to slip away like a thief in the night."

"It's not like that. You know I've got a hard-on for those two bitches that left me to take the fall for the guns and ammo show job. It's time for them to pay the piper."

"And what about me."

"I didn't want to drag you into it."

"Ahhh. How sweet. Bill doesn't want to drag his fuck buddy into it."

"Plus, if you came along, I'd be worrying about you all the time."

"Who was it put Deets in the cooler?" Jane demanded. "And another question: How's your Spanish?"

"What are you talking about?"

"You need me along for the ride because I speak Mexican like a fucking native. Lived there for ten years with my sorry-assed excuse for a husband Niles, where he worked at some feckless job at the Canadian embassy. Without me you'll never catch up with your precious Edie or the evil queen of S&M, Aunt Ida." Jane folded her arms triumphantly beneath her wayward knockers, thrusting them forward in all their lactational immensity. "Oh, and any part of the loot we recover we split fifty-fifty."

I'd been avoiding the dead obvious fact that mostly they spoke Spanish in Mexico. But now that was unavoidable. To get a line on Edie and Aunt Ida in old Mexico, I had to communicate in the local lingo.

Which was not in the cards for yours truly. I had as much linguistic ability as a dead cat. I could barely order a beer and a taco in a Mexican restaurant.

"How would this work exactly?" I asked.

"You take me with you or I rat you out to Deacon Dobbs."

"That's pretty cold," I said.

"It's a simple digital decision, Bill. A one or a zero."

Why was Jane blackmailing me? Why was she so determined to accompany me to Mexico? After almost six years there wasn't a chance in hell that Edie and Aunt Ida still had any of the loot from the guns and ammo show heist. Tracking them down was strictly motivated by my desire for revenge. And my relationship with Jane was mostly a matter of convenience and opportunity. But maybe, just maybe, Jane was scared shitless of being left behind at Compass House.

One thing I knew for sure. If I didn't cave, she would make good on her threat to add me to Deacon Dobbs' shit list.

A few moments later, I lay on my back on the bed, as Jane, straddling me on her knees, stuffed my prong up her prong hole and began to rock forward and back.

As I rode the wave of pleasure toward ejaculation, I vaguely wondered just how fucked up this Mexico trip was going to be. But then I stopped thinking about that and thought instead only about the sap rising in my dick. After that, it was only a matter of time.

*

It was pitch dark at four a.m., when Jane and I, each carrying a canvas sports bag stuffed to the gills with our worldly possessions, slipped out of Compass House like thieves in the night. We hurried up the street, keeping an eye out for a cruising late night cab.

An hour later we stumbled blearily down the aisle to our

seats on the Aeromexico Boeing 737 bound for Mexico City. I stashed my bag and then Jane's in the overhead compartment. Taking respectively seats A and B of our designated row, we buckled in.

Outside it was still night. Exhausted, I closed my eyes and fell into a fitful doze.

Next came the manly voice of the pilot over the PA system: "Flight attendants, prepare for takeoff."

The huge plane shuddered as it turned onto the runway and began to pick up speed, rumbling down the line in the fleeting late darkness, shivering to its very core as the metal behemoth struggled to shed its earthbound existence.

Jane's hand rested atop mine.

"Everything's going to be just fine," she said, as the 737 made its final thrusting leap skyward and, like a giant winged cock, burst into the dawn's early light.

Part III

Running Through the Jungle

1

Heading south! At last!

I sighed deeply. All those wasted weeks in Miami. But in the end I had broken free. No more Suki Wa crying hysterically in the kitchen because The Captain was AWOL and she had no sex life besides being ogled by Graydon. No more Deacon Dobbs and his cult of bounty hunters for Christ. And most importantly, no more murderous threats from my progeny. Mary Beth was over 18. She was on her own.

I was exhilarated, flying high. If I had been of the Muslim persuasion, I might have prostrated myself in the airplane's aisle facing more or less in the direction of Mecca and given thanks. After which, I would have been pounded to a pulp by a mob of my fellow passengers. Instead, I pulled the Aeromexico in-flight magazine from the seat pocket in front of me and flipped through it. All the articles were in Spanish.

I jammed the magazine back in the pouch and looked at Jane. She was hunched sideways against the window, eyes closed.

A sloe-eyed, olive-skinned flight attendance of stunning beauty and heavy hips rolled down the aisle pushing the refreshments cart.

I gave her a big smile. "Hi."

"Buenos dias."

Stupidly I imagined her saying: 'Coffee, tea or me?'

"Something to drink?"

"Double Jack and Coke," I said, smiling into her eyes, followed by: "Will you join me?" God, I was such an asshole.

But she poured two drinks. We agreed to meet later on in the galley.

For Spanish lessons.

I sipped my Jack & Coke. The flight attendant, whose name was Muriel, pushed the cart rearward, sipping hers. I turned my head, gazed upon her miraculous, aft-bound ass.

Beside me, Jane snorted and shifted her position. She looked cold, so I dug her

Everlast sweatshirt out of her sports duffel and draped it over her slumped form. Then headed for the back of the plane.

Two flight attendants sat, one on either side of the rear galley, gossiping, their hands in wild motion. The one I hadn't met looked like Jean Seberg in Breathless. I'm sure she would have been a fantastic fuck. But I was sort of committed to the one with the oily black curls falling to her shoulders and the owl-like black-framed glasses that she hadn't been wearing earlier. On further study I noticed her nose was thin and sharp. An unmistakable pencil mustache graced her upper lip. Had I made a mistake?

"Could I get another Jack & Coke? Por favor?" I stumbled over the 'por favor?.'

She looked at me with the coy lust of a slightly overweight gecko on a whitewashed wall eying a jittery June bug.

The movie star one ran her hand up the inside of my leg as far as it would go.

By the time she stood, blouse falling open, and thrust the dark tit of her breast in my mouth, my zipper was down, my cock consumed by the ebony-curled one. I thought of Jane. You snooze, you lose.

A sharp pain penetrated pitch darkness. My eyes opened. I had no idea where I was. Then I remembered. I was in the middle seat of row 19 on a jet plane bound for Mexico City.

Jane's finger fiercely poked me in the ribs.

"What!"

"We're landing."

The plane tilted. It had, as usual, been all a dream.

I looked past Jane. Beyond the scratched plastic of the tiny oblong porthole, yellow smog obscured distant mountains, enveloped serpent's tail-like a cluster of tall buildings nearer at hand.

As the topography of an endless city swirled below, something menacing swirled in my intestines. Somewhere I'd read about Americans getting the runs when they first arrived in Mexico. Montezuma's revenge it was called. Foreign microbes borne in the air, on the money passed from hand to hand.

Somehow I had contracted the interstitial illness in advance of arrival in Olde Mexico. Surely it was the piña colada and ham & cheese empanadas I scarfed down as we ran through the Miami Airport, plus the in-flight Jack and Cokes and little sleep. Regardless of provenance, it felt like my lower plumbing was on the verge of a core meltdown.

"Excuse me," I said, vaulting over the lap of the surprised aisle seat passenger. I scurried pell-mell to the back of the plane, where two flight attendants were already strapped into their fold-down seats.

"Senor, you must return to your seat immediately. The plane is in its final approach for landing," ordered my sloe-eyed, black-haired beauty. She gestured fiercely. But I was already inside the narrow confines of the unisex shitter, the bi-fold door closing behind me. With one hand I slammed the door lock to, the other fumbling with belt buckle, snap and zipper. Blue jeans and nylon skivvies around my ankles, I stumbled backwards over the shit hole. As the plane surged, my intestines exploded.

When I came up for air, someone was pounding on the bathroom door. "You must return to your seat!"

But I was lost amid the writhing chaos of my bowels.

I rode the shitter down until, with a shuddering skid, the

737 hit the tarmac and the roar of the reversed engines shook me out of my miasmic funk.

When I emerged from the lavatory, my fantasy flight attendant gave me an angry look. I had violated flight procedures. Refused to obey instructions. Put her job at risk. But for the moment at least my bowels were in a quiescent state. As I dropped back into my middle seat, Jane looked up from the Erica Jong novel she was reading. Fear of Flying.

"What happened to you?"

Before I could reply, the seatbelt sign pinged off and everyone leaped up, grabbed their bags and made a mad rush for the exit.

In the third world, where there is never enough to go around, life is all about bolting for the exit at the first burst of gunfire.

2.

Against all odds I was in Mexico City, standing in the middle of a teeming, roiling airport scene, otherworldly, alien, terrifying, with no f-ing idea where I was going or what was to become of me.

Everywhere I looked, eyes watched. Black, shining Indian eyes sizing me up as a likely mark, a gringo chump who'd just fallen off the turnip truck. Walnut-brown Conquistador eyes bright with blood lust. Ice-blue European interloper eyes filled with the Old World of the Holocaust and Freudian perversion. Federal cop eyes brimming with underpaid anger and corruption.

I thought about turning around and running back onto the plane.

"Come on," said Jane, pulling on my arm. "We need to find a ride into town."

"I need to piss," I said.

In the men's room I looked in the mirror. Who the fuck was that?

The face on the other side morphed into my father, in all his droll Atlanta lawyerlyness. From a time before that day when he stuck a shotgun in his mouth and blew the top of his head off. Since he was dead, we'd had more of a relationship than ever existed when he was alive and kicking, with his urbane courtroom manner and white-collar sleazebag clients. The brilliant, charming, obsequious Jew lawyer who had no time in his work or social schedule for a son.

In our afterlife relationship he annoyingly showed up at the most inopportune times. Who wants to have a conversation with a ghost in a crowded, smelly men's room in Mexico City's International Airport? His laconic gaze caused me to glance away. "Shit, Billy, look at you. The American samurai. What a fucking joke."

"Thanks for your support, Dad."

"Don't mention it. Word of advice: keep your eye on the money. I'm sure those two cunts are up to something down here, some devilish, high-stakes scheme to pay for their Southern Living magazine habits."

"I've got it covered."

"Sure you do. And watch out for that Jane number. She's a puzzle. A regular Rubik's Cube. Such women are dangerous."

"She makes me nervous," I confessed. "But she's one fuck of a fuck."

"Took the words right out of my mouth," said Dad, with a knowing wink that would have made the Marquis de Sade blush.

Suspicion exploded in my brain. How the fuck did Dad know Jane was a great screw? How did he even know about Jane? Was he spying on me in the dead of night? Or was something more sinister afoot?

Before I could undertake the most preliminary cross-examination, Dad vanished in a flash of light.

The reflection of my eyes in the lake-like surface of the mirror, caught me out in momentary madness. Droplets of sweat beaded my forehead. I leaned down and splashed tepid water on my face.

When I came out of the bathroom, I couldn't see Jane anywhere. Had she dumped me? Not likely. As her meal ticket, I still had the upper hand.

Then perchance had she been arrested? Or abducted? After all, Mexico was a seriously dangerous place. Anything could happen.

My first twinge of concern quickly dissipated. If Jane had fallen into the hands of desperate characters, maybe it was for the best. Especially if she was somehow getting off with my old man's ghost. If you figure that one out, call me.

A more generic sense of fear and dread pervaded my consciousness. If I was abruptly on my own in one of the most dangerous countries in the world, where I couldn't even speak the local argot, what I needed to do was to get my hands on some ordnance ASAP. Both my Taurus and the .25 caliber toy pistol were a thousand miles away under a loose floorboard in my old room with the lace curtains and the bath down the hall. Suddenly, I was feeling just a tad nostalgic for Compass House in all its depraved fuckedupness.

Next instant, fingers tugged at my sleeve. I jerked around as if I had been stung. Or someone was trying to steal my Timex. Jane's lips grazed mine. They were dry.

"Where were you?" I demanded.

"There you are," she smiled. "You were gone forever. I thought you'd had another bout of the Aztec two-step, so I went to take a pee myself and find us a ride. Make haste, Billy bong. There's a gypsy cab idling at the curb."

"You know I hate it when you call me that."

She kissed me again. We mixed saliva.

Leaving the terminal, we were mobbed by a dozen cab drivers, real and fake, offering everything from the best price for an eight-ball of blow to an afternoon of unimaginable delight with someone's kid sister. Jane waved them away.

The transport she had arranged was a Ford SUV, its black paint faded to matte by the sun's relentless rays and the virulent acid of the very air. Its driver, a giant burrito-bellied lout sporting a sagebrush mustache, hulked over the steering wheel. His pink and green cowboy shirt with fake pearl snaps lent him the air of a Mexican extra in an old Gene Autry western.

"I take you downtown Zona Rosa. Good price." A grin as fat as a sunrise split his jib. Trust no one, I thought.

We sped into the yellow fog of an ozone-filled Mexico City morning.

Freeways twisted, merged and diverged like the tail of the feathered serpent god Quetzalcoatl. The roads were packed but the traffic moved with bewildering speed. Cars, vans and pickups of every vintage, motor coaches, delivery trucks and lumbering eighteen-wheelers swerved across multiple lanes, dancing around and through each other at dangerous rates of speed. We streaked past an endless backdrop of cheap modern buildings and crumbling adobe, festooned with incomprehensible signage and swirls of razor wire.

The window on the front passenger side, where I rode, was missing. The result of a break-in or some oddball accident, I had no idea. Leaning the other way, facing the back seat, I studied Jane. Her face was puffy from the dawn flight. She'd put on some weight in the past few weeks. Nerves.

She addressed the driver:

"So, Luis, you know the Hotel Sevastopol?"

His brow wrinkled, then he grinned. "Si. I theenk."

"We go there," Jane said.

"I thought you spoke fluent Spanish?" I said.

"Oh, right." She looked as Luis: "Llevanos allí rápidamente."

"Ask him if he knows where I can buy a gat," I said.

"Hey meester. What kind you lookeeng for?"

Jane's eyes flashed death and destruction in my direction.

"My husband is making a joke," she said. "Please just take us to the hotel." The driver's onyx eyes examined her fake smiling face in the rearview mirror.

"Bill, you're such a joker," she said, her hand reaching out and squeezing my arm where it rested on the front seat back. Her nails gnawed into my flesh. "People might get the wrong idea."

The driver veered the SUV onto an exit. Then slowed for a red traffic light ahead, the first I'd seen. Two exit lanes merged into a three-lane boulevard. A dark sedan jerked to a stop beside us, just slightly ahead, so the passenger window behind the driver was parallel with my window. I glanced vaguely in the direction of this new arrival.

And freaked out of my gourd!

My hands flailed in the air. My eyebrows hit the ceiling. My eyes grew round and glassy. The tongue in my mouth turned to lead.

Framed in the open passenger window of the other car, a man/boy with a long, narrow face and nerdy glasses pointed a black Luger pistol at my head. Somehow Aunt Ida had gotten wind of my travel plans! This was her welcome-to-Mexico gift!

After an infinity of time, my tongue finally moved. A stream of air burst from my lungs. "Look out! It's a shooter!"

The young man's eyes locked onto mine. An insane smile crept across his lips. He pulled the trigger.

A stream of water arched across the narrow distance separating the two vehicles and splashed on my face.

Then the traffic light turned green and the car with the water pistol assassin sped forward.

Luis started to snicker. The snicker became laughter. Lighter female hilarity filled the background.

As the water dripped down my face, the smell of warm urine flooded the interior of the SUV like an olfactory nightmare. I had pissed myself. Something I hadn't done since my first week in I-rack, when I missed my own death by a twist of fate as infinitesimal as a black, curly pubis plucked from an androgynous groin.

When I looked at Luis, he was no longer laughing. A last girlish giggle tittered from the back seat, crashed and burned.

"Well," said Jane. "You have to admit it seemed pretty funny at the moment."

A horn blared from behind. Luis gunned the engine and the SUV shot forward, merging into the boulevard traffic.

3

We were dead in the water in an urban neighborhood of three and four story buildings, trapped in one of those famous third world traffic jams.

Bored, I watched a lithe young woman in tight jeans and a yellow T-shirt bearing the word IMAGINE and a photograph of John Lennon in cool shades as she wolfed a breakfast taco at a street stand.

For some reason I imagined her naked, dressed in naught but sandals and the feathered crown of Xochiquetzal, Aztec goddess of lust and fertility. I'd been reading up on my Mexican mythology. Hot sauce dribbled down her chest. The mind boggled. I wanted to hand her a napkin. Workers, loiterers, students, poets, pervs and the like strutted, swaggered and strode past her without a second glance. Was there something in the Mexico City air that affected only one in a hundred thousand hombres, that one being me?

When my dark-haired beauty abruptly returned to being fully dressed and, taco vanquished, licked with her longish tongue the last drops of hot sauce from her strawberry-shaped lips, I sighed and turned my attention to the passing architecture. It was a random mix of modern rectangles of glass and steel and colonial mansions and public buildings of hewn stone carved with gothic filigree, saints and gargoyles or decorated with elaborate tile patterns. The stonework was stained and defaced by exhaust fumes and airborne acid, the tiles crazed and pitted.

Jane imploded my reverie.

"Jesus fucking Christ, Luis," she said. "Can't you get us out of this?"

"Eees morning rush our."

"No shit, Montezuma. But you're an f-ing cab driver. You must know some shortcuts, some back alleys. For an extra twenty bucks."

"How much is that in pesos?" I said.

Luis chewed on this for about two seconds, spit out the window with inimitable savoir faire, jacked the SUV onto the sidewalk and stomped the gas. The clot of morning pedestrians burst out of our path as if a suicide bomber had walked into the middle of a rugby scrum. Or a hammerhead shark had been teleported into a school of tuna.

At the next corner we took a hard right onto a cul-de-sac shaded by Mexican limes and eucalyptus trees. At its end resided a stucco building in the el Zorro style, painted a pale vagina pink. Across its plaster front a sign had been painted in an aubergine color: Hotel Sevastopol – Hourly Rates. Stopping the SUV across from the hotel entrance, Luis put the gearshift into park, flicked the ignition to off and flashed Jane his wide-assed grin.

We'd paid an extra twenty gringo dollars to go two blocks at a dangerous rate of speed. As Lee would have said: "Such a deal…"

On a bench in front of the hotel, a moderately zaftig thirty-something señora, clad in a skimpy avocado-green halter-top that could barely contain its enthusiasms and an even skimpier black leather mini-skirt, lolled as if she had all the time in the world. One mini-booted leg was raised onto the bench seat and thrust sideways. Her undies were a field of white splattered with red, orange, yellow, green, blue and purple polka dots like birdshot from a Remington shotgun.

On the other side of the entrance to the Sevastopol, an equally moderately zaftig, slightly over-the-hill gal in a black negligee leaned against the stucco wall smoking a filterless cigarette. Black braids were twisted and tied on her head in the manner of Frida Kahlo. Her lips and the toes of her bare feet were painted in pinot noir. Her mammary glands evinced the stylistic influence of an Aztec earth mother goddess.

When Jane dismounted from the back seat of the Ford, the earth mother goddess leaned her head farther back and gazed at Jane down her short, puggish nose.

"If you're here because of the obituary in last night's paper," she said, "the position's been filled."

I strode around the front of the SUV and surveyed the scene with hands on hips.

"You, on the other hand," she said, looking me up and down and emitting a low whistle, "are welcome here any time."

"We're checking in," I said.

The bench whore, without breaking her pose, cocked her head in the direction of the Sevastopol's dusky interior.

I entered the dimly lit lobby, which was about the size of a casket for Sidney Greenstreet.

An ancient wooden reception counter, no doubt from a tree long extinct, ran down one side. A blood-red glow rose from the depths of the wood, oiled and polished by the touch of countless hands. A pair of orange molded-plastic chairs and a green ceramic pot full of lipstick-stained cigarette butts and the withered trunk and fronds of a mummified palm tree hugged the opposite wall. A pair of not especially clean, wintergreen-colored women's panties had been left higgledy-piggledy on the seat of one of the chairs, as if someone had needed to make a quick getaway. Black and white images flickered across the screen of a tiny TV set suspended on a metal bracket in one corner. The sound was off. A payphone hung on the wall in the opposite corner.

No one was watching the TV. In fact, there was no one about.

Leaning on the countertop, I tapped the service bell. It rang with a clear, crystalline note.

Next to the service bell, some peckerwood named

Rodriguez had carved his name into the surface of the exotic wood. Where the counter met the wall at one side, a nudie calendar showing Miss February and her perky tits hung suspended on a rusty nail. The calendar was two years and four months out of synch with reality.

A bevel-edged mirror, its surface crazed and streaked, filled the wall behind the counter. For the most part I avoided looking at myself as I waited for someone to respond to the bell tone.

A small disturbance erupted behind me. When I glanced around, it was only Jane and Luis. Luis dropped our sports duffels next to the dead palm and waited while Jane counted out a slew of pesos.

"Muchas gracias, señora. I'll see you around," he said, folding the peso notes into one of the pockets of his cowboy shirt. He handed her a card. "Give me a call if you get bored and need someone to show you a good time. I know all the hot spots."

Of course he spoke in Spanish, so I had no idea what he really said to Jane. But the exchange of winks was disturbing.

As Luis departed, he scooped up the wintergreen panties, twirled them a couple of times on his index finger before stuffing them into his pocket.

Jane stood next to me. Glancing at the calendar image, she made a face.

"So," she said. "Where the fuck's the goddamn management?"

A shadow flitted on the periphery. When I turned back to the counter, instead of my ravaged face in the mirror, I was met by the deeply lined, jowly visage of a dissolute dwarf. Standing on an upended orange crate, he met my eyes with cold indifference.

His get up suggested he'd been in attendance at an all night party of some social significance. White, ruffled shirt unbuttoned at the neck, undone black bowtie dangling from one side of the collar. Striped tuxedo trousers held up by royal purple galluses. Gold cufflinks in the shape of miniature Aztec sun gods.

He grimaced as the blue smoke from a cigarette held between puce pulp fiction lips drifted inevitably into his eyes.

"Reservation for Derringer," I said.

"Ah, señor Derringer. We've been expecting you."

The dwarf eyeballed Jane, who, gnawing on a torn cuticle, leaned with her back against the reception counter.

"May I help you, miss?" he asked.

"I'm with Derringer."

"Of course you are." The dwarf looked at me. "There'll be an extra charge for two persons in the room."

A key with a bronze tag appeared on the countertop.

"You're on the second floor. A quiet room in the back. And here's a coupon for twenty percent off any of our adult services. I'll have your bags sent up."

Grabbing my arm, Jane jerked me toward the rear exit of the lobby.

"Come on," she said. "I'm desperate for a shower."

*

In the room I flopped on the bed, sending up a cloud of dust. A roach scuttled for cover.In one corner a sink was suspended, with a mirror above it. The toilet and a tile shower occupied a closet-sized bathroom. There was a bureau with one drawer missing and a utilitarian wooden chair. The only light was a frosted-glass ceiling fixture in which a quantity of fly carcasses lay scattered like dirty little thoughts.

Jane unbuttoned her blouse and tossed it on the chair. Standing in skirt and bra in front of the mirror, she appeared to examine a purple bruise staining her pale skin on her right side just above the bra cup. Then she grew utterly still, hands at her sides. Her eyes unfocused. Perhaps she was examining her bruised and wayward soul. After a few seconds her eyes blinked, refocused on her tawdry surroundings, returning to the here and now from wherever she'd been.

"This place is a fucking dump," she said.

"We're on a budget," I said.

"I can't believe your pal, Lee, booked us a room in a brothel."

"He thought I was traveling alone."

"Well, don't let me stand in your way. Feel free to have at it with those two ladies hanging around out front or with anyone else who strikes your fancy."

Jane unhooked her pale pink lacy brassiere. I gazed at the resulting phenomena with mixed emotions. Longing and apprehension. What was it about breasts exactly?

"I can't believe I'm back in Mexico," said Jane. "It's totally scary."

"You mean all the cartel violence?"

"No, stupid. My own past is coming at me like a tsunami. I lived here for ten years with my dingbat husband. If it weren't for him, I would never have gone to prison."

"Tell me about it," I said, my mind drifting back five and a half years to that moment when Aunt Ida stood naked and revealed in the backyard of her Orlando three-bedroom ranch. If only Edie and I and the kids had never gone to Orlando.

If only I had never been born.

"Niles was my ticket out of a dreary Toronto suburb," said Jane. "Except he turned out to be a complete drip. He was a born bureaucrat. All he did was work. Eighty hours a week behind a desk was nothing for him. Whenever I wanted to fool around, he would fall asleep. But he moved up the ranks and before I knew it, we were living in Mexico City."

Jane's skirt fell around her ankles. Then her panties.

I was between a rock and a hard place. Exhausted from being up most of the night before and plunging head first into the deep alien waters of Mexico. On the other hand Jane's rear end was truly an object of beauty, a concupiscent inspiration even in the dimness of a crummy hotel room at the Hotel Sevastopol in the dark heart of Mexico City.

"Go on," I said.

"Ten years flew by and the next thing I knew I was forty. My life was over. Then one weekend when Niles was back in Canada sucking up to his boss, I thought I'd found love again. He was a Russian artist. His name was Gregory Gregorovich. Like someone out of a Dostoyevsky novel. With a dick to die for." Jane looked wistful, even nostalgic.

"Spare me the genitalia details," I said.

Jane tore the paper wrapper off a tiny bar of soap and selected a mangy white towel from a stack on the dresser.

"Aren't you all sweaty and grimy?" she asked. "You'll feel so much better if you take a shower." She stepped into the tile shower and turned on the water. Somewhere a pipe groaned and shuddered.

"So, then what happened?" I asked.

"It was lust, not love. We lived together for a couple of months but it didn't pan out. He wanted me to work and support him while he painted. I said fuck that. Niles took me back. I hated him for doing that. A few months later Niles had to go to Miami on business. I went along. One night I wanted to go out dancing, but Niles refused. I pitched a fit. He said I was being childish. So I ran him over with the rental car. That was childish. Vehicular homicide they called it. I took a plea for seven years, out in four."

I watched her lather soap over her breasts and stomach. It looked like fun. "Need someone to scrub your back?" I asked as I shucked off my clothes.

As I stepped into the phone booth-sized shower, it occurred to me that I didn't much care for dancing either. As long as Jane and I were traveling together, I needed to avoid rental cars.

It wasn't that I was afraid of Jane. But her story, whether true or not, was a tad nerve-wracking. For once I wanted to try to stay ahead of the curve.

Jane's soapy hand encircled my hard-on. Then her vagina swooped down and gobbled it up and we were off and running.

4

When I slid the postcard from Aunt Ida out of my wallet where it had lain hidden, folded in half, the corners foxed and dog-eared from five and a half years of incarceration, my hands shook. Anger boiled inside. I was a desperate man in a desperate moment.

Beside me Jane slept on. From outside I could hear the city waking up like a dog-tired whore in need of a fix drawing her hands across her face and staring into the meaningless dawn.

Aunt Ida the she-Devil had stolen my dear sweet wife and the money. I had taken the fall. But unbeknownst to Aunt Ida, that postcard had been a wolf gnawing at my entrails for all those days and weeks and months, keeping the wounds she had wrought raw and festering, ensuring that revenge was writ large in my dreams.

Now I was in Mexico City. And it was payback time.

I eased out of bed as quiet as a fucking mouse, so as not to disturb Jane . In the bathroom, I pissed up a storm. But Jane just flopped over onto her stomach, the sheet scrunched around her ankles. I gazed in awe at her verbose, yet charming ass. It rose before me like an excerpt from a pornographic Jane Austin novel. From between her open legs her twat winked at me like a mystical third eye.

Finally I broke away and, hugging jeans, shoes, shirt and wallet to my chest, slipped out through the door and carefully pulled it closed. The lock fell in place with a click as loud as a gunshot at a presidential inauguration.

Tiptoeing downstairs, I dressed in a jiff, passed quickly through the abandoned lobby and stepped into the daylight of Calle del Gato Muerte. The whores were gone. Only a broken longneck in the gutter and a cache of cigarette butts testified to the baser elements of human need.

Across the way, an oddly familiar black SUV hugged a graffiti-scrawled wall, illustrating in purple haze and Day-Glo orange a Latino couple copulating with comic book abandon. The driver's door of the SUV opened, disgorging obese Luis.

"Señor Biiill. Buenos dias. I ope your sleeeep was as fooll of pleasure as mine. I dreeeamed of seven vergins who wanted to maaake my daaay. Are you a fan of Cleeent Eeeestwood?"

"I think you're mixing your metaphors," I said.

"What ees your agenda todaay, señor Biiill?"

"I need to see a restaurateur about a lesbian succubus."

"I wiiill drive you, no?"

"No."

"But señor Biiill, I know all the gooooood spots. And I want you to meeeet my siiister."

"Only if you stop talking like that. Jane said you told her you went to a prep school in Ohio."

"OK," said Luis. "My sister works in an espresso bar. We can go there now. She has a Glock you can look at. If you're interested, she'll sell it to you for a good price. It belonged to an ex-cop, as in dead."

I got into the front passenger seat. It smelled of beef tacos and beer. A colorful polyester Indian blanket covered the seat. Across it lay a machete in a tooled leather sheath. Luis, looking something like a giant beach ball in a gaudy striped shirt, climbed behind the wheel.

"I need to go to a restaurant in the Zona Rosa called Emilio's House of Schnitzel," I said.

"I've heard of it." Luis hit the gas.

Luis' sister was as skinny, skanky and high strung as a

Siamese cat on the rag. "This is Mona," said Luis. "Mona, Bill." She pranced in jittery steps among the half-occupied tables of the modernistic coffee bar and back and forth to the barista working his knobs and valves behind the counter.

As we sipped our café con leches, Mona returned bearing a grease-stained towel. Drawing close, too close, she folded back the edge of the towel to display the ominous outline of a modern handgun. I smelled her sweat. Her teeth nervously chewed on her lower lip.

Suddenly I began to shake with the jitters myself. What if Mona was an undercover cop with a yen for oral sex. When I forked over the money, might she point the Glock at me and order me to get down on my knees. It was much too early in the day to engage in non-consensual cunnilingus. Or was Aunt Ida setting me up again? A vision loomed of Federales, armed to the teeth, swarming down upon us as I leaned in to make the buy.

I downed the rest of my coffee, burning my tongue.

"I can't do this now," I said. "I need to get to that address in the Zona Rose."

"This is the Zona Rosa," said Luis. "The restaurant you mentioned is just around the corner."

Mona looked pissed.

Luis looked nervous. Worried perhaps that Mona might put a couple of slugs in my gut just because I'd gotten her all hopped up about a sale for nothing.

"Gotta go," I said.

I was halfway down the block before Luis caught up.

We turned a corner onto a quiet side street of expensive shops, boutique offices and trendy restaurants in two and three-story modern buildings set side by side. A canopy of palms and broadleaf trees cast a cool shade over this vein of wealth and privilege.

Midway down the block, where Emilio's Casa de Schnitzel should have been, the burned out hulk of a building lay in contorted annihilation. Twisted rebar, charred beams, piles of shattered bricks and cement, the empty metal frame of a window staring at nothing. The ruins had lain undisturbed for a long while, for several scrub trees had taken root amid the carnage, while spray-painted graffiti covered the cement block firewalls separating the ruins from the buildings on either side.

My heart stopped. My gut churned.

"No!" I wailed, falling to my knees. "This can't be how it ends."

"Now I remember," said Luis "There was a fire here a couple of years back. A Molotov cocktail thrown through the front window. The newspapers said it was a vendetta carried out by one of the cartels. Now the property is tied up in insurance litigation."

Luis pulled me back to my feet. Together we staggered across the street, where I collapsed at the shaded sidewalk table of a wine bodega.

A gay-looking waiter sporting a monocle and a waxed mustache, and dressed in a blue and white striped French sailor's tunic, appeared and asked if we would like to order a bottle of wine.

"Why not," I said.

For the rest of the day I sat there, drinking rotgut red and brooding over this latest twist of fate, my eyes roaming the ruins for some sign, some cabalistic message telling me what to do now. Occasionally I used the bodega's tiny washroom to take a piss or a dump. Anon the fake French waiter Raoul sat with me over a glass or two, chattering nonstop about his endless stream of failed affairs with likeminded bum fuckers.

My revenge fantasies lay in shreds at my feet. What had I expected to find? Surely not Aunt Ida noshing on a plate of schnitzel. But maybe someone who, when I showed them the photographs, remembered her and Edie sitting at the bar.

Someone who had heard a casual conversation between two knockout broads about moving to Mazatlan. Or opening a Texaco station in Taxco. Or a guayabera shop in Guadalajara.

152

What I had found was an empty ruin. As empty as my very soul.

Luis brought Jane by. She took one look at me and said:

"I'll see you later. I'm going shopping."

She was gone for hours. Days.

As dusk settled, it came to pass that I saw movement amid the ruins. Was I hallucinating? Probably. With the high altitude, untold glasses of cheap vino tinto and little sleep, who wouldn't be? Still, I had to check it out.

Crossing the street, I scrambled up a pile of rubble. On the far side a madman dressed in rags squatted, playing a Jew's harp, a paper thin, ragtag dog resting at his feet.

When I approached, the dog growled and bared its teeth. I sat down away from the dog, my hands raised in a peace offering.

The madman stopped playing his tune and looked left and right with a crystalline craziness as irrefutable as the existence of God to a believer. When he looked at me, I saw hanged men dancing behind his eyes.

"Are you Bill?" he asked.

How the hell did he know my name?

"They told me someone named Bill might come here."

What the fuck!

"I'm Bill," I said. "Who told you I was coming?"

"They said if you showed up I was to give you a message."

Was this for real?

"What message?"

He reached into the pocket of his stained and frayed trousers and handed me a dirty slip of paper folded in half. I opened the paper and read in Aunt Ida's script:

Bill. If you're reading this, you're shit out of luck. Edie and I have left town.

But they had been here! And sooner or later, maybe with the help of Lee Kiev's Mexican agent, I would find them!

Back at the Sevastopol I showered and shaved. Then screwed Jane twenty-four ways to Sunday. And vice versa.

5

The dwarf, whom the whores called el pequeño Rififi, knocked and, without waiting for a response, entered. He bore a tray laden with two platters of enchiladas Suizas, a plate of steaming corn tortillas, and a pitcher of top shelf margaritas. The latter a combination of silver tequila, Cointreau and freshly squeezed lime juice that would have made a 1939 Ziegfeld dancer tingle down to her toes and drop her drawers.

I stood pissing in the sink because the toilet wouldn't flush. The management had promised a plumber would be dispatched in short order. But that was five hours ago. The room smelled like a latrine. In desperation Jane opened all the windows and swiped a fan from one of the whores' cribs down the hall.

In bed Jane sat with her back against the headboard, reading a Mexican movie magazine. A spliff smoldered between her compressed lips. Our room gecko shimmied across the ceiling until it was suspended directly above the spiraling resinous smoke. Then inhaled deeply. Or was I, as usual, imagining shit?

Little Rififi's jaded eyes wandered presumptuously over Jane's soft shoulders and salaciously plump, buck-naked knockers.

"Get you kicks on Route 66," I improvised, shaking the last couple of drops from the end of my supersized johnson.

"Put the tray on the bed and scoot," said Jane without looking up.

Little Rififi's face contorted into a gangsterish sneer, but he did as he was instructed. As the door clicked behind him, Jane leaned forward and began to fork huge bites of enchilada dripping with cheese sauce into her mouth, occasionally stopping to slurp from her margarita glass or use a rolled tortilla to wipe up extra sauce.

"That guy's a shitbag," she said between mouthfuls. "Better get some of this, Bill, while it's still hot." She motioned with her fork at the fast-disappearing late lunch.

I made a face. I had as much appetite as a boa constrictor that, while warming himself on the tarmac, had been run over by an freight truck.

If I'd been thinking straight, I would have realized, after the madman passed me Aunt Ida's note, that I had no chance in hell of finding the evil duo. The two of them could be shacked up, enjoying the pleasures of mutual cunnilingus, anywhere in the whole wide world.

But delirious from the 7,350-feet-above-sea-level altitude of Mexico City and an overabundance of sex with Jane, I was fixated on the idea that Edie and Aunt Ida were still in Mexico. Dangerous, exotic and kinky, Mexico was made for Aunt Ida.

I'd been trying all afternoon to reach Lee Kiev's supposed Mexican agent and impresario. If he was hot on the trail of William Burroughs' suitcase abandoned in Mexico more than a half century ago, surely finding a couple of current-day, lesbian-leaning gringo sluts would be a snap. But each time I dialed the number Lee had given me, it rang and rang and rang. And nobody picked up.

Plopping down on the edge of the bed, I picked up the handset and dialed the number one more time. On the fourth ring a female voice that should have belonged to a small time New Jersey gun moll said: "¿Bueno?"

"Is this Fritz?" I asked.

"Who wants him?"

"I'm a friend of Lee's," I said.

"Lee?"

"You know. Lee Kiev. In Miami."

"Hold on."

A muffled CRASH! cascaded over the phone line as though the gun moll had fumbled the handset at her end of the conversation, dropping it onto a tile floor.

Next moment, a raspy, feverish male voice burst over the line.

"Fritz at your service. You are a friend of Lee's. Lee and I go back forever. What did you say your name was? Of course he told me you were coming. The stars are moving into alignment. The entrails bode well. You must tell Lee it is just a matter of time. And money."

Stars in alignment? Entrails?

"We need to meet," I said. "To discuss the Burroughs suitcase and another matter."

"Whoever you are, please don't mention that name over the phone. This is not a secure line. Someone may be listening. Speak only in generalities."

It had never occurred to me anyone else might be after the suitcase. Lee had never even hinted at such a possibility. He had presented it to me as a done deal. I was just a courier picking up a package and bringing it stateside.

But, hey, I guess even in the world of antiques, curios and curiosa, it was dog-eat-dog.

"Right," I said. "About the...the thing of mutual interest, we need to talk. I'll come to your office."

"No, no. It's too dangerous. Let me think."

The line went silent. Behind me Jane pushed away the tray of now empty dishes. She belched.

"Excuse me."

"You're getting fat," I said.

Jane shot me the finger.

She clambered out of bed and into a pair of racy, wintergreen-colored panties.

I wondered if they were the same ones Luis had liberated

from the chair in the lobby the day we arrived? And if so, how had Jane come into possession of them?

Fritz's voice burst anew through the handset: "Still there?"

"Still here."

"Meet me in an hour at the Church of St. Simon of the Desert in Polanco."

"Where's that?"

"Ask any cab driver."

"How will I recognize you?"

Fritz's voice boiled over: "I'll have a fucking parrot on my shoulder!" The phone connection flatlined.

Jane leaned close to the mirror over the sink, putting on green eye shadow to match her panties.

"I have to go out. Meet this guy Fritz at some church," I said.

Jane glanced around at me. One eye was outlined in wintergreen, the other not, so she looked like the dog in The Little Rascals series. Except her nose wasn't wet.

"A church? What's the deal with that?" she asked.

"He thinks people are watching his office, bugging his phone. Maybe this Burroughs suitcase deal is bigger than I realized. Maybe I should ask Luis to bring his machete and wait around while I'm in the church."

"Forget about Luis," said Jane. "I'll go with you. Remember, trust no one." She added as an afterthought: "And you should ask Lee for more money."

"Fritz told me to come alone," I lied. I figured if things started to go south, I didn't want Jane distracting my attention.

Her gaze darkened. Trust no one! Had it occurred to her I might be planning to grab the Burroughs suitcase, dump her and skedaddle? I could read her like a book. Sometimes.

Stepping close, I kissed her with a certain affection. "Be of good cheer," I said. My free hand gave her left boob a reassuring squeeze.

Dressing quickly, I was halfway out the door when Jane

called after me:

"While you're there, I hear they're running a special on absolution." She was almost as funny as Aunt Ida.

*

When I exited the hotel, Luis was not around.

The cab I hailed on the main drag took me to an older, upscale neighborhood of stone and stuccoed single and two-story homes on the far side of Chapultepec Park. I stepped forth on a tree-lined, cobblestone street that exuded nary a whiff of danger, except for the heavy iron bars covering every window. A bearded gent in a tie and sports jacket walking a pit bull on a leather leash nodded at me as I stood contemplating the scene.

Across the way the low rent Church of St. Simon of the Desert squatted like a hunchbacked beggar. Above its raw, unkempt façade of rough stones and mortar, a two-tiered bell tower poked skyward like an erection waiting for the hand of God to jerk it to fecundity.

The man with the pit bull disappeared around a corner. The street was completely empty, surreal in its conjuring of the lost world of an earlier century.

I pulled open the church's heavy, iron-studded door far enough to slip inside. A wave of cold air redolent of mildew, damp plaster and melting candle wax rolled over me. Stumbling across the shadowy atrium, I banged into the sharp corner of a wooden table spread with religious tracts and nearly tumbled face first into a font of holy water.

I stood at the back of the nave, letting my eyes adjust to the dim, tomb-like light, scanning the row upon row of pews that marched like an army toward the sanctuary. Dank aisles obscured by stone pillars ran up either side. At the end an ornate, gold-encrusted altar shone dully in flickering candlelight. There was no sign of anyone that might be Fritz. In fact, there was no sign of anyone.

Was I early? Or would Fritz be a no-show?

It occurred to me there might be treachery afoot, that Fritz had ratted me out to Aunt Ida. As if on cue, a greasy, sharp-toothed rodent snickered along the seatback of a nearby pew, rising on its hind legs to sniff the air in my direction, before it scampered into darkness, its tiny claws tap-tap-tapping on the stone like a miniature blind person.

Get a grip! There was no way Fritz knew Aunt Ida. The Burroughs thing and the Aunt Ida thing were completely separate.

I would make one circuit of the sanctuary. If Fritz didn't show by then, I would go back to the hotel, call Lee and tell him things were not working out, that his agent had gone squirrelly.

My shoes echoing with each step, I advanced up the center aisle, glancing to left and right at various side altars dedicated to an abundance of saints, virgins and reformed hookers. Nearing the altar, I gulped and stopped dead. Someone sat in deep gloom at the end of one of the side pews. Nobody moved. Neither I nor the shadow figure.

A derelict had crept in from the street and fallen asleep, I thought.

I walked aggressively toward the figure and, when two feet away, lit a match.

In the flair of light, the blood on the man's white shirt appeared as a black, amoeboid stain. Blood and brains as dark and viscous as blackstrap molasses dripped from the shattered upper left quadrant of his cranium. One remaining eye gazed out of nothingness into nothingness.

My own blood roared in my temples like a juggernaut.

Don't just stand there!

Then the match burned my fingers. I dropped it and darkness fell.

6

Beating the match to the floor, I hunkered down, hugging the darkness, waiting for the shot to ring out, which would mean I was already dead. It didn't.

The guy with half a face was a fresh kill. In all likelihood the shooter, equipped with night goggles, had watched my every move from the moment I entered the church. And I was still alive! Which meant what? The possibilities were endless: 1. I wasn't on the hit list and, unlike the jihad cowboys who were happy to take out anyone and everyone who happened to be in the wrong place at the wrong time, professional killers avoided collateral damage whenever possible. 2. The triggerman had only one bullet. 3. He or she had a dentist appointment but would do me later. 4. He or she was toying with me like a rock 'n roll star with a starry-eyed teen groupie from Des Moines, but I wouldn't leave the church alive (or a virgin).

My anus puckered at this last possibility. I'd learned in I-rack it was risky to stay in one place too long. In my best imitation of a crab that has seen the pot of boiling water on the stove, I busted butt to the other end of the pew. Then lay still, cheek pressed to cold, gritty stone, and listened for something. A beetle or some other insect whirred. Again rat claws tap-tapped on rock. In the remote bowels of the church, a toilet flushed. Dust motes danced a silent jig in a slice of sunlight slanting through a high window. A chunk of plaster, corroded by dampness for decades, gave in to the force of gravity and fell to the floor with a dull clunk.

From far away in the back of the church came the whine of a metal hinge under pressure. Since there was no telltale echo of footsteps coming forward into the church, I figured someone had just exited through the same bank of doors by which I had entered. That someone would be ordinary and unremarkable in every respect, except their eyes would be colder and emptier than any pair of eyes you ever gazed into. Sniper eyes. I had seen them before in I-rack.

Feeling a little further away from death, I sat up and blew out a puff of air, rubbed my fingers over closed eyelids as if I'd just awakened from a nightmare.

There was no point in lamenting the past, but I did anyway. I was without a doubt a genuine, A-1 horse's ass. This was Mexico. Shit happened here on a regular basis. Bad shit. Yet I had come unarmed to a meeting in a totally weird venue with some Mexican hustler I'd never set eyes on. Ever since I came back from I-rack and spent time in the VA psych ward, my sense of self-preservation had been waylaid.

I should have bought the Glock from Mona when I had the chance. Or borrowed Luis' machete.

Having gotten that out of my system, I turned back to the dead guy. I figured there was a 1:500,000,000 chance that, after he snapped at me over the phone, Fritz came down with a migraine and blew off our meeting, and the dead guy was someone else.

When I tried to go through the dead man's pockets, he fell over sideways. I jumped about ten feet.

The Mexican driver's license in his wallet confirmed what I already knew. Lee Kiev no longer had a Mexican agent.

The wallet also contained a credit card, a few thousand pesos, a lottery ticket, a slip of paper scrawled with a phone number and a fuzzy snapshot of a naked woman lying ass end up on a chaise lounge made of tubular metal.

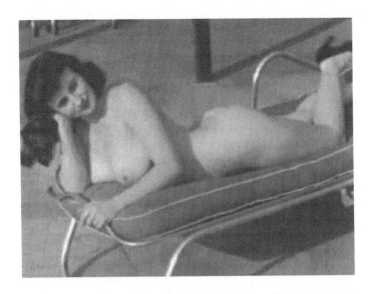

I pocketed everything except the credit card and driver's license.

All this had taken way too much time. I needed to amscray before some sodomite priest or grieving nympho widow wandered in, spotted me rifling through the deceased's effects and gave my description to the cops.

Leaving the church, I strolled up the street casual as hell. Totally cool on the outside. My balls in a sweat. Imagining the assassin drawing down on me from anywhere with his soundproofed sniper rifle.

"Helpless, helpless, helpless" played in a closed loop in my head. The Neil Young tune.

You can hear it now if you put your mind to it.

After a while I came into a commercial area and caught a cab back to the hotel.

When I walked through the door, Jane set down the Henning Mankell novel she was reading. She was still wearing the wintergreen undies. Nothing more, nothing less.

"So?" she said before I'd even taken my shoes off.

I sat down on the edge of the bed and, unlacing and

removing my two-tone tan and white brogues, rubbed my bare toes.

"You look...I don't know. Scared shitless, maybe."

"Scared?"

"Yeah, scared," said Jane.

I reached for the bottle of Presidente brandy. Poured an inch into a dirty water glass, my hands shaking like a junkie's. Somehow I got the glass to my mouth.

"Fritz is dead," I said. "Blown away."

"YOU'RE SHITTING ME!"

Jane jumped up and began pacing back and forth, her hands jittery as feeding bats at dusk. "Calm down," I said. "Do you want to know what happened?"

"Not really."

She found a coral-colored bra and, leaning forward, let her breasts cascade into the cups. Arching her back, she snagged the hooks behind. "Okay. Tell me what happened."

"I need to call Lee," I said.

Jane's teeth toyed with her lower lip. Drew blood.

"Do you want to fuck first?" she asked.

Her cunt smelled like old fish heads but tasted like homemade strawberry pie. When I shoved my dick in, I died and went to heaven. Jane screamed. Fuck yeah! I thought. I was alive!

*

You couldn't call long distance from the phone in our room, so afterward I went down to the lobby to use the payphone. Jane came along and sat in one of the orange plastic chairs with her movie magazine, pretending she wasn't listening.

I'd bought a cheap calling card at the local farmacia. When I dialed the access number and entered the special code, I kept getting a busy signal. I wasn't sure whether I was entering the code wrong or the Mexico City circuits were clogged up or Lee was actually on the phone talking to someone.

Finally Jane grabbed the card out of my hand.

"Here. Let me do it." She went through the whole rigmarole, listened for a moment, then handed the handset to me. "It's voicemail."

"Lee," I said after the beep. "It's Bill. I've been meaning to call you since we got here, but it's been crazy like you wouldn't believe. Anyway, there's a big problem with Fritz. We're at the Sevastopol. Room 205. Call me as soon as you can."

I hung up.

"You didn't leave the number," said Jane.

"I don't know what it is."

Jane handed me a matchbox with a pair of fat red lips on the cover. Above the lips were the words HOTEL AMORES. Beneath, it said Hotel Sevastopol, with a street address and phone number.

"Now you give me this?"

Jane turned away with a shrug.

"I'm for ordering a pitcher of margaritas and getting shitfaced," she said.

"Don't you want to get something to eat first?" I asked.

"Okay."

We walked up to the main drag to this little pizza stand we'd found. Luis was already there, sitting on a stool in front of a slice of pepperoni. We decided to make a night of it. Let Luis show us some hot spots. There was nothing else we could do.

We were in a place called Club Bleu and the midnight hour had come and gone. My head throbbed as if it were an oil drum on which someone was beating with a heavy stick.

The bar at Club Bleu, where we had taken up residence, ran down a long, narrow room with lots of indirect twilight-blue lighting along the edges. No expense had been spared in the high-end glitz department. Mottled, faux-gold wall coverings, life-sized 3D images of naked trollops set in wall niches, black leather and chrome bar stools, an underlit blue onyx bar that glowed like a hovering alien spacecraft.

The joint was nearly empty. On a platform behind the bar, a pair of not-quite-nude dancers swished and swayed to Mexican hipster vibes spun by a dark and brooding DJ. It was hard to take your eyes off the dancers.

"Stop looking at them and pay attention to me," said Jane. Her voice was slurred. She wrapped her arms around me and mashed her lips to mine. Her tongue toyed with my fillings, darted like a reef fish into the space where an infected molar had been extracted when I was in prison. After a while she lost interest and, turning back to the bar, slurped half of the banana daiquiri waiting there. Jane's sweet tooth trumped her desire to project the image of a badass bar fly. Next moment she was deep in an incomprehensible conversation with Luis.

On the stage the two dancers intertwined like incestuous vipers. I kept seeing them with half their skulls blown away, gore and carnage dripping down their lascivious flesh. The dance of the dead. Or the undead.

The offing of Fritz had spoiled the party. I'd come down to Mexico for some good old-fashioned tit for tat (or was it tat for tit?) and to make a little dough transporting exotic goods back stateside. Now everything tilted at an odd angle. Everything was up in the air.

Trust no one! I had laughed when Jane said that. But now, with Fritz's murder, whom could I trust? Fear ground in my gut. Living in a rented room in beautiful downtown Newark or South Central L.A. suddenly sounded a lot safer than sticking around in Mexico.

I drank off the iceless dregs of my sippin' tequila. The need to take a wicked piss bobbed like a cork to the top of the list in my alcohol-clogged brain.

"I need to take a leak," I said to no one in particular.

Jane leaned sideways against the bar, threw her head back and with shaking fingers placed an unlit cigarette between her lips. I didn't have a lighter or a match.

"When did you take up smoking?" I said.

"Ever since you told me about Fritz."

The barmaid, in a see-through blouse unbuttoned to her navel, came to the rescue, leaning across the bar, her hand holding one of those expensive gold lighters you see in gangster movies. Like an afterthought, the nipples of her saggy breasts grazed the surface of the bar.

"Fuck Fritz," I said and walked away.

The bathroom in this self-indulgent dump was all white Italian marble, stainless steel and mirrors. It looked a lot like Mary Beth's house in Miami without the furniture. A bank of urinals stretched for a mile or so. I picked one, unzipped and let her rip. My mind a blank, I stood wholly absorbed in the pleasure of emptying my bladder.

Next moment someone entered the space immediately to my left. A zipper unfurled with a rasping sound. I grew as edgy as a house cat in a Chinese restaurant. There were at least twenty empty urinals and the guy had taken the one next door!

I looked left.

The stranger's sly, jaundice-tinged eyes appraised me as if I were a slice of dubious roast beef being served up in a cafeteria catering to welfare scammers and methadone freaks. I took in the remaining details in a single sweep: four inches shorter than yours truly, duded-up in a brown tropical suit and open collar pink shirt, sunken cheeks of a career bureaucrat, an out-of-plumb nose that made his face lopsided, forehead scoured by worry, closely cropped salt and pepper hair. A dry smile as thin and papery as a molted snakeskin slithered across his lips.

"It's a pleasure to meet you in person at last, Derringer."

I'd seen his type before. CIA, military intel, Interpol, whatever. Spook wannabes of one sort or another.

I shook my member and tucked him away.

"Whatever you're selling," I said. "I'm outa spare change at the moment."

The worm zipped up, walked to one of the marble sinks and, turning on a blast of water, washed his hands with vigor.

"You're a wanted man, Derringer."

"And this is Mexico."

"It is indeed. One cell phone call and you'll be kidnapped off the street, beaten senseless and eventually dumped back in the US of A at some flyblown border crossing. From there it's a short ride back to Oopawalla for another five to seven."

The worm had turned, even as he dried his hands on a stiff linen towel plucked from a stack on the counter and leaned close to the mirror to examine the onset of a zit. I felt a chill in the air.

"Or we could talk turkey." He paused, waiting for some reaction, then snorted and spat nastily into the sink. "I believe you know a certain Ida Truluck, formerly of Orlando, Florida?"

My mouth must have dropped open, for that snakeskin

smile returned to the speaker's lips.

"You mean Aunt Ida?" I said.

"The very same."

The worm swayed back and forth with nervous exaltation.

"Aunt Ida, as you call her, is at the present moment a player in a new and enigmatic organization in the drug wars, a group calling themselves the Mayan Cartel. They're holed up in an estancia near the Puuc Hills south of Mérida on the Yucatan Peninsula. We need someone on the inside to find out what they're up to." Again the pause, as if I was supposed to say something incredulous like: 'You're out of your cotton-pickin' mind if you think I'm going to... !' When I didn't, he continued.

"A few miles east of the estancia, there's a little burg called Boca del Diablo where Aunt Ida likes to go sometimes to play pool, drink and let down her hair. Your past relationship should make it easy for you to hook up with her when she's in town. Get an invitation out to the ranch."

I wondered what the worm thought my past relationship with Aunt Ida had been. That we were old lovers with fond memories of our time in the sack together? A typical spook-craft fuckup that they would get it all wrong. Have no clue I was out for Aunt Ida's blood, carve my initials on her chest.

I must have looked confused. At one time I had been a gung-ho patriot. Now the stars and stripes waving in the depths of this stranger's eyes filled me with foreboding.

"So, Derringer, what's it to be?" my nemesis asked. "Oopawalla or Aunt Ida."

Did I want to take a vow of poverty and move to the slums of Mumbai or discover a diamond as big as the Ritz buried in my back yard? Did I want to be sucked off by the world's most beautiful woman or step in front of a speeding bus?

I wanted to laugh out loud. And bury my fist in his face.

"How do I get to this Boca del Diablo?"

"A plane ticket will be delivered to your hotel room

tomorrow."

"I'll need two tickets," I said.

"If I were you," said the worm. "I wouldn't take Jane along. It's bound to make things more complicated."

I needed Jane to watch my back. And provide me solace.

"I don't go without Jane."

"Fine. But she travels on your nickel."

He handed me a white business card. In embossed script it read: Pandemonium Import / Export with a telephone number beneath.

"If you need to get in touch with me, dial this number and ask for Mr. Burke. I'll call you back."

He walked out of the men's room whistling "I'm a Yankee Doodle Dandy" from that old James Cagney movie.

8

Things were getting a tad schizoid.

On the one hand I couldn't believe my good fortune. At last Aunt Ida was within my grasp. I was so excited I was panting like a bloodhound. And screw that little turd Burke, or whatever his real name was. If he got in the way, I'd run him over. Or get Jane to do it.

On the other hand there was Fritz. Or the lack thereof. I still needed to talk to Lee about that. Maybe he would decide the Burroughs thing was off. Too risky. Though I didn't think that was very likely. I'd seen the gleam in Lee's eyes when he told me about Burroughs' lost suitcase. He really, really, really, really, really wanted to know what was in that fucker. And what were the chances that whoever wasted Fritz had a branch office in Miami?

The way I figured it, Lee was pretty much in the clear. It was I who had all the risk.

Then it occurred to me Burke might have had something to do with Fritz's murder. Or Aunt Ida.

Anything was possible, especially in Mexico.

Right now though, I was dog-tired and in no mood for Jane, who, as we drove in Luis' truck back toward the hotel, kept trying to get at my cock.

"Hey," I said, as I pulled her hand out of my fly. "Why don't you go for Luis' cock?"

"No, no, man," said Luis. "We could get in an accident. The cops would come. It could get very expensive."

"Cool," said Jane and promptly fell asleep against my shoulder.

Back at the Sevastopol, with Luis' help I got her upstairs into our room and undressed. I could see he was smitten with Jane's pulchritudinous bits, as she lay sprawled across the bed.

"One hell of a woman," I said harshly.

Luis backed toward the exit. "Adios," he said and disappeared

I stood at the door for a moment listening to the whores, who where having a party down the hall. It would have been fun to join them, but I had a big day tomorrow.

*

It was noon when I dragged myself out of the sack and down to the lobby to see if there was a message from Lee. Jane was still out for the count.

"Your party called back," said Little Rififi, wobbling atop his orange crate behind the front desk, a cigarette clamped in the corner of his mouth. "He was not happy to learn you had gone out on the town, rather than waiting for his call."

He flashed me a self-satisfied smirk, as if I had disregarded his sage advice to stick around last night for Lee's call and now would pay dearly for pissing off some higher authority.

"What time did he call?" I asked.

Little Rififi shrugged. "It was my night off. One of the girls took the message."

He passed me a greasy slip of paper containing Lee's phone number and nothing more.

"You made that shit up about Lee being pissed off."

"I make nothing up," asserted Little Rififi. Twin geysers of white cigarette smoke billowed from his nose, forming momentarily, as they swirled ceilingward, into a pair of languid tits, before dissipating into nothingness. "Is all true."

After shooing Little Rififi out of the lobby for some

privacy, I dialed Lee on the pay phone, punching in the calling card code without a hitch. Lee was in a good mood, ebullient even. Perhaps he'd gotten laid the night before by some Eastern European Jewish princess steeped in the cabalistic arts of love.

I told him in vivid detail about finding poor Fritz, his brains spattered from point A to point B.

Everything was going to be okay Lee assured me. Fritz had many enemies. This unfortunate turn of events had nothing to do with our project. Easy for you to say up there in Miami, I thought.

What I needed to do now, asserted Lee, was head down to the Yucatan...

I almost dropped the phone! Was it wild-assed coincidence that the owner of William Burroughs' lost suitcase and Aunt Ida were holed up within spitting distance of each other? Or was something rotten in Copenhagen? But, hey, synchronicity was the spice of life.

I got back to the room just in time to eyeball Jane as she eased into her bra and skivvies. It was always a treat, like watching the Flying Wallendas working without a net.

"What are you looking at?" she demanded. She had the look of someone who had had a dozen too many banana daiquiris the night before.

"You need to pack your stuff," I said. "We're flying to Mérida tonight."

"What do you mean?"

"I spoke to Lee. The Burroughs thing is still on. Now that Fritz is out of the picture, Lee's in direct communication with the suitcase's owner, some renegade fag poet left over from the Beat Generation. Lives on a remote estate in the Puuc Hills, wherever that is. We're to settle into this two-bit pueblo called Boca del Diablo. Once Lee finalizes the details long distance, he wires us the money, we make physical contact with the party in question and close the deal. Simple as pecan pie."

"Poet. Schmoet. It sounds like a weird setup to me."

"It's the best I can do."

"Swell. We're leaving just when I was hoping to have time to take in some of the sights."

"You can take a vacation after we get the suitcase. Besides, you used to live here. You've already seen everything."

Then I told her about Burke. And about Aunt Ida being part of a drug cartel operation just down the road from Boca del Diablo. Jane sat on the edge of the bed twirling her hair but saying nothing. A chill shook her shoulders, though the room was hot and stuffy. After a moment she sat up straight; rolled her neck from side to side as if to get rid of a kink. Then she stepped into the bathroom and began applying garish lipstick to her languid lips.

"Well, shit," she said over her shoulder. "If we're going on a suicide mission the least you can do is buy me lunch at the House of Tiles."

*

By the time we left the Sevastopol, the noontime frenzy of Mexico City was in full bloom. Everyone was rushing to get home to their wives, husbands or whomever for a nosh and a frisky fuck before catching a snooze during the heat of the day. Traffic was in gridlock, so we walked. Crossing through Alameda Park where the trees were dying of ozone poisoning and public indifference, we trucked up Avenida Juarez, turned left on a side street and there it was in all its baroque splendor, la Casa de los Azulejos. The ornate, blue and white tile-covered, 18th Century palacio of a wealthy Mexican family, now reduced to the flagship location of a restaurant chain.

"Isn't this place amazing," said Jane, gesturing at the vast, two-story, glass-roofed courtyard in which we sat, surrounded by tourists yapping away in every known language and a couple of unknown ones. On the courtyard walls a famous artist had painted a garden scene with peacocks. A stone fountain, out of order at the moment, silently took up most of one wall.

"Absolutely fucking amazing," I said, glancing over the plastic-coated menu.

"No need to be harsh."

"I must be hungry."

I imagined dead Mexican revolutionaries from another century hanging from the second floor balcony overlooking the courtyard, their black tongues like exclamation points.

"What're you having?" asked Jane.

"Thought I'd go for the cheeseburger and fries. Nothing but rice, beans and blackened iguana steaks once we hit the Yucatan jungle."

"Have you ever eaten iguana?" said Jane.

"No," I said. "But I did see that movie Night of the Iguana with Ava Gardner. She was incredibly hot. For an older chick."

"Don't change the subject. Mexicans prepare iguana fifteen different ways."

"Swell," I said. "I'll stick to chicken."

A tarty, slightly-gone-to-seed waitress decked out in faux-peasant garb conveniently arrived to take our order before Jane could make some further smartass retort that I could see forming on her pouty lips. The waitress brought silverware and napkins and poured coffee for me. Jane ordered huevos rancheros and told the waitress to bring a Bloody Mary while we were waiting for our meal. I took a sip of java and made a face. Weak and tepid.

"Don't you want to do something with your life?" said Jane.

Now what, I wondered.

"For instance?"

"I don't know. Settle down. Open an ice cream parlor."

"All I want to do right now is catch up with Aunt Ida and drop kick her into the next county."

"What about Edie?"

"What about her?"

"Well, you're still married to her, aren't you?"

Jane's Bloody Mary arrived. She stared at it, perhaps hoping the answers to life's vagaries would rise like flotsam out of that pool of bloody fucking tomato juice and vodka. The Oracle of Delphi in a glass. What was with Jane this morning?

"If you're not going to drink it, pass it over. This coffee's crap."

"We could liberate the suitcase," Jane said. "Find our own buyer and unload it at a discount price. Move to Bali and open a beach bar."

"I don't think ripping off Lee would be a great idea," I said. "Besides, I don't see myself running a small business like a titty bar. I'm more of a big score kind of guy."

"As I recall, the last time you went for the big score, things didn't work out quite as well as you hoped."

"Practice makes perfect," I said.

Jane pushed back from the table and stood up, her face snarling.

"Maybe once in a while you should think about somebody other than Mr. Perfect. Besides, I wasn't talking about opening a titty bar. Just an ordinary have a few beers and a few laughs kind of place."

She kicked her chair fiercely and it crashed backwards onto the marble tile floor.

BANG!

"I'm outa here!"

As I watched Jane's fanny flounce toward the exit, our waitress set down my cheeseburger and Jane's huevos rancheros.

What was I supposed to do now?

"Anything else I can get you?" said the waitress.

"Everything's perfect," I said, giving her over abundant behind a friendly pat. Pulling Jane's plate of huevos rancheros to my side of the table, I picked up my fork and dug in. I was hungry enough to eat for both of us.

9

Later, we kissed and made up and caught the last flight out to Mérida.

Now it was the afternoon of the next day and Jane and I were deep in the Yucatan jungle. She drove; I was in charge of navigation.

An impenetrable wall of trees loomed over the narrow tarmac road along which we traveled. Walk a hundred feet in and you'd never find your way out.

Here and there flowering vines in cascades of yellow or blue broke up the monotony of green shading into black. An occasional bird, sometimes large, sometimes small, sometimes medium, flew out of the forest, crossed in front of us and disappeared into the other side, as if it had never existed. The light of day faltered, giving way to impending night.

I wondered if naked pygmies lived in the jungle. But that was stupid. Pygmies lived in Africa. There weren't any elephants here either. Only an occasional marauding band of feral pigs or the shadow of an unseen jaguar. All jungles were not equal. Some were more exotic than others. This second-rate Mexican jungle offered up the debris of dead civilizations and the twisted offspring of randy conquistadors and native princesses.

But it did have Aunt Ida, a rara avis indeed, holed up on some backwater ranch with a bunch of crack-crazed psychopaths of the Latino persuasion.

In my daydreams of revenge she wore jodhpurs, knee-high lace up leather boots because of the snakes and a too-petit great white huntress' blouse. A killer smile rearranged her ruby lips. Mrs. Francis Macomber came to mind. From the Hemingway story.

When the occasion arose, I would have no trouble shooting Aunt Ida through her black heart with the silver bullet I'd brought all the way from Miami Beach. A gift from Lee.

We'd been driving since the crack of dawn. Lunch of vegetable and rodent stew at a roadside snack bar hovel lit fireworks in my gut.

For the last couple of miles human toil had pushed the jungle back from the road to make room for fallow, weed-infested fields, others planted with regimental rows of corn or convoluted melon and squash vines.

"Where the fuck are we?" Jane asked.

She downshifted our rental, an old school VW Bug with the lawnmower engine in the back. Front bumper bent and rusty. Tires bald. A twisted rag making due for the missing gas cap.

We got a great deal. Paid cash up front for two weeks. Figured it was going to take a while to glom onto the Burroughs suitcase and finish the other business.

Afterward we would chill at the beach, drink ice-cold beer and ogle nearly naked women. At least I would.

There was nothing like crystal clear seas and ice-cold beer. Did I mention scantily clad women?

Ever so slowly Jane eased us over a metal speed bump. We'd quickly learned Mexican speed bumps were nasty. Even at a moderate speed, this one would have ripped our front end to bits.

"I think we made a wrong turn about three hours ago when we left the interstate," I said. I stared at the rental company map. "This map doesn't show any detail. I might as well be looking at a blank sheet of paper."

Jane gave me a dirty look.

"We're coming into a town. We can get directions."

In the field to my right, the burned-out skeleton of a car lay black and twisted as a giant spider that had been flash-fried in napalm.

"Check that out," I said.

"Maybe they had an engine fire," said Jane.

"Or died in a fiery crash."

Wooden shanties and cement block bungalows began to appear, some along the road with fields behind, others dimly seen in the shadow of the jungle. An Indian woman lay in a rope hammock on a front porch while a child suckled her vast milk chocolate tit. From the road ahead an old man astride a burro and smoking a cigar approached and passed us by as if we were invisible.

Miraculously, a sign appeared: Boca del Diablo. Pop. 5,843.

By pure chance we'd wound up where we wanted to be. Or maybe destiny and the gods were at work.

Minutes later we circled the main square. A cathedral on one side and a smattering of businesses that looked mostly closed on the other three. In the middle a park with palm trees, where a few ne'er-do-wells napped on benches or gazed listlessly at the passing scene. On one corner an Indian woman offered up colorful rebozos and other trinkets. The afternoon sun beat down like a dominatrix in a sweat.

"That's our hotel." I pointed to the stuccoed façade ahead bearing the name Hotel Colonial.

We pulled through an arch into a courtyard. A skinny Mexican gigolo in tight black pants ran his hands through glistening obsidian hair that looked like it had come from a Jell-O mold and offered to replace Jane in the driver's seat.

"I'll park it myself," she said.

It was a swank setup. Two stories, a lobby with a couch and two wingback chairs in red leather, a real dining room with linen tablecloths. The public areas had authentic-looking beamed ceilings. A tasteful sepia-colored nude etching hung by the check-in desk. The central courtyard, surrounded by a covered portico, incorporated a pool surrounded by potted palms, flowering cacti and gravel paths.

"How'd we end up at the Taj Mahal?" asked Jane. "I was so looking forward to staying at another cheap-assed bordello."

Lee had prepaid for the room. I signed us in as Mr. and Mrs. William P. Derringer.

"What does the P stand for?" asked Jane.

"Don't ask."

"I already did."

There was no way I was going to tell her it stood for Percy.

"This is swell," I said, waving expansively. "You're going to love it here."

"I hope so," said Jane.

Ahead of us a genuine bellhop, spiffy as hell in a uniform and cap from the pages of The Great Gatsby, carried our cheesy canvas luggage up stone stairs to the second floor. He turned a heavy skeleton key in a giant door lock.

"You're going to cream your pants over this room," he said.

I gave him a hard look. Had he really said that?

The door swung wide to reveal a whitewashed, high-ceilinged space. A heavy mahogany four-poster bed draped with mosquito netting dominated the room. A Victorian loveseat, a bureau and a gaudy antique escritorio made up the remaining furniture. French doors looked out onto the plaza.

After we were left alone, Jane opened the French doors and stood gazing outward. The zócalo had fallen into a blurred gloomy state as if draped in gauze. Here and there neon signs flickered on.

"I don't like the looks of this place," said Jane.

I shrugged. What was not to like? Sitting in the straight-back chair to the writing desk, I unpacked my bag. My eyes rested on Jane and nowhere else. She wore a flower-print dress falling to mid-thigh that looked like it could have belonged to her grandmother, if her grandmother had been a hooker. The fabric oozed over her flesh like melted butter over popcorn.

Having been in close quarters with Jane for a longish time, it was second nature to imagine her starkers. The dazzling curves of her rump, like a UFO. Musky crotch, muscular thighs the better to strangle you with my dear, cute calves and ankles, flamboyant feet and toes made titillating with turquoise lacquer. The arch of her back, her rugged spine, supple shoulders and an egret's neck, the veneer of blond tresses, black roots beneath. And the boobs. Who could forget the boobs?

The victim of an immense, implacable desire, I longed to insinuate my hand between those legs. Entwine my fingers in her black, wiry pubis. Inhale the anchovy paste scent of her slit on my fingertips.

She turned and caught me starring at her.

"Don't you ever think about anything else?" she said.

"What?"

Jane bared her teeth.

"I'm exhausted," she said. "I need a bath and a good night's sleep."

In short order she disappeared into the steaming vapors of the bathroom. There was no invitation to scrub her back.

I needed some air.

Around the zócalo the shops had reopened in purple twilight. Children and mothers crowded in front of an ice cream store. In several beer gardens sinister, mustachioed riffraff lounged and drank, smoked hand-rolled cigarettes and spat.

The smell of grilling pork from a street stand made me suddenly hungry. I bought three tacos and wolfed them down. My stomach happy, I strolled on, my hands nervously jingling the coins in my pocket.

In my head questions and doubts sloshed back and forth like flotsam on the evening tide. Was Lee bullshitting me that Fritz's death had nothing to do with the Burroughs suitcase? When I came face to face with Aunt Ida, how would the lust versus revenge thing play out? How did I really feel about Jane? I was working myself into a lather of nerves that would keep sleep far at bay.

From out of the night, a tumult of shouts and screaming arose at the other side of the plaza. With a nerve-jangling roar, a motorcycle sped pell-mell down the street. Gunshots rang out.

All too familiar with that sound, I dove for the gutter, hiding behind orange peels and cigarette butts.

BOOM! The motorcycle made full frontal contact with a stone wall and exploded in a fireball, dazzling my vision into momentary blindness.

When I got to my feet, the ruined Harley was still burning. Someone sprayed it down with foam fire retardant. A little ways away, a crowd stood in a circle.

I approached. Peering over the Mexican gapers, all of whom were four or five inches shorter than me, I saw a crumpled body.

"Qué pasa?" I said.

An old man with a white beard and deep-set piercing eyes looked at me and laughed. He reminded me of Walter Huston as Howard, the grizzled gold prospector in Treasure of the Sierra Madre.

"Just some cabrón," he said in English. "Lots of drifters in town these days. This one tried to hold up the farmacia. The owner doesn't take no shit from nobody. Shot the thief twice in the back."

A police car with a swirling blue light came around the plaza and stopped. The rubberneckers pulled back from around the dead man. The body lay like a broken doll that had been crushed and distorted in a bad dream.

"Can I buy you a drink?" I said to the old man. I almost called him Howard.

"The dead always make me thirsty," he said.

10

Get your ass down to the Yucatan and hang loose, Lee Kiev had said. Wait for my call.

Like a Yiddishe cockroach flying under the radar, Lee was working his magic, spinning his cabalistic voodoo to pry the mysterious Burroughs valise from the grasp of its conflicted owner. Residing all these years in the heat and humidity of the tropics, I figured the end result would be a moldy, bug-infested, weather-stained junker signifying nothing. But there was no accounting for the quirkiness of human obsession.

My Aunt Ida fixation being a case in point.

Speaking of which, I needed to get the skinny on the ranch where she and her Mayan Cartel buddies spent quality time harvesting drugs and torturing DEA spies and infiltrators. My plan was to become a fly on the wall at the pool hall in Boca del Diablo where Aunt Ida came to play eight-ball, get shitfaced and blow off steam.

My friend Sierra Madre Howard, whose real name was Pablo, was a wealth of information. There was only one pool hall in Boca del Diablo. Manny's Bar and Billiards. Three ragtag pool tables covered in worn green baize, a reeking pissoir in the back, a beer cooler that was pretty much on the fritz pretty much all the time, and a scattering of tables and chairs that had seen better days.

For the next four days Pablo and I sat at a table in Manny's front patio, drinking room temperature Carta Blancas on my nickel, watching out of one eye the occasional spicy señorita, mongrel Indian or rail-thin yellow dog that passed down the street; the bickering, talentless pool players out of the other. Waiting for the appearance of Aunt Ida.

*

Day One.

"The robber who was killed the other night," I said to Pablo, as we tapped beer bottles for luck. "You said he wasn't alone. That more and more drifters were appearing in town."

"Many bad men come now to Boca del Diablo, looking for work with the foreigner."

"The foreigner? What foreigner?"

"The new owner of Hacienda de Sade, the largest land holding in the area. They all want to work for the German. Everyone says Frau Stein is very well connected with the PRI, our ruling political party, so there will be no trouble from the military or the gringos. I've never seen her but they say she is a flamboyant beauty. Like Marlene Dietrich. That she swims naked in the Olympic size pool at the hacienda."

"What goes on at Hacienda de Sade?" I said.

"The usual for Mexico. Drugs, orgies, murder and mayhem."

It sounded like I had struck gold. Hacienda de Sade was where I needed to be.

"Are there any Americans at the hacienda?" I asked. There was no point in beating around the bush. "Specifically a woman named Ida Truluck?"

"Is this one a friend of yours?"

I took a swig of beer, wiped the back of my hand across my lips, smiled conspiratorially. "Not exactly a friend."

"Alas, I am not aware of anyone by that name associated with the German."

"I've heard she comes into Boca del Diablo on occasion," I said. "To play pool."

Pablo gave me a blank shrug.

The day drifted from one beer to another, punctuated by the click of cues against the cue ball, the rat-a-tat-tat of colliding pool balls and the muttered curses of the players. At one point a woman came in from the street. Her blond hair shimmered as she stepped from sunlight into the shadowy interior. Was it Aunt Ida at last? An adrenalin rush sent my heart vaulting over the vague moon hanging listlessly in the heat-stroke blue of the endless tropical sky. But it was only a hooker hungry for business. She cadged a cigarette and stood smoking for a while, but there were no takers. Before long it was three o'clock in the afternoon. I remembered I'd promised to meet Jane for lunch at the hotel at noon.

"Shit."

How had the day gotten away from me?

I found Jane lying on her back on an inflatable float in the deep end of the hotel pool. She wore rhinestone-studded sunglasses, a wide-brimmed straw sombrero, maraschino cherry lipstick and three postage-stamp-sized triangles of semi-transparent-when-wet white cloth pretending to be a bathing outfit. It was enough to make your spit dry up and your dick tingle.

Spying me, she waved. Then with a great splashing and casting off of water, swam to the chrome-plated ladder and clambered up onto dry land.

"Thank heaven you remembered our date," she said. "A girl could starve to death around here."

She teetered and swayed forward in a haphazard collision course, her lips missing mine, grazing my cheek. One hand thrust against my groin, the other grappled around my shoulder. Boozy breath assailed my nostrils. I saw the empty Bushmills bottle, the ice bucket and a smudged, lipstick-sullied glass on a low table next to a poolside chaise.

As I held her from pitching forward onto the stone pool deck, a look of utter panic washed over her face. Her mouth opened wide like a landed fish gasping for breath and she spewed her liquid lunch over my brand new lime green Asics running shoes and the cuffs of my linen trousers bought in a trendy Mexico City boutique.

*

Day Two.

Jane, feeling like warmed-over dog poop, lay in bed moaning like the ghost of Christmas past. I fetched her a bicarbonate of soda; made her drink it all down. Making a wretched cow face, she fell back on the bed, sunk in a swamp of boozy, female sweat. Which was where she wallowed for the rest of the day, relieving me of any lunch obligations.

Hanging out at Manny's, Sierra Madre Howard aka Pablo and I were running out of things to talk about. Luckily Manny's had a set of dominos. Pablo gave me a quick rundown of the rules. I lost the first six games. I was sure Pablo was cheating but I couldn't figure out how.

"Do you want to play one more?" Pablo asked.

"Fuck off," I said.

The owner of Manny's Bar and Billiards, Manny Valdez, fat, pigeon-toed and unloved, resided on a stool behind a counter next to the beer cooler, from whence he doled out cue chalk, shots of tequila and nihilistic commentary on life's fatal twists and turns. I handed him a twenty-dollar bill and a photo of Aunt Ida, but he vehemently denied she'd ever crossed his doorstep.

How could that be?

His was the only pool hall in Boca del Diablo and Burke had said...

Then it occurred to me, just as Burke and his sycophants had gotten it wrong about my relationship with Aunt Ida, they could have fucked up about her affiliation with the Mayan Cartel. For all I knew, she and Edie were halfway around the world, lounging on Waikiki Beach, drinking Mai Tai cocktails paid for with the residue of my share of the guns-and-ammo-show loot.

But I couldn't give in to despair now. Not when I might be so close.

Determined to leave no stone unturned, I made the rounds of Boca del Diablo's bars, bodegas, cafes, tacquerías, pulquerías, newsstands, farmacias, pawnshops and juke joints. I left behind a trail of twenty-dollar bills, Aunt Ida's mugshot and the promise of a greater sum for legit info leading to her whereabouts. Though my Spanish was for the shits, pointing at Aunt Ida's photogenic kisser plus the etching of Old Hickory and the words In God We Trust seemed to get my point across.

"Gran recompensa. Gran recompensa." I kept saying. "Si? Si?"

But no one had seen hide nor hair of Aunt Ida.

Or so they claimed, their eyes glazing over or darting to the four corners of the room. Then I had a revelation. Of course. It had to be. Everyone in Boca del Diablo was scared shitless of Aunt Ida. And of Frau Stein.

Exhausted, introspective and thirsty, I walked back to Manny's.

Both Manny and Pablo were happy to see me. And my wallet. I bought a round of beers and tequila shots and we watched the evening redness wash like blood over the cumuli towering in the western sky.

An omen of the coming apocalypse?

Fuck that. That was the kind of bullshit thinking Jane loved to embrace. It probably just meant she was about to get her period.

As the color of the clouds faded to Pink Cataba wine and then merlot, a thick trail of black smoke spiraled upward in the distance.

"Looks like a fire," I said, pointing. "Maybe someone's burning trash."

"Is the campesinos," Pablo said. "They are demanding land reform. That the government divide up the big estates. Sometimes they block the roads leading in and out of Boca del Diablo. Set old tires on fire, even a vehicle or two. The estancia owners hire mercenaries. There are retaliations, shootings. People are burned alive. Is no bueno!"

"How do they feel about gringos?" I asked.

"More or less, not so good. But I don't think any gringos have been killed yet."

"Swell," I said.

"Is bad juju," said Pablo with a frown. He crossed himself. "Stay out of the countryside and there will be no problemo."

11

Day Three at Manny's. More of the same.

Jane stood at the bathroom mirror examining her gums. I slipped up behind and nuzzled her neck, one hand grasping a squeezable bun. She arched away from me.

"Jesus Christ, Bill, can't you see I'm doing something?"

I ground my teeth. Ignoring her, I went about my morning ablutions: the first piss of the day, messaging a little gel in my hair, slathering on plenty of Old Spice deodorant. Jane leaned in close to the mirror again, raising her upper lip with one finger.

"Do you think I've got periodontal disease?" she said.

"Maybe you should floss more often."

At breakfast in the hotel dining room, she toyed with her two sunny side eggs and refried beans until they looked totally inedible.

She wanted me to be personally responsible for her malaise, whatever it was.

"I need to go for a run," I said. "Get some physical activity."

I had washed Jane's puke off my Asics and wore them now, along with wine colored Harvard University nylon running shorts and a Bob Marley T-shirt

I finished my black coffee and chugged a large glass of ice water.

"I don't think they give you purified water by the glass,"

Jane said. "You have to ask for bottled water. Otherwise they just give you tap water. It's risky."

"Why didn't you tell me that before?"

"Before what?"

"Before I drank the glass of water?"

"You have the constitution of a refrigerator. It won't be a problem."

I was so glad Jane thought of me as a major appliance. But was I generic contractor grade or a Sub-Zero?

I stood up and began to jog in place.

"See you for dinner?"

"I'll save you a seat," Jane said.

She banged her hand on the table. SLAM!

The waiter on duty and the maître d'hôtel glanced over at us for an instant, shrugged and returned to their endlessly fascinating conversation. There was only one waiter because the hotel was almost empty. The violence in the surrounding countryside had pretty much spooked the tourists.

"This town gives me the creeps," Jane said. "And I'm bored stiff."

"Hang in there a little while longer. I'm very close to getting a line on Aunt Ida." I said. "Maybe what you need is a good fuck."

"Whom should I see about that?"

I wasn't prepared to answer that question beyond the obvious, so I turned and jogged out of the dining room. Traveling at a moderate pace, I passed through the lobby, crossed the zócalo and followed a haphazard pattern of town streets. After a while I found myself on a lonely country road with pastureland on either side where a few skinny cows munched away.

I felt great. My breathing was easy and those little LSD-like endorphins had me as mellow as a missionary after a hard day's work among the heathen. I'd been running for almost forty-five minutes. It was time to head back. Just another hundred yards to a four corners. Maybe there would be a store where I could buy some water.

I jogged up to the intersection and stopped. There was no sign of a mini-mart or roadside taco stand. Two men stood on one side of the road. One with long, black hippy hair, the other with pigtails. Both wore rumpled work pants and checked shirts. Red and blue bandannas, respectively, tied around bull-like necks. Faces as stoic as stone. One had a ragged scar the color of dead moonlight running down the side of his face. A pair of cigar store campesinos.

"Hola." I called out. "Is there agua?"

They looked at me as if I was from Mars or someplace equally ridiculous.

Upon further examination I noticed an assault rifle hung off the shoulder of the man with pigtails. The other man had a blue steel revolver in a worn leather holster strapped to his hip. Yikes! This was not cool. What had Pablo said? Stay out of the countryside and you won't get into trouble.

My mouth, dry from running, instantly became Death Valley at high noon on a summer day. My tongue was a rodent pelt.

I spread my hands wide to show I was just a guileless gringo, weaponless and non-threatening.

The two Mexican bandits, or whatever they were, remained as stolid as a pair of cement pylons.

"Adios, amigos," I said. "I hope everything works out for you."

Still smiling like an idiot savant, I made a U-turn and headed back the way I'd come. At any moment I expected a bullet to slam into my carcass, leaving me dead or dying on the side of this empty road in the middle of nowhere. A sorry-assed end to the grand arc of my existence.

The curve of the road carried me out of sight of the two bad hombres, and my feet, as if possessed, broke stride in a fantastical jig to celebrate my good fortune at not receiving a bullet in the back. After a while I stopped dancing and ran flat out, hell bent for leather.

When I arrived back in the center of town, I was lathered in sweat to a fare-the-well, my bad knee throbbed and a crick in my left side felt like a heart attack in progress. As I streaked through the zócalo, the loafers and hangers-on rose from their territorial benches and applauded.

The return of the gringo loco!

*

Day Four.

I awoke early, sore as hell from my marathon run.

Unable to face another breakfast of Jane's refried beans irony and huevos fritos sarcasm, I whisked into my duds and tiptoed out the door and down to Manny's, even as Jane moaned and rolled onto her stomach, revealing yet again her bounteous bottom.

There would be time for that later.

At Manny's I ordered a Pacifico lager for breakfast, turned down a game of dominoes with Pablo and sat leafing through a motorcycle magazine I found on a shelf in the pissoir. I couldn't read the text, which was in Mexican, but the glossy photos of custom hogs also featured hot biker chicks. Gals you wouldn't want to meet in a dark alley. But whose finer points, viewed in Kodachrome in the light of day, held a certain vicarious masturbatory appeal.

"I've been thinking, señor Bill," said Pablo.

Thinking! I thought. We had reached a whole new level of discourse.

"I believe I erred when I told you Manny's was the solo pool hall in Boca del Diablo. Before you came there existed another. But the owner was stabbed to death more than one month ago by a bad man just like the one who tried to rob the farmacia. I apologize for my omission."

I was on my feet, magazine discarded, wound up with excitement. I clutched Pablo's arm.

"You've got to take me there right now."

"I was thinking maybe a little drink first," said Pablo.

After a little drink, Pablo led the way through a twist of

narrow back streets until we stood in front of a metal-shuttered storefront. In faded letters painted on the stuccoed façade above, were the words Salón de Billar. Some neo-Basquiat artist had painted on the locked steel shutter a frightening, devilish thing with rotting teeth and spiraling, hallucinatory eyes. Torn paper and other unnamable trash filled the corners of the space between the street and the bottom of the shutter.

"Is closed," said Pablo. "No more in business."

I must have looked majorly disappointed because Pablo continued: "No worry. Manny's still open. Plenty of good times with Manny."

Was this the place where Aunt Ida came to let down her hair? Toss back tequila shots, quarrel and break a few heads? There was no one to ask. It was ancient history. Aunt Ida didn't exist in Boca del Diablo except as a figment of my obsession. As a name on the lips of that lunatic Burke.

One more dead end.

"Story of my life," I said to no one in particular.

Suddenly I had a great yearning to have lunch with Jane. Some ordinary boy-girl conversation over grilled trout almondine, garlic toast and a glass of chilled Chardonnay.

When I walked into the hotel room, Jane, naked from the waist down, was on her hands and knees, rump cast high in the air, backed toward the closet door mirror. A little weird.

"What's up?" I asked.

"If you must know," said Jane, "I'm checking to see if my pussy's still attractive."

"Let me know if you need any testimonials," I said.

I unlaced my Asics and lay down on the bed with my hands behind my head to watch. Jane moved her tail end this way and that, her head twisted awkwardly sideways to glimpse the reverse image of her nether region.

Ennui and the early hour at which I had awakened weighed on my eyelids. My eyes closed.

Minutes or seconds passed. I awoke in darkness, disoriented. Something like steel wool covered my nose and mouth. My head was held firmly between Jane's milky, blue veined thighs, her twat thrust unabashedly in my face. There was nothing to do. Nowhere to go.

Slowly, delicately, then faster and faster, I licked, slurped, nibbled, grazed, guzzled, munched, chomped, browsed and gobbled. Above me Jane gyrated, wriggled, jostled, impelled, writhed, heaved, flounced, convulsed, pitched and yawed. A full-court press. A feast for all seasons. An endless summer.

I was lost in a primordial time zone. Jane's cunt spread open like a great, fleshy star portal, sucking me back into the immense darkness, the infinite sea of the womb, where I curled once again into a fetal ball. Fear, hate, anger, self-loathing, loneliness, despair, helplessness, every evil emotion fell away like chaff before our roaring erotic wind. Aunt Ida forgotten. William Burroughs dust. The horrors of Oopawalla and the horrors to come obliterated. Dachau, Belsen, Auschwitz nothing. The Bataan Death March nothing. Pol Pot, Idi Amin and Mao Tse-tung nothing.

Somehow I found myself naked, my cock huge and stalwart as the Eiffel Tower. Jane impaled herself on it. Time stopped and then time sped up. Entwined, we labored like beetles pushing balls of shit up an endless hill. Over and over we sought to reach the summit. And failed.

Gasping for breath, we made one final effort.

"GREGORY, YOU COCKSUCKER!" screamed Jane.

Who was Gregory? I wondered for a nanosecond.

Then I came, spurting for an eon vast globules of viscous, pearlescent sperm across Jane's stomach. In accordance with our agreement, I had pulled out at the last second. With near simultaneity, waves of climactic tremors wracked Jane's body and she howled like a Canadian poet in a typhoon.

Afterward, I lay spent, undone, drenched in sweat and all manner of other effluvia. Jane crouched in my arms, her eyes starring at nothing.

I thought about asking whether she preferred this or trout almondine. But on further consideration, it seemed like a stupid question.

When dusk fell, we roused ourselves from torpid sleep. While Jane took a bath, I ordered room service.

BADA-BOOOOOM!!!!!!

An explosion rocked the zócalo. Several panes in the French doors of our room shattered. I dove behind the bed. "What the fuck was that?" Jane yelled out from the bathroom.

Surely there were no Sunni jihadists operating in the Yucatan. Maybe a gas main had burst.

From the French doors I could see a building burning at the far end of the plaza. As I watched the chaos, a fire engine arrived and began the task of extinguishing the blaze.

The waiter who delivered our room service order told us someone had thrown a bomb in the front door of the farmacia previously involved in an attempted robbery the day we arrived. The pharmacist and his wife were vaporized. The waiter said my friend Pablo, by pure chance passing by the farmacia at the moment of the blast, bled to death when flying glass severed an artery in his throat.

So much for staying hunkered down in Boca del Diablo while the countryside roiled with revolution and counter-revolution, drug lords and Marxist peasants.

"Poor Howard," I said.

"Who's Howard?" said Jane.

12

"Let's go on a picnic," said Jane, stretching her arms high above her head and pushing her chest forward, solely to drive me wild. She was, of course, naked, standing in front of the open French doors for all the world to see.

Pretending to still be asleep, I lay in bed with one hand over my eyes.

"Rodolfo's been telling me about these ancient cenotes," she said. "They're sinkholes in the limestone bedrock filled with ground water. The Mayans considered certain of them to be sacred. They sacrificed virgins at these special cenotes to appease their gods. Nobody does that any more. Nowadays people just go there to swim."

"Thank God for that," I said. "I'd hate to see you at risk. Although, if they were still sacrificing virgins, you wouldn't really qualify."

"Fuck you, too, Bill."

Rodolfo was the hotel concierge. He was always chatting Jane up, complimenting her on her cleavage and other sterling attributes, winking and smiling nonstop like some demonic Eveready bunny, trying to finagle her into a little-used back corridor of the hotel for a quick grope. He cultivated a 1930s Mexican bon vivant air: pencil mustache, monocle, hollow cheeks, longish slicked-back hair and a single gold tooth in front. I'd threatened him with bodily harm on several occasions. But it didn't seem to do any good.

"I wish you'd stay away from Rodolfo," I said. "He pisses me off."

"Oh my, is big bad Bill getting jealous?" Jane puckered and made kissing noises. "Not to worry. Rodolfo's harmless as a fly."

"Yeah," I said under my breath. "A fly with a big, hairy dick."

Jane stood at the bathroom sink brushing her teeth.

I climbed out of bed, yawned, scratched my balls and farted with gusto.

"That was attractive," said Jane over her shoulder. She came and stood in the bathroom doorway, toothpaste dripping down her chin, hands on waist. "Seriously, Bill, if I stay cooped up in this hotel for one more day, I think I just might cut my wrists."

"Okay, okay," I said. "Take a chill pill. We'll go check out one of these cenotes."

We'd been in Boca del Diablo for a week. So far, no sign of Aunt Ida. And I hadn't heard a peep from Lee Kiev since I'd spoken to him in Mexico City, though I'd sent him a pithy telegram: IN BOCA. AWAITING INSTRUCTIONS. BILL." Before we went down to breakfast, while Jane was putting on blush and pomegranate-red lipstick, I dialed Miami on the room phone. The call deep-sixed to voicemail.

"Lee. Bill. Long time no hear. Things are getting dicey here in Boca. That's del Diablo, not Raton. The local pharmacist just got blown up in some Mexican revenge fantasy. The peasants are in revolt. The landowners are arming to the teeth. Hope I fucking hear from you soon about the Burroughs hook up, so we can get the heck out of here."

At breakfast Jane was jubilant about our forthcoming excursion. She ate two flour tortillas spread with melted butter and honey and drank two cups of black coffee, smacking her lips and carrying on a mile-a-minute conversation in Mexican with the waiter. The waiter kept blushing. What was she saying to him exactly? In stoic silence I ate my usual: two fried eggs, refried beans with a splash of hot sauce and a cerveza Pacífico with a wedge of lime. I added the waiter to my hit list, after Rodolfo.

Finally, wiping her lips on a linen napkin, Jane turned her attention back to me.

"I can't believe you actually agreed to go on a picnic to the cenote," she said. "This is so exciting." She clapped her hands. Leaned across the table and ran a sharp-nailed finger down my cheek and along the curve of my jaw.

How could I have not agreed?

Rodolfo had told Jane about a certain remote cenote that was never visited by tourists. He gave her a map, drawn on a sheet of hotel stationery, showing how to get there. The hotel kitchen packed us box lunches. On the way out of town we bought a 12-pack of Tecate, ice and a Styrofoam cooler.

We headed south on a narrow blacktop road. It was a different road from the one on which I had taken my run, but it looked exactly the same. Jane studied Rodolfo's map, while I drove and puffed on a fat spliff rolled from the local schwag. In my mind's eye I held Rodolfo in a headlock, my hard fist punching him in the face until my knuckles became raw and blood dripped.

We met no other traffic going in or out of Boca del Diablo. Where the jungle had been burned back and hacked away, the countryside opened in long, bucolic vistas. In the far distance you could see the undulating profile of the Puuc Hills, like the body of a woman covered in green silk. I sank into a daydream in which a giant eco-goddess, her body sheathed in greenish-gold scales, went on a rampage until she was brought down by tank and rocket fire. Attack of the 50 Ft. Eco-Goddess.

"Turn here," Jane blurted.

Shit! I swerved wildly, narrowly avoiding putting us in the ditch and ending up in a thicket of prickly pear. To our right a sandy track curved into the scrub and disappeared over a slight rise. A weathered wooden gate, once upon a time painted a rich turquoise, blocked access to this dirt road to nowhere. A large sign nailed to the gate read: Propiedad Privada NO PASAR. Beneath the words a skull and crossbones had been painted.

Even I could figure out what that sign said.

The sign was splattered with bullet holes, a humorous retort by some local wag.

Jane jumped out of the Bug and opened the gate, which was unlocked.

"Let's go," she said, sliding back into the passenger seat. "The cenote's just a mile or so up ahead."

"Are you sure we should be doing this?" I asked. "I don't want to stir up the natives."

"Rodolfo said all the locals go here. It's not a problem."

Well, I thought, if shitbag Rodolfo said it was okay, it must be okay! I shrugged and drove through the gate.

Next stop: the cenote.

It actually was an incredible sight. An almost perfectly round puncture in the landscape maybe 200 to 300 yards across with rugged limestone walls overhung with jungly foliage and filled about fifty feet below the rim with the clearest aquamarine water I had ever seen. It was impossible to tell how deep the water was, as the blue fell away into darkness, as if it was somehow an entrance to the Mayan underworld.

Where I parked the VW, there was a small crumbled ruin of oblong stones, the remnants perhaps of a Mayan temple from which ripe maidens were thrown to their doom to bring rain or victory in war or fertility or whatever else it was that was in short supply. A primitive wooden stairway and ladder led down into the sinkhole, where a rough-hewn dock jutted into the cerulean pool.

"I told you it would be spectacular," Jane said. She bounded out of the car, scrambled down the rickety steps and the even more rickety ladder. "Last one in is a dinosaur turd," she called out.

It doesn't take a lot of smarts to guess who ended

up as the dinosaur turd. But it was worth it to stand there and watch.

At the bottom of the ladder, Guess T-shirt, mini-skirt, lacy black bra and sensible panties slumped to the deck. Jane's mind-boggling, blitzkrieg, take-no-prisoners physique walked to the end of the dock. There, feet together, toes slightly over the edge, arms horizontal to either side like a crucifix, she hesitated. Was she suddenly fearful of the aqueous abyss? Did she see the faces of dead virgins rising from the deep?

My eyes counted the fourteen black moles strewn helter-skelter across her back and buttocks like spare change. My kind of spare change.

She brushed aside the horror at the heart of the cenote and, raising her arms above her head, dove artfully, an arc of flesh and light. A tiny splash rose were her body sliced into the water as she disappeared into the endless blue. A lump of spittle stuck in my throat. She was gone. Lost to me forever. Kidnapped by some evil Mayan spirit that lived in the cenote.

Next moment Jane came up for air, bursting through the surface, tossing back her hair. She beckoned to me.

"Don't just stand there like a lump of shit. Get the beer cooler and the lunches and come on down. I'm starving."

I was, for a brief moment, a happy man. Maybe we could move from the hotel to the cenote. Build a little shack of mud bricks with a roof of sticks. I could learn Spanish; plant a vegetable garden. We would grow a little pot for our own use and maybe a little extra to sell for hard currency.

Then I started worrying about Lee. After he didn't hear from me, what if he wanted his money back? Would he send a professional collector after us? One skilled in inflicting pain, breaking fingers and kneecaps? The idea of living off the grid was a crock. There was no escaping your debts and obligations. In a lifetime you could never pay all you owed. You died a pauper.

Besides, Jane was high maintenance. She'd never go for

living in a hovel.

Thinking thusly, I climbed down the ladder into the cenote, overloaded with the beer cooler, our box lunches and a pair of beach towels. As I neared the bottom, Jane's hand reached up and gave my cock a friendly fondle. Dazzled by the glint of sunlight on water and Jane's provocation, I lost my grip. Laughing, we tumbled to the dock. Box lunches, towels and cooler fell around us. In no time we were fornicating like feral hogs checked in to the bridal suite at Motel 6.

As afternoon settled in, a sliver of shade eased over the dock. Jane spread the towels one on top of the other for cushioning and so the person on the bottom didn't get splinters in his or her ass.

I was sleeping on my stomach when a sound woke me. My eyes pinged open. The hard object pressed against the back of my neck sent a chill up my spine. The twin barrels of a sawed off shotgun is what it felt like. Adrenalin churned through my blood. My armpits reeked with fear.

"Don't anybody move," said a voice I knew like I knew the Devil's spawn.

A southern drawl version of Tony Perkins in Psycho.

Who did he mean by "anybody?" I wasn't just anybody. I was somebody. But since I wasn't suicidal, I didn't move. My dick shrank to the size of a peanut on a good day.

"That means you, sweetie," said the voice of Deacon Dobbs, the bounty hunter and Sunday preacher I had left a million miles behind in Miami.

I gave five to one odds he was talking to Jane. But one could never be completely sure about these things.

"Stand up real slow and put on your clothes so's you're decent in front of the Lord."

How the fuck had Dobbsie found us out here in the middle of nowhere? Someone at the hotel must have tipped him off. Rodolfo. The waiter. Just about everybody at the hotel knew we had gone to the cenote.

And how had it come to pass that he knew to look for us

at the Colonial Hotel? It was a long way from Miami to Boca del Diablo. Someone wanted us out of the way. Not Lee. Not Burke. Maybe whoever killed Fritz? Or was it possible Dobbs worked for Aunt Ida? That I was getting too close for comfort?

The sawed-off dug into my neck.

"You're wanted dead or alive," he said. "How I take you back matters more to you than me." He was lying, of course. We'd jumped parole but we hadn't killed anyone. After coming all this distance, he wanted the pleasure of shooting somebody.

"Now your turn, Mr. Bill. Stand up and put your clothes on. Don't look around. If you do, I'll blow your nads to kingdom come."

Being very partial to my nads, as I pulled on jeans and a Corona T-shirt, I looked straight ahead where Jane, in bra and panties, leaned provocatively on one hip. La Femme Nikita came to mind. Though it was ninety degrees out, her tanned skin was covered in goose bumps.

I turned my head partially in Dobbs' direction. "How much do you want?" I asked.

"Want for what?" he said.

"To leave us be."

"You don't understand. I'm here to save your souls. Now both of ya get down on your knees and face me."

We complied.

Deacon Dobbs looked wasted, as if he were sick unto dying. His flesh sagged. The whites of his eyes were bloodshot, his irises bleached of color. He wore swamp-green, pseudo-military fatigues that did nothing to disguise his huge hog belly.

He motioned with the sawed-off.

"You first, missy. Get down in the water. I'm goin' ta baptize your sorry-assed soul."

On her knees Jane moved to the end of the dock. Dobbs stepped forward, raised one combat-booted foot and thrust it against her chest. With a garbled groan, she pitched backward, ass over elbow, into the water. My mind seethed with righteous hate. I retracted like a metal spring, ready to launch myself on Dobbsie, beat him until he moaned to be released from this life. But Deacon Dobbs was on top of it, swinging the shotgun left handed in my direction, his steely, colorless eyes daring me to come to Jane's aid. And die trying.

I willed myself to stay put.

Jane fought her way to the surface, splashing and flailing wildly as if in a panic. Maybe she was cramping. "Help! Help!" she pleaded, raising arms and hands toward Deacon Dobbs. "I can't swim."

With the sawed-off leveled at my face, his eyes darting back and forth between me and Jane's folly, Dobbs knelt down on one knee and reached out toward her. Their hands met, locked, struggled mightily, their faces contorted with rage and determination and, in the case of Deacon Dobbs, after a while, disbelief and fear.

Wipeout!

In the end Jane won, wrenching Deacon Dobbs forward, pulling him into airspace. Going down, he could have pulled the shotgun trigger and taken my face off. But he hesitated, and then it was too late, as he catapulted into the water, his weight and momentum sending up a vast spray.

The Deacon struggled toward the dock, Jane fighting him all the way like a scrappy mongrel dog. Her feet found purchase on a submerged support for the dock and, as he grabbed at the rough planks, she rose above him and bore downward on his forearm with all her weight and fury. I heard the bone snap.

The shotgun was gone, sunk to the bottom of the cenote.

I reached out and pulled Jane up onto the dock. She was shaking, consumed by emotion. I held her until she stopped.

Deacon Dobbs had disappeared.

Twice he bobbed up, eyes bugged out like Peter Lorre in The Man Who Knew Too Much, one hand lashing at the water. The other hanging broken and useless. His mouth gaped, taking on water.

In a rage I ripped loose a plank from the dock and brought it crashing down on his skull. He went under for the last time.

A trail of bubbles marked his descent to hell. A red stain in the water spread outward until it became nothing.

Dobbsie's bible lay abandoned on the dock. I kicked it into the drink, where it sank like a stone.

Jane took off her wet undies, making a spectacle of herself yet again, before donning a grape leather mini-skirt and T-shirt and beginning the long climb out of the cenote.

13

After the business with Dobbsie, things with Jane suddenly cooled. Listless, she lay for hours in our hotel room with the blinds drawn, a cold compress across her forehead. When I nuzzled her neck, she pulled away. "Not now," she said, when I made a grab for her snatch.

Jumpy was her general state of being.

There was still no word from Lee. No sign of Aunt Ida. Maybe it was all bullshit.

At breakfast the second day after our ill-fated cenote picnic, Jane sat stone still, gnawing on a cuticle, staring into the distance.

"So, what's up?" I said, in between mouthfuls of fried egg and refried beans.

Jane rubbed her eyes, then shook her head, as if she had just awakened from a dream. She looked at me as if I were a stranger.

"I'm creeped out. I need to get out of here for a while."

"What are you talking about?"

"I don't know why I came with you to the Yucatan. The fucking jungle gets on my nerves. I should have stayed in Mexico City. Looked up some of my old friends."

"We had a deal," I said.

"Oh. A deal? Is that what you call it? I thought it might have been something more."

"You knew I had obligations," I said. "Things I had to do."

"Stick your to-do list up your ass, Bill. I almost got killed the other day out there in the boonies. And for what? I want…" She put her hands over her face. Drew them away. "I need to go up to Mérida for a few days. Come up for air."

Our waiter, the one and only waiter, came by and offered more coffee. We declined. Could he get us anything else? Nada. Should he bring the check?

"Charge it to the goddamn room," I said. "Like you've been doing every day since we got here."

For an instant he looked like he might fly into a rage and attack me with a butter knife. Or something sharper. The moment passed unrealized, and with a nihilistic third world shrug, off he went.

"Give me some money," Jane said. "You owe me."

Weariness afflicted me. My breathing grew shallow, stuttery. Someone, it seemed, had sucked all the air out of the room.

Was this adios? Sayonara? Auf wiedersehen? The end of whatever? I thought of Mary Beth pointing a gun at my heart. Of Edie disappearing through the door to Aunt Ida's bedroom back in Orlando. The cell-like room at the VA psych ward in Atlanta where nightmares of Armageddon ran roughshod through my head. None of it made any sense. But all of it hurt like hell.

I gave Jane all the money I had in my wallet, a little over five thousand pesos. She caught the two o'clock bus to Mérida.

"Call me," I said, as she boarded the bus.

I went up to the room to put on my bathing suit and get the James Bond thriller I was reading. Diamonds Are Forever. A couple of Jane's dresses still hung in the closet. Some mismatched slinky underwear occupied the top drawer of the dresser. Were these a sufficient reason for her to return from Mérida? I doubted it. Was I?

The red message light on the room phone blinked at me. I dialed the operator but nobody picked up. When I went down to the front desk, Rodolfo squinted at me through his monocle as though I were a blue giraffe with yellow spots and a hard-on. He handed me a slip of paper with Lee's phone number written on it.

Lee answered on the first ring.

"Bill, where have you been?"

"I was seeing someone off at the bus station."

Silence. When Lee resumed, his tone was clipped, breathless.

"We're moving on the Burroughs thing at last. I've got someone coming down from Mérida with the do-re-mi and some armament in the next couple of days. He knows how to get to the suitcase owner's hideaway. It's deep in the jungle. I don't think there'll be any trouble. But you need to be prepared for the worst case scenario."

Armament? Worst case? Suddenly the whole operation sounded very uncool.

"It's a good thing you took Jane with you to Mexico," continued Lee. "I did a quick background check. She's a tough cookie. Murdered her husband. In a prior life she was involved with some sort of Russian mobster down in Mexico. Always good to have a gun moll as backup."

"Your sources must be giving you bad info," I said. "Jane hardly qualifies as a gun moll. In a fit of depression she ran over her husband with their rental car."

"Didn't she shoot someone at that halfway house where you were staying in Miami?"

I'd forgotten all about the Deets affair. "That was a one-off," I replied. "Nothing you could rely on. Besides she's gone up to Mérida, so she probably won't be back in time."

"Is something wrong?" asked Lee.

"Just the usual."

Another silence. In my mind I could see Lee's heavy shoulders rise and fall with centuries-old Jewish fatalism.

"On second thought, it's risky to count on a skirt in a tight spot," said Lee. "You can never be sure whose side they're going to come down on."

"Jane's no different then anyone else. When you're up

against it, it's every man for himself."

"That woman is distorting your perspective, Bill."

"Let's just get this behind us," I said.

I wondered if I should mention to Lee the appearance and disappearance of Deacon Dobbs. Or the existence of the enigmatic Frau Stein. Screw it! It would only add to the tension that hung in the air like a severed head.

"I'll call you as soon as I know the exact date and time of the meet," said Lee.

"Roger that," I said into the dead handset.

On the way down to the pool, I ordered a pitcher of Mexican margaritas, a cabalistic combo of fresh lime juice, Cointreau and a shitload of ultra-smooth 100 blue agave silver tequila.

Time passed. One, two, maybe three days.

I was drinking heavily and smoking pot in between.

Jane didn't call, as far as I knew. At one point I accused Rodolfo of not giving me her messages. Grabbed him by the throat and slammed him against the wall. From somewhere he pulled a gun on me. Lucky for him, the hotel manager stepped in before things really got out of hand.

I wondered if Jane was having fun in Mérida. Whether she was getting her head straight. Maybe she had already gone back to Mexico City, bedding down with someone suave and debonair from the good old days.

On day three I'd had enough of the Hotel Colonial. It was time to knock off the booze, eat healthy.

A mango juice and smoothie stand on a back street plaza, where I'd made inquiries about Aunt Ida, came to mind.

As I approached the juice bar, two finely wrought ladies in the trade offered me warm smiles of encouragement, their Crest-polished ivories and sweat-oiled skin gleaming in the crystalline light of morning. I guessed both were in their early twenties.

One, dressed in blue striped shorts of the skin-tight variety and a matching halter-top, leaned with her back to the counter on which wooden bowls of limes, mangos and bananas were set out. One foot languidly scratched the calf of her opposite leg. A Swarovski bauble glinted from her exposed belly button. Strands of wispy jet hair outlined a Mayan face traced verbatim from a temple ruin a thousand years old.

Her ivory-complexioned pal, outfitted in a frilly-skirted pale pink dress that hugged her upper body like a second skin, gazed wantonly over her shoulder in my direction. Her elbows rested on the counter as she waited to be served. Her thinness stood as staunch and steadfast as a flamenco dancer.

Both were barefoot and libertine.

"Hola," said the Mayan beauty, slurping her fruit drink through a straw.

"Hola to you," I said. "And hola to your friend."

I knew already I was a goner.

The electric whirr of a commercial blender ripped apart the opportunity for further repartee. The mulatto juice man handed the flamenco dancer a tall glass filled with fruit slush the color of blood oranges.

"So," I said, "What's your favorite fruit drink?"

With less than zero tourists thronging the streets of Boca del Diablo, times were tough. I negotiated a two-for-one, all day rate and, after sucking my way to the bottom of an extra-large banana mango smoothie, we headed back to the hotel. My mood was ebullient. Screw Jane and the bus she'd left town on! As Conchita and Inez and I walked arm in arm, an old nursery rhyme my mother sang to me danced in my head.

I went to the animal fair.
The birds and the beasts were there.
The old baboon, by the light of the moon
Was combing his auburn hair.

The funniest was the monk.
He sat on the elephant's trunk.

The elephant sneezed, and fell on his knees
And what became of the monk, the monk, the monk, the monk …

(Repeat until bored.)

As a kid, I had reinvented myself as the monk. That seemed as true in the present as it had then. Now, as then, I wondered what would become of me.

As we paraded through the lobby, Rodolfo, seated at the concierge desk reading an existential Mexican comic book, glanced up and did a well-worn double take. Before he could raise an objection, we bounded up the stairs and into the room.

The bed was a sandless beach of sweat-stained sheets. Dirty glasses, tar-stained roaches and half empty bags of queso-flavored potato chips and lime & chili chicharrones covered every surface. While the girls freshened up, I hung out the "do not disturb" sign, neatly straightened the sheets and pillows and gathered up the glasses, roaches and snack bags. Pouring myself a shot of tequila, I sat on the bed and sought to prepare myself for the forthcoming storm of lust.

Moments later, the bathroom door swung wide and Conchita and Inez pranced forth naked as a nudist colony. It was enough to make you salivate and stand on your head, clap your hands and bark like a seal, snort and squeal like a pig in shit. They stood, flawless, fecund, rococo. Mirror opposites flaunting their wears. Conchita, a voluptuous, epicurean feast, her jiggly-wigglies cascading like a Niagara Falls of flesh, swayed on hips made to give birth to the world. Lanky, long-limbed Inez stalked egret-like and elegant, her pointy tits threatening danger.

In seconds the duo shucked off my clothes, exposing me like an ear of sweet corn. Oddly, my schlong remained limp and unmoved.

"Es muy pequeño," smiled Inez. "¿Por qué?"

"You no like sex with woman?" asked Conchita.

"Hey," I said. "I'm paying the freight here. You ladies

need to strut your stuff. Get the old pocket rocket to salute."

It was a long, arduous day. Despite Inez and Conchita's best efforts, Mr. Softy remained as flaccid and unforthcoming as a bowl of oatmeal. The more languidly my dick lolled, the more blame I cast.

The stress of the impending Burroughs deal. The near death experience with Deacon Dobbs. Too much booze and pot. My feud with Rodolfo. Burke and his threat of deportation. The nightmare of Fritz's shattered skull and gore-spattered corpse. My utter failure to track down Aunt Ida. The lack of red meat in my diet. The roiling, breeding, ravenous, blood-sucking jungle on every side like the very heart of darkness.

In the end I decided it was all Jane's fault. I had come to count on Jane being around. And now she wasn't and my life had turned topsy-turvy.

At one point we ordered sandwiches, chips and salsa and two bottles of el cheapo Mexican white wine and had a nude picnic in the room.

On the shank of the afternoon, my half-hard cock finally coughed up a watery trickle of jizz, much to the excitement and relief of Inez and Conchita. To celebrate we took a group shower. Then collapsed together on the bed. My dick had suffered an Indian burn. Exhausted, depleted, sucked dry as an insect corpse, I fell into a doze.

When I jerked awake, Inez and Conchita were sitting at the escritorio going through my wallet.

"WHAT THE FUCK IS GOING ON HERE?!"

"We were only curious," said Inez.

"Yeah, right," I said.

Inez held up a photograph. "We found this."

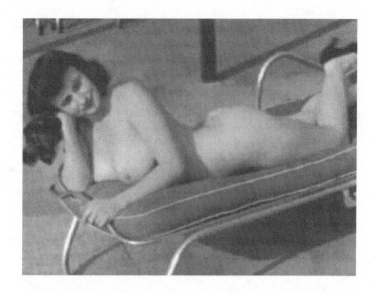

I ripped it from her grasp. It was the snapshot of the nude woman on the chaise I'd found in Fritz's wallet back in the church in Mexico City.

"How is it you have this fotografía of señora Stein?" asked Conchita.

"What did you say?"

I stared again at the fuzzy image of a dark-haired buck-naked wench loitering on her stomach, provocative yet bored, one pump-clad foot raised jauntily in the air, one lollygagging boob exposed.

"It is the señora Stein," said Conchita. "The owner of Hacienda de Sade."

"How do you know that?" I asked.

"She gives parties. We are invited. We go there."

"You mean orgies," I said.

Conchita laughed. Inez winked and wrinkled her nose.

I remembered another piece of paper also from Fritz's wallet. A piece of paper with a phone number on it. Was it possible?

Grabbing my wallet, I dug out the worn and creased slip

of paper and dialed the number written on it.

"Hello. Hello? Who's calling?"

If I were deaf, dumb and blind, I would have still recognized that lilting country twang. Holy Toledo! It was Aunt Ida, the Devil incarnate! Knock wood!

Her voice rose in anger. "Who the fuck is this!"

I cut the line. Ran helter-skelter for the toilet and vomited lunch. Back on the bed, I lay shaking as if struck down with the ague.

There was a knock at the door.

The door opened and Jane walked in. She looked from me to Conchita. To Inez. Then back to me.

"This is a fine kettle of fish," she said. "I leave town for a few days and the place turns into the fucking Mustang Ranch." Before anyone could react, Jane stepped to Inez's side, leaned down and kissed and tongued the magenta rosebud nub of Inez's left tit.

My cock grew instantly rigid as a 2x4, while my mind dialed 911. This couldn't be happening!

14.

"Luis! What the heck are you doing here?"

I'd gone down to the dining room to get more ice for the party we had going in the room, me and Jane and Inez and Conchita. And there he was, obese Luis, looking, to put it mildly, tattered around the edges, sitting in one of the red leather wingback chairs in the lobby.

His double chin sagged. Eyelids drooped like water-soaked brown paper bags over swollen, bloodshot eyeballs. Dried spittle clung to the corners of his mouth. His skin, beneath two days of salt and pepper scruff, had the color of a dead fish underbelly. A battered aluminum briefcase that Muhammad Ali might have used as a punching bag rested on the tile floor next to the chair.

"You look like a pile of bat guano," I said.

He smiled wanly.

"Just got in from Mérida half an hour ago. Been running around like a crazy person. No sleep for three days. But here I am." I must have looked puzzled for he patted the briefcase with one beefy paw. "I'm the money guy."

"You work for Lee!?" I said, almost falling off my chair, though I was standing up.

"Strictly on a per diem."

"In Mexico City?"

"He had me pick you guys up at the airport. Just to keep an eye on you. Make sure you didn't get in too much trouble. Lee's a very careful guy. Always working the odds."

"But Jane… Was she…"

"Nah. She didn't have a clue. I had her picture in my pocket. Picked her out of the crowd when she came outside the terminal looking for a cab."

I was not reassured. There were too many players, each with their own lunatic agenda. Too many coincidences. Everybody was working for somebody else. Or the opposite.

What was really going on here?

Suddenly it was even possible Jane and Luis had something going on the side. It was her idea to go up to Mérida, when she could have gone to Cancun or Cozumel and chilled out on the beach. Maybe she felt sorry for Luis, that he was so overweight. So pathetic. Or was she thinking about cutting me out of the Burroughs deal?

I wanted my money for the Burroughs delivery and my revenge. And then what? Something would come to me. It always did. I just wasn't 100 sure about Jane any more.

"By the way," said Luis. "That guy Burke is a scumbag. You should stay clear of him."

"Lee knows about Burke?"

The answer to that question was as obvious as the profession of the young Latina in black bra and butt-cheek-exposing red mini shorts who sometimes leaned against the wall outside of Manny's, a cigarette clenched between glossy puce lips. The spiraling smoke made her squint and twist her mouth, so for an instant her face was that of the crazy old woman she would become sooner rather than later.

Luis' eyes narrowed to slits. The lids tumbling down like a curtain falling at the end of Act 2 of a three-act melodrama. Intermission. But the audience was restive, anxious for the final plot twist they knew was coming. In a rush they leaped up and made for the bar in the lobby, reaching in their pockets and purses for cigarettes and matches, money for a weak drink.

Luis stood, shoulders slumped with exhaustion. Picked up his briefcase.

"I need to get some sleep," he said. "The Burroughs deal

goes down tomorrow. We need to get an early start. A long drive south of the Puuc Hills. The roads down there are crap."

What I needed was a bucket of ice and a fresh drink. And another snort of blow.

*

Crap was an understatement. The road we'd been on for the last two hours was a thrill ride to Hades, a raw streambed littered with boulders the size of ostrich eggs. Shark's teeth razored up from the hard laterite surface, ready to slice our tires to shreds. The VW Bug jounced and hiccupped, skidded and shuddered until I thought it would break apart like a ship crashing on a coral reef.

My head thrummed from the previous night's festivities, my intestines reeled. The long, rolling vistas of the Puuc Hills were miles behind us. Like hog intestines, the unpaved washboard road twisted and twined through barbwire jungle.

When we came around the next bend, marked by the fiery hothouse blooms of a Royal Poinciana, Luis whispered:

"Pull over."

Ahead, in the middle of nowhere, a two-story, white stucco house of modernist lines had been built on a modest rise in the land. Six brick columns supported a balcony on three sides shaded by a wide roof overhang. One side of the house was connected to an older adobe structure whose red tile roof, bell tower and heavy wooden, double doors fortified with wrought iron fixtures suggested the restored remains of an ancient mission. Behind reared the ravenous maw of the jungle.

As Jane and I stared at this apparition, Luis' arm brushed my shoulder as he handed me a snubnosed Smith & Wesson .38 revolver.

"Just in case things get dicey," he said.

The .25 caliber Saturday Night Special he offered Jane looked like it had been shoplifted from a 1940s film noir melodrama.

I thought of Miss O'Shaughnessy in The Maltese Falcon. Jane and Miss O'Shaughnessy were blood sisters.

"You're shitting me," said Jane. "I'm not carrying a gun. People with guns end up shooting themselves in the foot. Or worse. If the deal goes south, I'll just take my clothes off. Make love, not war, baby. Besides that thing couldn't hurt a house cat."

"Best I could do on short notice, sweetie," snapped Luis.

Jane grabbed my right arm with both hands and cuddled up.

"Bill will protect me," she said.

My lips peeled back from clenched teeth.

Luis ratcheted a round into the firing chamber of a black polymer Glock 9mm and thrust the weapon behind his back into the waist of his black jeans, where it nuzzled contentedly in his Grand Canyon butt crack.

Armed and dangerous, we exited the VW and walked toward the house. Out in the open, the tropical sun beat down like a demonic child armed with a truncheon. No one seemed to be about. Were they expecting us? Or had they all driven over to the local cenote for a dip?

Briefcase at his side, Luis led the way toward the church-like structure.

As we drew close, one side of the double doors opened inward and an ebony-haired Indian woman stepped forth. Her face was hard but attractive, with full, pouty lips unadorned with lipstick. Her wood ash-colored eyes were overhung with eyebrows as thick as strips hacked from a rare wooly mammoth pelt. I guessed early thirties.

She was rigged out in a silky black blouse vicariously open to the navel, black calf-length skirt and cowboy boots. A cartridge belt cinched her waist. A heavy gold necklace and gold bangle earrings completed her get up, casting her as a refugee from a faded Kodak snapshot of Emiliano Zapata's band of brothers from the 1910 Mexican Revolution. My gaze might have been transfixed by the rising convexity of her mostly revealed breasts and the firm, nutmeg-toned flesh of her stomach but for one additional detail. Two-handed, she held before her a revolver of archaic, but still lethal, design. At the moment it was pointed at the ground. But my nads still shriveled.

"It's been a while, Luis," she said.

"Indeed it has. How've you been, Gretchen?" When Gretchen responded with silence cold enough to freeze your heart, Luis gestured toward Jane and me. "These are my associates, Bill and Jane."

This was weird, I thought. Now we were all on a first name basis.

Gretchen tightened her lips. Clearly she was having none of this make believe camaraderie.

"My father's waiting," she said.

The interior of the mission consisted of one large hall rising up two stories to a vaulted ceiling painted with entwined vines, bodacious nymphs and satyrs sporting uncircumcised hard-ons. In front on a low proscenium, resided a seated, blissfully smiling Buddha at least ten feet high, carved from some greenish stone.

Rows of tatami mates covered the stone floor. Zodiac signs and other mystical looking symbols decorated the white-painted stucco walls. Aqueous light tumbled from high windows. The air was hazy with incense.

A booming male voice exploded from speakers mounted in the upper corners of the room.

"Leave your weapons on the table at the back of the room."

"We come in peace and harmony," said Luis.

"Just do what I fucking told you to do," said the voice of god-like authority.

After an exchange of raised eyebrows, Luis and I complied.

From behind the Buddha a male nurse slash caretaker type in a white uniform pushed forth a wheelchair containing a gnarled and wizened ancient swathed, despite the blistering heat and crotch-rot humidity of the Yucatan summer, in a hand-woven wool blanket.

Dr. Jacobi, I presumed.

The attendant wheeled the old fart forward to a low table situated in front of the Buddha. From there Jacobi considered us from eyes buried in dark, wrinkled flesh like fisheyes implanted into a pair of dried prunes. A wispy Fu Manchu mustache and beard failed to hide the cadaverous hue of his complexion, the emaciated folds of flesh that made him look like a death camp survivor.

Gretchen stood to one side, her pistol residing in the cartridge belt circling her waist.

We approached obsequiously. At least Luis and I did. Behind us, Jane swaggered.

Words dribbled from Jacobi's lips like the whisper of dry seed husks rubbing together.

"Show me the money."

Luis knelt on one knee and set his briefcase on the low table, unsnapped the twin locks and folded back the top half, exposing stacks of gringo twenties and fifties in colorful bank wrappers. It looked to be a tidy sum. A hundred grand was my guess. Under other circumstances I might have let loose a high-pitched whistle.

If Lee was prepared to pay that kind of dough for a crummy suitcase, he must be charging his client a shitload and then some. Too bad I hadn't negotiated a bigger fee.

The male nurse stepped forward and rifled through the contents of the briefcase, punching numbers into a small calculator. Jacobi was taking no chances.

His eyes hungrily followed every action by the attendant.

I glanced over my shoulder at Jane. She stood in a casual slump, feeding Chiclets between her lips. When she began to chew, a wave of mintiness wafted up my nose. Her cyborg eyes were jacked up, taking in every body movement, every detail, every nuance.

When the count was completed, the male nurse leaned close to the shriveled figure and whispered in his ear. The poet's thin lips twisted this way and that, as if he were sucking on a piece of hard candy. One fisheye closed.

It was a signal!

They were going to rip us off!

Gretchen pointed her ancient firearm at Luis and fired. But despite his 300 lbs., Luis was no longer where he had been. The bullet embedded itself in the wooden table.

Catapulting across the table, Luis tripped up the hired help, sending him sprawling on his ass. Luis followed up by beating him senseless with repeated blows of the barrel of the Saturday Night Special that had previously resided in Luis' sock.

A bunch of fucking amateurs. No one had bothered to frisk us.

Before Gretchen could react, Luis jammed the Saturday Night Special in Jacobi's ear. The nasty old man began to wheeze like a bagpipe being blown by a terminal emphysema patient. "Tell Gretchen to put down her weapon," hissed Luis.

The oldster was speechless.

Gretchen's eyes danced a tango of indecision.

A knife appeared in Luis' hand. He drew it across Jacobi's wattled throat. A line of blood appeared where the blade, honed to perfection, nicked the skin.

"We just want the suitcase," said Luis. "The money's yours."

Why did Luis say that? I wondered. Jacobi and company had intended to rip us off. Murder us. Now the shoe was on the other foot. We had every right to take the suitcase and the money.

The male nurse groaned, tried to rise onto hands and knees. Failed. Luis' sneaker-clad foot caught him in the chin and he was out cold again. In the wheelchair Dr. Jacobi made a gurgling noise and slumped sideways.

"Okay, okay," said Gretchen. She set her weapon on the floor. "I'll get the suitcase."

"And the notarized affidavit," said Luis.

It didn't look like much. An ordinary old beat-to-shit leather suitcase, its sides swaybacked, its brass locks and fittings tarnished. In one corner two faded but still readable travel decals proclaimed: *Visit Sunny Mexico and Cuernavaca: City of Silver.*

"It's locked," said Gretchen. "The key was lost a long time ago."

"Doesn't matter," said Luis. "I'm supposed to deliver it unopened. It is what it is. Caveat emptor and all that crap." He grasped the worn leather handle.

Wait a minute, I thought. I was the one who was supposed to deliver the suitcase to Lee, not Luis!

I tensed, about to pounce, when Jane's hand smacked the back of my head. She always knew my intent, like the next routine in a well-worn sitcom. One of those big 1930s Hollywood nightclub flashbulbs went off in my brain. Now was not the time to become embroiled in a dispute with Luis.

"And the affidavit." Luis held out his hand toward Gretchen and drew it back grasping an ornate legal document affixed with gold ribbons, seals of authority and flamboyant scrawls. That must have cost a pretty penny, I thought. An arm and a leg.

Luis studied it, his lips moving. "Reads okay to me," he said. "But what do I know. I'm no lawyer." He shrugged. "If Lee wanted a legal opinion, he should have had his legal beagle here."

He looked at Gretchen.

"And the rest."

She pretended to look puzzled.

"Don't be coy," said Luis. "The deal included a full release of claims by Dr. Jacobi, on behalf of himself, his heirs and assigns, and the original Burroughs' letter granting your father a lien on the suitcase, for consideration received. He was desperate for cash so he could split the scene down here before the Mex authorities changed their minds about locking him up for murdering his spouse."

"You sound like a freakin' lawyer to me," I said.

"I flunked out at the end of the first year."

"What school?"

"Yale."

"You're kidding? I went to Yale for a couple of years. When were you there."

"Let's talk about this another time," said Luis.

Satisfied at last that he had all the necessary documents, clutching the crummy suitcase to his bosom, Luis backed toward the massive double doors by which we had entered. Jane and I followed suit. Jane scooped up the two pistols we had left on the table.

Bang!

A chunk of the green Buddha splintered into the air. As usual Jane was going wild in the streets.

"Don't come after us!" Jane shouted. "Don't even fucking think about it!"

But Gretchen was already on her knees beside the body of her father, who had half-slid, half-fallen out of his wheelchair and lay in a heap on the floor. Maybe he'd had a heart attack. Maybe he was dead. In which case Gretchen was rich as well as hot. And the nurse attendant was shit out of luck in the job department.

Outside, we scampered like March hares across the clearing to where we'd left the Bug in the shade of a vast tropical tree. At any moment I expected the shadow of Lucifer or another winged predator to pass over us before the inevitable strike.

Scratch that metaphor. What I was really worried about was Gretchen or the male nurse standing in the doorway of the Buddhist temple, bearing down on us with a high-powered sniper rifle.

It didn't happen. But I had to worry about something.

By the car I patted my pockets for the ignition key. Once, twice, three times. It wasn't there! I yanked my pockets inside out.

"Shit," I said. "I can't find the key."

Luis gave me a death stare.

Jane pointed through the window. The key resided in the ignition slot, where I'd forgotten to take it.

"Good thing we're off the beaten path in the middle of this shithole jungle," she said. "If we were in downtown Mexico City, we'd be looking at an empty parking space. Have to make a dash for the subway."

"Are you done rubbing it in yet?" I said, hands on hips. "Because then we can get in the car and vámonos."

"Oh, poor baby's all upset. Let mommy make it better." Next moment her lips devoured mine, her tongue thrust halfway down my throat, her leg grinding against my groin. Did we have to do this now? With Luis watching?

I eased her gently away from me.

"Sorry," said Jane. "I get horny as hell in a tight spot."

After that, we jumped in the Bug and hightailed it outa there.

Half an hour later I pulled over while Jane scooted behind a bush to take a pee. The humidity must have been a hundred and fifty percent. Sweat poured indiscriminately down my neck, chest, back and crotch. Above, thunderheads boiled in the narrow slice of sky visible from our low down, jungle-enshrouded vantage point.

"Looks like rain," said Luis.

"Do you think they'll come after us?" I said.

"Nah. They got the money. We're home free. Jacobi's dying. That's why he was willing to do the deal after all these years. Wants to provide an inheritance for his daughter."

I didn't believe him. I figured they were hot on our trail. We needed to haul ass.

Jane scooted back into the passenger seat. "Forgot tissues," she said, apropos of nothing.

"Hope you didn't use some poisonous leaf," said Luis.

"You're kidding," said Jane.

Luis shook his head. "Lots of bad shit out there. That's why they call it a jungle."

I started the engine.

"Hold up," said Jane. "Aren't we going to look and see what's in the suitcase?"

"Sorry. No can do," said Luis. "Lee was very specific about not opening the suitcase. Part of the premium price he's charging the collector is for the thrill of discovering the unknown. Like opening an ancient tomb that's lain hidden for a thousand years."

"No one will know," said Jane.

"Lee will know," said Luis.

"What? He has supernatural powers?" She blew out a dismissive puff of air.

"There's no key," said Luis. "If I pick the lock, there'll be scratches. It would be obvious to anyone that we'd taken a peek. Maybe even removed some item of value. The client would be very unhappy, pissed even. He or she might back out of the deal."

"Luis is right," I said. "Lee was very specific. 'Don't open the fucking suitcase.' were his very words. That's it. End of discussion. Besides, we gotta get moving."

"Jesus, Bill, lighten up. Lee Kiev's a thousand miles away as the crow flies. It's not like he's lurking behind the bush where I just peed."

"If we open it, he'll know and I'd never get another job in Miami."

"There's a warrant out for your arrest in Miami. I doubt you'll ever work there again," said Jane. "Frankly, you guys are a bunch of pussies."

On that note, I jammed the stick shift into gear and resumed our trek back to Boca del Diablo, pushing the Bug to the limit on the raw road to perdition.

*

Back in the vicinity of the Puuc Hills, the Bug started limping on one side.

What now!

I pulled up and got out just where an ancient Mayan road

stretched toward the northwest through open countryside. The right rear tire was flat. I opened the trunk, which, in old school VW Bugs, is in the front. There was a jack and a lug wrench. But no spare!

When we rented it, I hadn't bothered to check.

But who checks for the spare? I mean, what kind of rental car doesn't come with a spare?

Up to now the day had gone more or less as planned. At least we weren't dead or dying.

At the moment, however, we were clearly in deep doo-doo.

"What kind of a piece of shit is this?" demanded Luis. He kicked the flat. The hubcap came off, rolled a couple of feet and fell over on a rock. Clang!

I chanced to glance toward the horizon. Along the parallel lines of the ancient Mayan roadway, a cloud of dust churned into the air. A large black automobile was the cause. It was maybe a quarter mile off and closing fast. From the outline and the grillwork, it had to be a classic Mercedes Benz sedan.

I wondered what kind of car Lucifer would drive.

15

It all happened in a flash.

As we gawked at the black Mercedes pounding toward us like a charging rhino, chased by a cyclone of dust, behind us came the rumble of a hopped-up truck engine, running on methamphetamines. When we sprang around, a machine gun mounted in the bed of a cobalt blue Dodge Ram pickup stared us in the face and took our breath away. It was an older Soviet PK model. The militias in I-rack loved them. One burst would cut you in half faster than a chain saw.

The mestizo in the Bart Simpson two-tone baseball cap manning the machine gun was not smiling. I raised my hands in the spirit of fellowship. And surrender. Luis and Jane followed suit.

Where had these pricks come from? The pickup must have been lurking behind the Mayan temple disguised as a pile of rubble that we had just passed. A man and a woman in blue-gray camouflage fatigues descended from the cab, frisked us (found Luis' Seal-style combat knife, kneed him in the nads, laughed as he rolled on the ground) and bound our hands behind our backs with plastic restraints, to which I was instantly allergic. My wrists broke out in a rabid rash.

Jane started to hyperventilate. There was nothing I could do. She closed her eyes and calm descended upon her. By then the fat-cat Mercedes had arrived, together with the cloud of dust. We waited for the dust to settle. For the other shoe to fall.

*

Contrary to popular myth, revenge is rarely sweet. More commonly the moment of retribution brings on stomach-churning indigestion and heart palpitations, nerve-grinding fear of discovery by law enforcement and self-loathing at one's ability to commit mayhem in the name of an eye for an eye. But when the smoky, rear passenger-side window of the Mercedes retracted into the doorframe to reveal Aunt Ida's nightmare visage, I felt an express train sugar rush of desire to commit murder surge through my bloodstream.

But alas, my fingers numb from the tightness of the restraints binding my wrists, a hapless fool, I was helpless to do anything except peruse her every sordid detail.

Time had beaten Aunt Ida to a pulp. Left her lying in the dirt, her face bloody.

A mere six years had passed since the big score that sent me to rot in hell in Oopawalla Prison. But in that short time period, blight and corrosion had descended upon Aunt Ida like some post-modern end game.

The face that looked out at me was gaunt, wasted. A hollow woman. Gone were the rambunctious, bottle-blonde tresses; replaced by a sheenless, mouse-brown mop tied back in a ponytail. Her sassy, fuck-me-if-you-dare smile had fallen at the corners into a permanent frown of discontent. Only the bottle-rocket eyes, hidden now in deep, haunted sockets, remained unchanged, ready to explode with anger or delight, satire or sadism.

Yet, despite the ravages of time and drugs and gall and whatever else had consumed her, Aunt Ida was still one hell of an eyeful, in a Countess Dracula sort of way. Lips as red as fresh blood. Swaths of orange and gold make-up curving above her eyebrows like the shadows of devil's horns. Her jutting, overconfident chin. Heavy gold earrings raped from a Mayan tomb hovered like strange insects at her earlobes. She was naked above the waist except for a bra made of two silver seashells from which her dream-breasts spilled like the waters of the River Lethe.

With a gulp I realized Aunt Ida's cooze still held sway over me. That I would throw everything away to drown in the waters of forgetfulness that flowed from that orifice. The past was water over the dam. But my schwantz and I, the eternal optimists, still had high hopes for the future.

A black hair, emerging like an insect appendage from one nostril of her upturned nose, broke the spell.

"Bill?" said Aunt Ida. "Is it really you? Someone told me you died in prison. Wishful thinking, I guess."

227

"Always the smart-ass," I said. "I'm surprised no one's taken out a snuff contract on you."

"But you still pine for me. I can see it in your eyes."

I blinked, caught at the still point between lust and murder.

A bound and trussed Luis was heaved into the bed of the pickup. Jane disappeared into the cab between the driver with a hard-on and his hard-as-nails sidekick.

Aunt Ida beckoned for me to sit next to her in the spacious backseat of the Mercedes. With the blade of a stiletto, she severed the bonds holding my wrists. A wiry, clean-shaven young man with a high-pitched voice, who filled the roles of palace eunuch and aide de camp, prepared a pitcher of gin fizzes.

"For old time's sake," said Aunt Ida. I recalled the gin fizzes served on that fateful afternoon when Edie and I and the kids arrived at Aunt Ida's tawdry, two-bit ranch home in suburban Orlando, back before the shit hit the fan. We clinked glasses. It was not a happy memory. You can't go back.

"Who's the chick?" asked Aunt Ida., as she slurped down her frothy drink and lit a spliff as fat as a pregnant python. I'd never really thought of Jane as a "chick."

"Nobody really. Just some adventuress I hooked up with in Mexico City."

Was I protecting Jane? Or distancing myself from her?

Aunt Ida contemplated my poker face, turning my answer over in her mind like the two sides of an ancient coin. A coin that still held the possibility of upending expectations by landing on its edge.

"Let's cut to the chase," she said. "Do you want to fuck me or kill me?"

"Are those my only choices?" I said.

"I've been dreaming about you ever since you called me from the hotel."

"How did you know it was me? When I dialed the number I found in a dead man's pocket and you answered, I never spoke."

"I've known about you from the day you arrived in Boca del Diablo." Aunt Ida winked. "And since you've come this far, you may as well come for a visit to Hacienda de Sade. Spend the weekend. We let down our hair on the weekends."

Inez and Conchita claimed there were orgies at Hacienda de Sade. With any luck I would find out the veracity of their story. And I could do a little spying for that douchebag Burke, get on his good side. Later on I might need the assistance of his friends in high places, if any trouble arose when I garroted Aunt Ida.

Yes. Notwithstanding my never-ending infatuation with her ace-high anatomy, my plan to put an end to her earthly existence had never wavered. To right the wrongs that had been done to me. But I needed to pick the perfect circumstance. If I screwed up, there would be no second chance. Aunt Ida was an extremely dangerous motherfucker.

"Do I have a choice?" I said.

"Not really," said Aunt Ida.

"Well, now that we're reunited, maybe there's a niche somewhere in your organization that I can fill. It's the least you can do after leaving me in the lurch back in Orlando."

"Don't get your hopes up," said Aunt Ida. "This is just a short term invitation."

Then I remembered the Burroughs suitcase. It was under the front seat in the VW, along with Luis' ordinance. Were they going to leave the VW behind? Let the local peasants strip it down for parts? Some rube would find and keep the guns, toss the rat's ass suitcase in the local landfill.

"What about my rental car?" I asked.

"That piece of shit?" said Aunt Ida. "You know, Bill, you've really come down in the world since I last saw you."

"That may be," I said. "But I need to return it to get my deposit back."

"I wouldn't worry about getting your deposit back."

"You can't just abandon the car in the middle of nowhere."

"My people will bring it to the estancia," Aunt Ida said. Her eyes flashed with devilish glee. "The car and the Burroughs suitcase."

How the fuck did she know about the Burroughs suitcase!?

Sweat beaded my forehead. I could feel a boil swelling on my ass.

*

Time sped up. Or slowed to a crawl.

In a gin fizz and weed induced haze we traveled onward through déjà vu jungle. In time the harsh light of day sloughed into a shadow land of approaching dusk, haunted by ghosts and sharp-fanged monsters. Were we entering hell's anti-chamber?

We came at last to a cast-iron gate beneath a stone arch decorated with carved doodads shaped like giant chess pawns. On either side of the arch, a basalt griffin stood guard, gazing blindly into eternity.

Beyond, a gravel avenue, lined on either side by rows of royal palms, led up to a vast and eccentric structure, its weathered and mold-stained stone illuminated by the final rays of the setting sun. Hacienda de Sade.

Its façade consisted of two levels of long stone porticos anchored by towers at either end and a third tower in the center pierced by a passageway leading to an inner zone. Rows of Greek columns, too numerous to count in my snockered condition, held the porticos aloft.

The structure, Aunt Ida informed me with gloating pride of ownership, was the dream made flesh of some deranged Eighteenth Century Spanish nobleman and amateur architectural whiz-bang banished to the New World for unmentionable crimes. By serendipity he had teamed up with a Mexican robber baron with no taste and a bottomless wallet, who wanted a one-of-a kind palacio to party down in with his underage bride.

I turned to Aunt Ida: "How did you find this place?"

"Would you believe Century 21?"

As the sun fell off the edge of the world and darkness descended, we drove up the palm-lined avenue. Between each set of columns of the hacienda's second story, torches flared into life, illuminating standing figures, alternately male and female, naked to the waist and armed with assault rifles. As we drew near, the figures snapped to attention, raising their armament in a half-assed, quasi-military salute. Lucifer's army of the night.

Entering the arched central passageway, we passed beneath the edifice and into a wide courtyard crowded with all-terrain vehicles parked helter-skelter. Humvees, military style Jeeps, pickups, dune buggies, dirt bikes, quad bikes, you name it. On the far side of the courtyard a park-like expanse with pavilions, man-made waterfalls and grottos surrounded an Olympic-sized swimming pool. An even larger three-story, neo-classical extravaganza overlooked the pool from the far side. More torches. More half-naked guards.

A raven-haired, Mexican beauty opened the passenger door of the Mercedes. Cartridge bandoliers crisscrossed her shallish but stunning breasts. A zigzag scar like the Devil's birthmark defaced one cheek from hairline to chin. That must have hurt like a motherfucker! A .45 in a leather holster rested on her camouflage-fatigued hip.

"End of the road," said Aunt Ida. "Georgina will show you to your room, where you can freshen up. Dinner is at ten."

Dazed and depressed, I stumbled after Georgina as she swayed audaciously across the pool area and into the chateau, if that's what it was. We climbed a marble stairway and, at the end of a long corridor decorated with faded, flaking murals, she opened a door and motioned for me to enter. As I took in the platform bed facing a mirrored wall, a second mirror on the ceiling over the bed and the white leather & chrome Barcelona chair, the deadbolt slammed into place behind me. I was Aunt Ida's prisoner.

I flopped on the bed and stared at myself in the ceiling mirror. I looked like crapola.

None of this was really happening. I had fallen into a psychotic episode. The vengeful waiter at the Hotel Colonial had slipped a super-powerful, slow-acting hallucinogenic drug into my breakfast lager. Somehow I had been transported to an alternate universe where everything was majorly out of alignment. I was Icarus and I'd flown too close to the sun.

"FUUUUUUUUUUUUUUUUUUUUUUUUUUUUUUUU UUUUUUUUUUUUCK!!"

Now that I'd gotten that out of my system, I needed a plan.

A. Find out where they were holding Jane. B. Find out what had happened to Edie. C. Pop Aunt Ida. D. Reacquire the Burroughs suitcase. E. Together with Jane, get the hell out of Dodge.

But first I needed a shower and a drink.

I stood under the streaming water until it turned from hot to tepid, toweled off and poured an inch of Patron silver into a hand-blown Mexican rocks glass. The bottle of tequila resided on a shelf next to the carefully folded white linen pants and pale blue linen shirt that were my size and a flawless fit. Clearly Aunt Ida and Frau Stein had been expecting us.

My single window came with iron bars and a view of the swimming pool. The underwater lights in the pool had been turned on but no one was swimming.

I poured a second drink, a double, and picked up a glossy travel magazine someone had left on the night table by the bed. The lead article was about Paris in the fall. Not a bad idea.

I was on my fourth tequila, and just reading about a bistro where Ernest and F. Scott used to drink and whore and quarrel, when I was interrupted by a knock on my door. The lock retracted and the door opened. It was Georgina, repackaged in a black bodysuit with a plunging v-neck. The

232

.45 was still strapped to her waist.

"Is it dinnertime already?" I said.

She didn't crack a smile. No sense of humor. Or maybe her English wasn't that great.

Georgina led the way. Going down the marble staircase proved much more difficult than going up it two hours before. Having eaten nothing since breakfast, the Patron had gone to my head. Partway down, I tripped and stumbled into Georgina's arms. She was soft and malleable, but when I made a grab for the .45, she body-slammed me into the wall. Her booted foot caught me in the chin. Propelled me like a rag doll down the last four steps.

I lay on the floor, bruised and bleeding. Georgina didn't offer me a hand up.

Our welcome to Hacienda de Sade dinner was staged in a banquet hall suitable for several hundred guests. When we entered, there was only Jane and Aunt Ida, seated at one small Louis-the-something-or-other table set beneath one glittering cut glass chandelier. The rest of the auditorium-sized room was as murky as a Jack-the-Ripper fog. A pair of Dobermans paced in and out of the shadows, their eyes contemplating me with a lean and hungry look. The chandelier light glinted off their rows of shiny teeth.

Jane waved. "Over here," she called. Her voice echoed.

A transparent white lace top displayed her upper body to concupiscent perfection. I wondered what covered her bottom half.

Aunt Ida, retro and ridiculous in a purple and gold, Ming-the-Merciless outer-space getup with a turned up collar, gave me the once over.

"There's blood on your shirt," she said. "And your lip's swollen."

"To be completely forthright, you little cunt Georgina kicked the crap out of me," I said.

"That'll teach you not to fuck with my assistant," Aunt Ida said.

Jane chortled into her napkin.

The table was set for four. I took the seat that put Aunt Ida on my right and Jane on my left. To my surprise Georgina took the fourth seat.

"Isn't Frau Stein joining us?" I said. "I've heard so much about her."

Aunt Ida's eyebrows beetled.

"Frau Stein has a headache."

"Ah."

A tuxedoed waiter served tortilla soup. I asked for a Corona but settled for a glass of Chardonnay. I turned to Jane.

"Did they give you a nice room? Or are you chained up in the dungeon?"

"It's okay. One flight up from here, with a pool view. And bars on the window." Jane looked at Aunt Ida. "I'm sure you realize you can get into a lot of trouble holding people prisoner against their will."

Aunt Ida laughed uproariously, slapping the table with her hand. When she had recovered, she said: "You're too much. Both you and old dick-for-brains Bill. This is Mexico, the most dangerous country on the planet. People disappear every day. There's only one reason you're sitting here and not rotting in a shallow grave."

At this point the waiter interrupted and removed the soup bowls, even though I hadn't finished. Then he handed out plates of thinly sliced grilled meat and French fries.

"The dinner is a prix fixe, I'm afraid," said Aunt Ida. "I hope you don't mind."

"Beef, is it?" I said, digging in with knife and fork. The meat was tough and the French fries cold and soggy, but I was really, really hungry.

The waiter brought white bread, little plastic and foil containers of butter, a bowl of pickled jalapeños and more vino. The vino wasn't bad.

Aunt Ida likewise ate with gusto. Jane picked.

Finally I set my utensils on my empty plate, swallowed another mouthful of wine and said: "Okay, I give up. Why is

234

it that Jane and I are still among the ravenous living rather than out there with the decomposing dead?"

"I probably shouldn't have mentioned it."

"But you did," said Jane. "You can't leave us hanging."

Aunt Ida and Georgina exchanged glances. Georgina departed.

The waiter brought a tray of over-ripe looking fruit, then also disappeared. Overall the meal had scored a D-minus.

Only the dogs remained, nuzzling up to Aunt Ida as she scratched them behind the ears. Their sterling white teeth sent a chill deep into my gut. Aunt Ida cleared her throat.

"Okay. I don't know what you've heard about Frau Stein. What rumors are making the rounds. But she's engaged in some very delicate scientific experiments."

"What kind of experiments?" I asked, curious as a lapdog sniffing his first snatch.

"I don't know the details," said Aunt Ida. "But it's something to do with raising the dead."

"What a crock!" I said.

"I wouldn't shit you, Bill."

"Yes you would."

"Would not."

"Would too."

I was getting hot under the collar. Ready to throw a punch.

"Stop!" said Jane. "You're giving me a fucking headache."

Aunt Ida leaned in close, her voice dropping to a whisper.

"The experiment is at a critical stage. She needs a certain very rare blood type."

"I have a rare blood type," said Jane. Her forehead wrinkled. She rose from her chair, fingers massaging her temples. "This is crazy. You're saying you've brought us here because I'm to be some kind of modern day human sacrifice. My rare blood drained from my body as part of some lunatic experiment. Well, no fucking way, Jose!"

"I think she only needs a pint or two," said Aunt Ida.

But Jane was raging out of control. She grabbed a steak knife. Lunged at Aunt Ida. Aunt Ida was up out of her seat, backpedaling like crazy. Her chair spinning away, crashing to the floor.

Now was not the time to whack Aunt Ida. I wanted to know more about Frau Stein and her experiments. Burke would eat this shit up. Besides Aunt Ida had a gun.

A very large chrome-plated semi-automatic had appeared in Aunt Ida's shaking hand. It was aimed at Jane's abdomen at point blank range.

Springing up a millisecond after Jane, I wrapped my arms around her, grasping her knife hand, squeezing her wrist until her grip faltered. The knife clattered harmlessly on the tile floor. My lips touched her ear. "Cool it or you will be dead," I snapped, as I eased her back into her seat.

The crisis had passed.

But our welcome dinner was over.

Georgina reappeared and escorted Jane and me back to our executive platinum cells. Jane was silent, brooding. Our rooms turned out to be next to each other.

As the clang of the closing cell door echoed behind me, I poured myself a Patron and stood by the window.

Raising the dead? Ha. What a joke. Undeniably, Frau Stein had gone off the deep end. Was completely and utterly unzipped.

Movement outside the window caught my eye.

A plumpish Biblical Eve-wannabe walked to the edge of the swimming pool. In the phosphorescence of the underwater lights, her nudity shown with the otherworldly whiteness of a mystical albino virgin. Her lush black hair tumbled below her shoulders, just as it had in the photograph I'd found in the wallet of Lee's murdered agent.

Frau Stein mounted the diving board, walked intently to the end, gave a tiny leap and spiraled into the air in a trick dive that cut the water like a razor blade.

She surfaced, shaking a rain of droplets from her hair,

treading water in the deep end. I knew what that was like. I'd been treading water for longer than I could remember.

Turning away from the window, I tossed back the last of my drink and climbed between the satin sheets. I was still alive and tomorrow was another day.

16

It was more or less dawn when the topless Georgina roused me from a dead sleep. She did so by whacking my bare ass with a riding crop. I hadn't heard the cell door open or the stomp of her paratrooper boots across the tile floor.

"Hey!" I said, leaping up and covering my dangling privates with both hands. "What's the deal here?"

I would have strangled her but for her .45 caliber pistol pointed dead center at my groin. A shit-eating grin split her face in two. She had a sense of humor after all. At my expense.

"Rise and shine, gringo."

I looked at my watch. Fuck! "It's six o'clock in the goddamn morning. Can't a guy get some rest around here."

"You're favorite aunt is downstairs. I wouldn't keep her waiting."

"You're a real card, Georgina. But she's not my aunt."

This time I led the way down the marble staircase. Georgina wasn't taking any chances on a repeat of last night's little dustup.

Outside, instead of breakfast by the pool, a dappled gray horse chomped at the bit in anticipation of my arrival. Aunt Ida, in de rigueur olive-drab riding duds, was already mounted on a nervous palomino that was making mincemeat of the flowerbeds.

Even when my old man had scads of cash and hobnobbed with Atlanta's gentry, I never ran with the horsey set. But I'd ridden a few times at summer camp, so I mounted up without too much difficulty.

"Thought you'd like a tour of the operations," said Aunt Ida.

"On the top of my list," I said.

"Now who's being a smart-ass?"

"No. Seriously. It is. Followed by a climb up the main pyramid at Chichen Itza."

Aunt Ida took off at a fast canter.

I urged my horse to follow.

Aunt Ida wasn't fooling me with all this casual banter. This was some kind of cat and mouse game. She'd hated my guts from the get-go. And now that I had tracked her down in the middle of the mother-raping Yucatan jungle, it was just a matter of time before she gut shot me and then delivered the coup de grâce.

We exited by the same passage beneath the outer hacienda structure by which we had arrived the previous day. The horses' hooves made a deafening clatter on the stones of the inner courtyard, where I spied our VW Bug ensconced between a camouflage-painted Humvee and a Mercedes all-terrain vehicle. The flat tire had been repaired.

I wondered what had become of the Burroughs suitcase and Luis' assortment of handguns. For that matter, what had become of Luis? Too many questions. I picked the one that seemed most important.

"Can I ask you a question? How the fuck did you know about the Burroughs suitcase?" I asked, trying to get my horse to trail Aunt Ida's palomino down a sandy track while avoiding a tangle of ass-biting prickly-pear cactus.

"Frau Stein…Gunda heard through one of her informants that a fixer in Mexico City was looking to acquire it for a client. She had read in a privately circulated memoir that its contents might include a previously unknown hallucinogen discovered by Burroughs on a trip to the Yucatan backcountry. A drug the Mayans used to travel back and forth in time."

"Wow. No shit. A time travel drug. What will they think of next."

"Gunda dreams about going back in time. To Germany in 1938 to attend one of the Nuremberg Rallies."

"She's a Nazi?"

"Her grandfather was. Worked for Goebbels. Or maybe it was Mengele. I can never keep it straight."

"So? When you opened the suitcase, did you discover a glass vile of some time-warping substance? Or was it crammed full of dirty underwear and nudist magazines with the pages stuck together?" I asked.

"At the moment it's sitting unopened on the credenza in my office. Gunda's a little preoccupied by the arrival of your friend and her special blood."

Aunt Ida pulled up at the edge of a vast field. Alternate rows of spiky agave cactus and bushy marijuana plants stretched as far as the eye could see. Near at hand stood several long sheds with slatted wooden sides that opened like vertical shutters.

"There's an underground irrigation system," said Aunt Ida. "Those sheds are where we cure the pot. We're a wholesaler to the cartels."

"So you're in the agribiz," I said.

"I never thought of it that way," said Aunt Ida.

We rode on. The sun climbed the sky, its heat flaring like a gas grill on high, scorching the landscape and the back of my neck. I could have rung a gallon of sweat from my shirt. My mouth was a dry wadi through which imaginary camels trudged.

"Any chance of a glass of iced tea?" I asked.

"Buck up," said Aunt Ida.

The next field was a sea of orange. Opium poppies.

"A bit of the hard stuff," said Aunt Ida. "Grows like a weed down here."

"With an operation on this scale, you should be able to retire soon," I said.

"A lot of our net cash flow goes to pay for Gunda's

240

experiments. The equipment she requires is very expensive. And the raw materials."

Raw materials. I wondered what that involved.

"I never thought of raising the dead as a money pit. But then again, other than Jesus, I'm not sure many people are in that line of work. Gunda must be pretty much on the cutting edge."

Leaving behind the mega fields of agri-drugs, we pointed our quadrupeds back toward the estancia, whose eccentric profile I could just make out on the horizon. A dusty byway led through fallow land from which the jungle had been recently hacked and burned off.

Twenty yards ahead, a man burst from a scraggly clump of second growth banana palms and bounded pell-mell across the road, heading for a thicket of scrub trees that offered some cover. A pair of dune buggies pitched and bounced in pursuit, churning up clouds of dust. They careened to either side of the fleeing man, swirling around him in tightening circles, cutting off any chance of escape. The man lurched wildly this way and that, but without hope.

Aunt Ida drew up her horse, swung an AK-47 style carbine from a saddle pouch and sighted on the fugitive. I heard the pop of the high-powered cartridge. The runner pitched backward into the dirt, dead or dying.

"Shoot first, ask questions later," I said.

"Just another DEA spy. We kill two or three a week."

A warning flare burst aloft in my head. An image of the great white in Jaws rose out of the deep waters of my id. Aunt Ida was mucho dangerous!

Back at the ranch, lunch was served. A buffet had been set up by the pool, along with several metal tables decorated with Mexican beer logos and shaded by colorful umbrellas.

I asked for iced tea but settled for the same white wine they'd served the night before.

The lunch crowd consisted of the same happy foursome as at dinner. Frau Stein was again indisposed.

I pulled up a chair next to Jane. Georgina stood at the

buffet, piling her plate with tacos and pico de gallo. Aunt Ida had stepped away to consult with a minion about something or other.

"I still can't fucking believe they want my blood," Jane whispered out of the side of her mouth.

"Don't worry," I said. "I'll think of something."

"Right."

"I promise."

"Can't we just clear the fuck out of here?"

"We could if the guards all fell asleep and they forgot to lock our cell doors at night."

"Well, tough guy, I found something out while you were horsing around with Aunt Ida. During my morning stroll I checked out our VW parked over there. It's unlocked and the keys are under the floor mat."

"Good work. Is there any gas in it?"

"Fuck you, Bill."

"No need to get hostile."

"Maybe I should cozy up to Aunt Ida. You told me she likes women."

I gave Jane a look.

"Don't give me that look. If it wasn't for your twin obsessions, Aunt Ida being one of them, we'd be somewhere else. Like maybe running a beach bar in Bali. Getting a good night's sleep. Eating lots of organic vegetables, tofu and whole grains."

"Yum."

Georgina sat down next to Jane.

"I didn't catch that," she said.

"I said 'Yum'"

"Oh." She jammed half a taco in her mouth, followed by a tortilla chip loaded with pico de gallo. Drank down half a Corona longneck.

"Hey," I said. "Where'd you get the beer? They didn't have any last night."

"It's all about who you know," said Georgina. She chomped the second half of the taco. Six more to go. "When you have a chance," she said, "let me know what you want for dinner tonight. Your most favorite thing. We probably won't have it though. Sysco's two weeks late in its provisions delivery. I think the Federales and your DEA are trying to starve us out. Something stinks to high heaven and I don't like it."

"You're on some neocon bureaucrat's shit list," I said.

"The boot of oppression," said Jane, "is about to drop kick you in the pussy."

The conversation meandered.

Aunt Ida returned.

"Here's that iced-tea you wanted," she said. "Sweetened. Right?"

I took the glass and went on with my story. I was telling Jane and Georgina about an Arab I'd met in Baghdad who had four daughters, ages sixteen to twenty-three. He was mystified why I couldn't marry them all. Take them back with me to America, away from the daily mayhem and murder.

I took a long drink of the iced tea. It was sweet and cold and bitter all at the same time.

Seconds later my head began to spin.

I blacked out, falling head first into a wormhole to another universe.

*

And awoke in a nightmare.

What the…!

I lay spread-eagled across my bed, naked from stem to stern, and all the other parts as well. Someone had bound my hands and feet tightly but not torturously to the four corners of the bed using strips of blue velvet.

My head was elevated on a stack of pillows, giving me a panoramic view.

The silver backing of the mirror that covered the opposite wall dissolved like melting quicksilver, morphing into a floor-to-ceiling sheet of transparent glass. The empty room on the other side had to be Jane's.

A portable massage table had been rolled into the middle of her room. Jane stepped from the bathroom and looked right at me with no reaction. She moved in a slow motion stoner haze. A hand-painted, silk robe of oriental design wilted from her soft shoulders to the floor. The goddess of lust. Aphrodite. Bettie Page. Eva Mendez. Jane Ryder. I wanted to lick every inch of her. Run my calloused fingers between the lips of her vagina 'til she wailed like an orang-utan in high heat. Lose myself in the old in/out, in/out, in/out.

I called her name: "Jane."

But no sound reached her.

Bum side up on the massage bed, she waited.

Aunt Ida entered from upstage right, rigged out in a silver sliver of a thong and fluffy pink slippers with stiletto heels. From a dark green bottle olive oil drizzled onto Jane's body. Aunt Ida's hands went to work, kneading and pinching. Using high art, she cajoled, squeezed, stroked and beguiled. Her body leaned over Jane, her distended nipples brushing Jane's rump, back and shoulders. Fingers insinuating into every crease, chamber, niche, cleft and orifice.

I slammed my eyes shut. Opened them wide. Thrust my head aside. Stared fixedly ahead. Gnashed my teeth until my jaw ached.

IT WAS JUST A DREAM! A BAD FUCKING DREAM!

Alas, it was not a dream.

Aunt Ida had stolen Edie, the jewel of my life. Mary Beth and Ben were emotional paraplegics.

Now she had Jane in her sights and her hand up Jane's crotch. Her middle finger in my face.

And like a rodent caught in the paregoric gaze of a predatory snake, I couldn't take my eyes off the intertwining twosome.

Thongless, Aunt Ida slithered between Jane's spread legs.

Rose above her, a dark beast of macabre rapacity. Old Scratch herself. Jane's body arched upward, as if stung by an electric current. Their bodies blended together, body parts rubbing, pressing, oozing.

My cock quickened, thickened. Pulsed wildly.

How pathetic was that.

As my drugged brain gasped, Jane and Aunt Ida transmogrified into two colossal, single-celled creatures. Amoeboid shape-shifters. Hallucinatory refugees from an orgasmic, off-world elsewhereness. They mingled, merged, conjoined, the flesh of each dripping, seeping, percolating into the other, copulating backward, fucking themselves into a single, indescribable, androgynous entity.

The glass barrier grew opaque, resumed its mirroresque state, the phantasmal scene banished to unreliable memory.

Georgina walked into the room. Smirked at my engorged phallus quivering like a dowsing rod over an unknown aquifer. When she tickled the knob with the tip of a peacock feather, my semen burst aloft in geyser-like profusion.

As my dick shriveled, all hope seemed to wither with it.

I no longer knew what was real and what was the opposite. A lot of evil was on the loose and I wasn't sure how it would all turn out. It would be the shitstorm of the century. Let it come down, I thought.

In the meantime the only answer was to put on a bold face. After Georgina untied the blue velvet cuffs, under her watchful eye I pissed, showered, shaved, brushed my teeth, flossed, cleaned the wax out of my ears using a bobby pin, engaged in the usual snorting, hawking and spitting.

Georgina informed me cocktails would be served in Frau Stein's laboratory. I had a splitting headache. But I wasn't in a strong position to request a rain check.

"Frau Stein would be very unhappy," said Georgina. "And I would be in a lot of trouble."

"I certainly wouldn't want that to happen," I said.

The lab was in the basement of the chateau. And what a basement it was!

The space or room disappeared into a horizon of gloom, falling into the ultra-darkness of craggy niches and side passages. On all sides massive stone walls caked with lime rose up around us. Cavernous vaulted ceilings receded into pools of shadow. Through the vastness moved a cool, dry wind, producing an eerie whistling sound as it wafted through hidden tunnels and sinkholes and around murky irregularities in the stone masonry. Rusted chains of unknown purpose hung down, swaying ever so slightly in the underground wind.

We descended by a bannisterless stairway of over a hundred roughhewn stone steps, irregular and cast in chiaroscuro except for dribbles of light from occasional low wattage industrial lamps bracketed to the wall. I sought Georgina's arm for support but, being familiar with my treacherous ways, she pushed me ahead of her.

"Nice try, gringo," she said with a laugh.

The floor, when we at last reached it, was poured concrete of recent vintage. We walked to the center of the room where several banks of head-high steel cabinets, like mainframe computer cabinets, stood along one side. Two men in white, mad-scientist coats moved back and forth adjusting dials, reading gauges and leafing through printouts. Opposite, like something out of Twenty Thousand Leagues Under the Sea, a tank of riveted sections of iron with a glass window insert rested on cement underpinnings. Observable through the window, a humanoid figure, vague, indistinct, floated in a watery green liquid, its lurid color reminiscent of lime Kool-Aid or worm guts.

The entire setup exuded an aura of raging madness that made the hair on my neck prickle with anxiety.

The usual semi-nude militiamen and militia-gals skulked on the periphery. I noted they all carried Israeli Galil SAR assault rifles. Another info tidbit for Burke, if I ever ran into him again.

An ovoid desk strewn with papers, graphs, sharpened yellow Ticonderoga No. 2 pencils and several open laptops occupied a pivotal point midway between the banks of computer equipment and the holding tank.

A drinks cart with glasses, an ice bucket and a variety of intoxicants was parked next to the desk. Jane, barely decent in an off-the-shoulder little black dress, and Aunt Ida, indecent in fire engine red capris and a white see-through camisole, were already hard at it in the grog-swilling department.

Staggering toward me, Jane sought to implant her lips on mine. Missed. And ended up nuzzling my neck.

"Bill. Glad you could make it to my farewell party. This place is a hoot. Aunt Ida's been filling me in on Frau Stein's big plans. You won't believe all the crazy shit that's going on here. And the bottom line is, I'm going to die!"

Jane gripped my arm, her nails like piranha teeth. I would have scars. Her eyes started to roll up. I slapped her left cheek. Then the right. Not too hard, but enough to bring her back to the present.

From somewhere came music. An old Roy Orbison tune, "Dream Baby." Or was I imagining that part? I took a hard grip on Jane's used flesh and moved her around in a slow box step.

"Okay," I said. "Tell me everything."

"Tomorrow they're doing a test resurrection. If it works, the day after its gramps' turn. And I'm toast. Nice knowing and fucking you, Bill. We had some laughs, some tears. What more could I have asked for in this vale of tears?"

"Don't get maudlin on me. Gramps who?"

"Over there, you nitwit." She nodded at the aquarium. "It's Frau Stein's Nazi grandfather floating in the frigging tank, in some sort of suspended animation. Wolfgang von Putz III, Obergruppenfuhrer and all around assistant asshole to Herr Josef Goebbels. While visiting Prague's red light district on New Years Day, 1945, a prostitute (and part-time partisan) stabbed him five times and left him for dead. His minions packed him in ice, shipped him to Montevideo via Zurich and the Algarve. The South American Nazi underground put him in cold storage, where he's remained in stasis until now."

Tears trembled in Jane's eyes. She squished against me. "Hold me close, Bill."

I held her, swaying ever so slightly until the music stopped.

Aunt Ida came over and handed me a glass filled with amber liquid and ice cubes. Thank God it wasn't a gin fizz.

"Cheers," she said.

"After that iced-tea you gave me, I don't know if I should drink this or not," I said.

"No tricks this time."

That first sip! The world's greatest fucking bourbon. Or close to it. Some high-end, small batch stuff they'd no doubt brought in for Jane's funeral. Burned my throat like a line of blow snorted from a pole dancer's tits.

"How the heck are you?" I said to Aunt Ida. But for my iron will, I would have jammed my fist down her throat then and there. And died seconds later in a spray of bullets. Instead I took another sip of bourbon, rolling the limited edition hooch around my tongue, savoring its piquant sexuality.

For an instant I imaged a Kentucky sportswoman, pink, buxom, lascivious, sprawled au naturale across dazzlingly white, late afternoon sheets. Two tall mint juleps sweating on the bedside table. "Well, sir, if you see somethin' y'all want," she said. "Y'all should take it before someone else does."

At that moment a bodaciously top-heavy figure draped in a white Greek goddess outfit and holding an oversized bronze mask in front of her face, stepped into the mix. A pudgy hand moved the mask aside. Frau Stein in the flesh. A Rhineland naiad a little past her prime.

And what was I to make of her outré entrance? A game of peek-a-boo? Or something more trippy and fruitcakey?

Beneath the gauzy linen, her red bra and panties were the identical fire engine red of Aunt Ida's capri loungewear. Très kinky. Her black hair brushed her pale, liebfraumilch shoulders. In the front a swath of hair swooped down across her forehead, covering her right eye like an eye patch, then twisting ribbon-wise down her cheek to the corner of her mouth. The mask depicted the same hairdo in bronze.

"Good evening," said Frau Stein. She sounded a bit like Marlene Dietrich doing Boris Karloff. "You are Bill, ya?" Taking the beer glass filled to the brim with a dark foamy brew offered by Aunt Ida, she took a long pull. Wiped the suds from her upper lip. "I only drink Guinness. It eez healthy for you, no?"

I'd known a few megalomaniacs in my time, especially in the military. The one thing they loved to do was talk about themselves and their grandiose plans.

"Nice setup you've got here," I said.

"Ah. You like it? I think it eez somewhat primitive but ze best ve can achieve under ze circumstances. Mexico eez Mexico, n'est-ce pas. "

"As you say." I reached for the bottle of bourbon. "So, what's the next step?"

"Ze next step?"

"You know…" I waved my hand holding the bottle, taking in the computers, the aquarium, the desk, the whole megillah. Then poured two inches into my glass. "What are you up to with all this shit?"

"Ze vorld eez in chaos. It eez vaiting for a new messiah. My grandfather eez the promised one. To bring a new vorld order."

"Cool," I said. "Bring on the old bastard."

"Unfortunately, he eez in a state of limbo. Closer to death than life. His body must be reanimated. A very delicate undertaking. Vun wrong move and…"

"Dust to dust," I said, cracking a broad grin. "Maybe you should call in a team of crackerjack scientists from M.I.T. for a second opinion."

Frau Stein's hand struck me full in the face. My drink went flying.

"This eez no laughing matter, schweinehund."

I stared cross-eyed at the unblinking eye that was the barrel of a Luger semi-automatic pistol an inch away from my face. My heart dropped to my gonads. My gonads hit the floor.

Slowly I raised my hands, palms forward, in the universal gesture of peace and surrender. "Just kidding. I'm sure you've got everything under control."

"Yah. Everything eez under control."

Frau Stein's hand holding the Luger dropped to her side. My heart resumed a semi-normal beat. Saliva once again moistened my lips and silver-tipped tongue.

"Zere are more zen seventy trillion cells in ze human body. With zese powerful computers ve catalogue zem all and make sure zay are in alignment when ze life-giving electric surge jolts through ze body."

The setup was sounding more and more like Bride of Frankenstein revisited. What kind of crazed zealot believed in shit like this in our modern age? Then again…

I decided to keep an open mind.

Frau Stein drew me by my arm to a smaller oblong tank that I hadn't noticed before.

"At great expense I have acquired a perfectly preserved Mayan mummy. It has lain undisturbed in its burial chamber until a veek ago. She vas a high priestess. A sorceress."

Frau Stein lifted the lid of the stainless steel coffin. Inside, beneath a sheet of clear Plexiglas, lay a human shaped thing wrapped in crumbling strips of burlap-like cloth, boobs and all. A slight movement of air within the coffin, perhaps having to do with the preservation of the mummy, ruffled the loose threads of the burlap.

"It's dead, right!?" I said, more to myself than to Frau Stein.

"Zee scan ve ran revealed zet all zee cells are intact. Tomorrow ve vill bring life to her. A trial run, as you say in America."

She rubbed her hands together. Nerves.

"Zen, zee day after, it vill be Volfie's turn."

"Who's Volfie?" I said.

"My grandfather, Wolfgang." Frau Stein waved at the aquarium. "He is ze one in ze big tank."

"Nice."

"Unfortunately, your associate's blood eez necessary for Volfie's resurrection. All of it."

Wrong!!!!!!!

That was not going to happen. Nobody was draining Jane's blood.

I needed to get to a phone. I needed to call Burke.

Shortly thereafter the party broke up. Frau Stein had some additional calculations to make before tomorrow's trial blast off.

As we trudged back up the hundred or so steps, I turned my head and said to Georgina, who was bringing up the rear, "How about something to eat."

"I think there's some fish sticks and maybe even some chicken tenders in the cafeteria."

"May we please go there."

"It's in the other building."

"I'm not hungry," said Jane. "I'd like to go back to my room."

We went there first. When Georgina opened the door, Jane walked in without looking at me. Her face was a blank page. The door closed behind her. Georgina slammed the deadbolt into place.

Back outside, night had fallen. Georgina and I walked through the pool area toward the outer hacienda building.

It was now or never.

I leaned close to Georgina and ran my hand up the inside of her thigh. She tensed like a jungle cat, her hand darting to her holstered weapon. Then, by the illumination of an overhead light, she saw the lust in my eyes. I realized I barely had to pretend.

"Let's skip dinner," I said.

She laughed deeply.

"You think you can keep up with me, gringo? That

you've got the cojones that it takes?"

As prisoner and warder, we had developed a strange simpatico. The tension of the last forty-eight hours burst like a rocket to the moon. I jettisoned my clothes in a jiff. Georgina likewise.

At her command I held my hands behind my back. Using a switchblade that appeared magically in her hand, she cut my shirt into strips, which she used to harshly bind my wrists. I was still a prisoner. But a prisoner with a hard-on.

She kicked my legs out from under me and I tumbled to the raw stone floor of one of the pool area's manmade grottos. From whence we commenced to rut with nothing less than feral cat abandon. The gallons of sweat and love juice that poured from our bodies and the muffled grunts, squeals, moans and curses of our fornicating fury marked the passage of time. As Georgina came for the fifth time (I'd been counting the shudders), she heaved me out and away from her Amazonian loins.

"Jesus, it's hotter than Satan's steambath tonight," she said. In the starlight her brown body glistened as if dipped in cooking oil. Or wildflower honey. "I need to pee," she said. "You're okay, gringo. Más o menos. But don't get a swelled head."

The moment she stepped away, I wriggled my hands free of the bonds, which had loosened during our shtuping. Two seconds later, I held in my hands Georgina's cell phone, the shape of which I had observed in the rear pocket of her canary-yellow skinny jeans that lay crumpled on the ground.

Somehow I pulled the number Burke had given me out of a brain folder buried under piles of other pointless memories. I tapped it in on the virtual keyboard and waited. A ring tone reverberated in my ear. Yes! The call had gone through. It was connecting.

"Hi. You've reached Pandemonium licensed customs agents and brokers. We're not able to come to the phone right now, so…" Then came the beep.

"Burke!" I said in a breathy whisper. "It's Bill. Bill

Derringer. We're in Rancho de Sade. I've got the whole inside scoop, but they're going to kill us. You've got to extract us outa here by tomorrow noon at the latest. You won't believe the shit I've got for you. Our lives are in your hands. Do not tarry."

Georgina returned just as I slipped the cell phone back into her jeans pocket. We resumed fucking for another half hour, but at a more measured, even desultory, pace. Afterward we lay in the shadows cast by the decorative palms and other vegetation and, each absorbed in our own dark thoughts, observed the ice-cold stars. They brought no solace.

From far away, but still insistent, came the tireless boom-diddy-boom, boom-diddy-boom of peasant drums talking to the night.

I hadn't noticed them before.

Boom-diddy-boom. Boom-diddy-boom.

Boom-diddy-boom. Boom-diddy-boom.

17

I blinked awake. The residue of a thunder crack reverberated in my head. A car backfiring? Someone beating on my door with a baseball bat? Or was I flashing back to a roadside bomb incident in I-rack that had killed three of my buds and put me over the edge?

Opening one eye, I focused on the glowing hands of my wristwatch. The hour hand pointed at the twelve. The room was steeped in gloom.

Thakata, thakata, thakata …

There was no mistaking the sound of a chopper coming in fast and low. I was fully awake now. It had to be Burke!

Rushing to the window, I scanned my allotted quadrant of sky but couldn't see the whirlybird. But the courtyard and garden below were like a fire ant nest that had been stomped, kicked in and stirred with a stick. Soldier ants ran this way and that, first one direction, then another, then back again the way they had originally come, shouting and gesticulating stupendously and with great emotion in the Latin manner.

A mixed-sex team of cartel gangbangers commandeered one of the weaponized pickups, the man driving, the two women maneuvering the fifty-caliber machine gun mounted in the truck bed. They rode roughshod across the garden, the gun crew firing random bursts into the sky. Sometimes the trajectory of their rapid fire raked the chateau's façade.

A tumult of thunderheads filled the sky, changing shape

like bad dreams, endlessly devoured and reborn. From the direction of the agri-drug fields, a plume of smoke unfurled heavenward.

Behind me came the rasp of the deadbolt unlocking. Was it the delightful Georgina come to surrender to me and show me the secret passageway by which we would make our escape? Or was it my executioner sent by Aunt Ida? Made desperate by a sudden wave of fear, I took one last gulp of tequila and splintered the bottom of the bottle against the marble bathroom countertop. Clenching the jagged, face-destroying weapon, I leaped behind the door.

When the door swung open, the figure standing there was none other than obese Luis. The last person in the world I had expected.

"Luis!"

"Bill!"

"I though you were dead."

"I had the same idea about you. Isn't this Jane's room."

"Jane's is next door."

We went there. But there was no Jane. Some black lace undies I remembered from the hotel in Boca del Diablo lay abandoned on a coffee table. Nonplussed, we stood about, equivocal, undecided.

"I know where the Burroughs suitcase is," I said.

"We need to find Jane," said Luis.

"First Jane, then the Burroughs suitcase," I said. "My guess, she's in Frau Stein's laboratory." Or Aunt Ida's bed. I didn't say that. Instead, I said, "They're going to drain her blood. Use it to raise the dead."

"You're shitting me."

"God's truth," I said. I agreed that raising the dead was a bunch of horseshit. But draining Jane's blood was all too real.

"Do you know how to get to the lab?" said Luis.

"I think I can find it," I said. "But shouldn't we get some guns or something."

Luis handed me a military issue .45.

"Take this. I borrowed it from a pretty young woman with attractive breasts whom I met on the floor below. Part Mayan. And absolutely stunning."

Georgina.

"Was she wearing cheesy, pseudo-antique looking beads?"

"Roger that," said Luis, "By the way, what's with all the bare breasts?"

"Just a local fad," I said. I felt a great weight on my heart. You know how these jailhouse infatuations are. I couldn't believe Georgina had passed. "The woman…Georgina, she's dead?"

"Cold-cocked her. Tied her to the wrought-iron banister."

Relief drained over me, as if I'd just taken a wicked piss.

"Then she's probably loose by now and coming to kill us."

As if on cue, Georgina appeared in the doorway.

Her hands rested at her sides. She held no gun. No straight razor. No machete. And Luis was right. She was stunning! Except her hair was greasy and her eye makeup smudged.

"I'm surrendering," she said. "I seek your protection and pledge my undying loyalty. I told you before something reeked to high heaven around here. This place is going down."

I stared at Georgina. Then took a stab in the dark. "You work for Burke, don't you?"

"How did you know?"

"Everybody I've met in Mexico works for somebody else. And Burke told me he wanted to infiltrate the Mayan Cartel to find out what was going on." I shrugged. "Besides, I don't have any other guesses."

Georgina stuck out her tongue and made a face. "Us modern girls have to work for a living."

"We need to go," said Luis.

Roger that.

*

The door to Frau Stein's basement laboratory was unlocked.

I could barely face all those steps again. The metallic smell of an electrical fire hung in the air. But the emergency lighting was working. In its dull glow, I made out Jane pacing back and forth in a metal cage next to the aquarium. Last time I was here, the cage had been empty.

"There she is." I pointed.

As we stumbled our way down, Jane spotted us and started to jump up and down and wave. Her flamboyance was alerting the whole fucking world of our arrival. I motioned for her to cool it. Of course she didn't.

Whatever had happened between her and Aunt Ida was water over the dam. Besides, for all I knew it had been nothing more than a drug-induced hallucination.

We rushed up to the cage. I tried to hug Jane through the bars, felt her arms around me. Felt her stiffen and release her hold. "Who's this?"

I stood back. "You remember Georgina. Turns out she's a good guy."

"Don't turn your back," said Jane.

"We need to go," said Luis.

"We just got here," I said. Then to Jane: "Where's Frau Stein."

"There was some kind of fuck-up in the trial run of the resurrection. One of the computers shorted out and caught fire while she was trying to bring the mummy back to life. She put the fire out. Everyone else split. Now she's over there installing new circuit boards or something. I don't know what happened to the mummy. The thing sat up and then the computers blew."

A muffled explosion came from outside the chateau. The floor shook. Dust floated down. But the emergency lights held. In the wan light I saw that the aquarium tank had sprung a leak. It was only a matter of time before Wolfgang finally reached the end of the line.

"What's going on out there?" said Jane.

"I think Burke, the CIA and the whole fucking Mexican army is attacking the hacienda."

"Well then, you'd better get me the heck out of here." said Jane.

"Stand back and I'll shoot the lock off," I said.

"How about we use these," said Luis, holding up a ring of keys he'd found on Frau Stein's desk. The third one he inserted did the trick.

"I'm going to check out Frau Stein," I said.

She was crouched down in front of a flame-seared computer cabinet. A steel front panel had been taken off, exposing the fried innards. Frau Stein was talking to herself, snickering under her breath. It was a dry sound, almost like a cough. A screwdriver and an Uzi lay on the floor near her. Her grand experiment was down the shitter.

I stepped forward and retrieved the Uzi. Frau Stein didn't even notice. She was in another world. Having some kind of a breakdown.

I looked in the coffin-shaped container. The mummy wasn't there.

Maybe it had burned up in the fire.

Luis grabbed my shoulder.

"Come on. Let's go get the Burroughs suitcase," he said. "Then make like roadrunners and get the fuck away from here."

"Maybe I should put Frau Stein out of her misery."

"Leave it," said Luis. "There's something else in here. A ghost from another world. I can sense it. It will take care of Frau Stein."

How could he be so sure? When had Luis become so mystical? So extrasensory?

As we scrambled up the stairs, I glanced back. Stopped dead in my tracks. Holy jumpin' Jesus monkeys, there it was! The thing. The Mayan princess. Her anatomy was clear. Her skin smooth and richly dark as mahogany, her breasts firm and high, an ancient woven cloth covered her privates. She had the sharply slanted Mesoamerican nose and forehead taken directly from a temple bas-relief.

Next instant her flesh transformed, became cracked and desiccated, steeped for a thousand years in the cold, dry air of the tomb. Layers of papery skin peeled from her face and body. The eyes were blind scars. Fragments of rag fell away from her arid loins. From her head a few wispy strands of straw floated on the underground wind. Her hands, her brown skeletal claws, were around Frau Stein's throat, squeezing, squeezing, squeezing.

The others pretended they hadn't looked back. Had seen nothing.

Then we were back in the light of day, and I wasn't sure what I'd seen. "Did you see it?" I said. "The mummy. Frau Stein did it. Come on. You saw it too. I'm not the only one. I'm not making this shit up."

No one would look me in the eye.

*

Seen from the chateau's entrance, the exterior world was chaos. An Apache helicopter gunship hovered over the pool, overconfident, its 30mm canons busily blowing everything and everyone to kingdom come.

Behind a stone wall, a cartel soldier crouched, the firing tube of a heat seeking ground-to-air rocket resting on his shoulder. The flame of the igniting rocket burst from the back of the tube.

For an instant I was the gunship pilot, panning across the field of vision before him, suddenly fixating on the mercenary with the rocket tube on his shoulder. Unmistakable. Image and analysis merged in the pilot's brain. Strangulating dread gripped his face as if the hands of a zombie had encircled his throat. He tried to take the Apache up in some kind of evasive action.

The gunship exploded. Burning pieces of the sundered

bird and barbecued body parts scattered across the pool deck.

Whoa! Guess they weren't expecting that, I thought.

Luis leading, we pelted up the marble stairs. You know the ones. We'd been going up and down them for the last two days. This time we went all the way to the third floor.

The roof was gone except for a section at the back that was on fire. No one appeared to be trying to put out the fire. In fact we had the place to ourselves. The plume of smoke on the horizon had grown thicker.

"What's that fire?" I asked Georgina.

"It's the peasants burning the marijuana and poppy fields. That's what started everything. At dawn several hundred armed campesinos stormed onto the property.

The 30mm shells that had taken off the roof, had also taken out the back wall of Aunt Ida's office. The doors of a heavy metal cabinet had been torn from their hinges and scads of cash tossed around like confetti on Cinco de Mayo. I picked up one of the banknotes. It was a U.S. hundred-dollar bill, used. They were all used U.S. hundred-dollar bills.

"Holy shit monkeys!" said Jane. She set down Frau Stein's Uzi that I'd given her and, dancing a lurid little ass-shuddering ditty to some hip hop tune breakdancing in her head, threw handfuls of cool, hard cash into the air. Finding a box of plastic wastebasket liner bags, she began stuffing greenbacks into one of them. Georgina fell to her knees and began filling another.

Why not, I thought. Get back some of the money Aunt Ida had stolen from me after the gun show job.

Luis, unengaged, disinterested in the spectacle of greed, leaned against a doorframe, using a nail file to clean grease and smut from under his fingernails.

The half of Aunt Ida's office near the front of the chateau was virtually untouched by the gunship onslaught, except all the windows were blown out. Broken glass scattered everywhere. The Burroughs suitcase sat on the corner of her credenza just as Aunt Ida had said.

I grabbed it and tucked it under my arm.

Jane glanced up at me and stopped stuffing. "What the fuck are you doing," she said.

"Retrieving the Burroughs suitcase."

"No, no, no. This time we're opening it. I'm not dragging it around in the middle of this revolution or civil war or whatever the fuck it is unless there's really something valuable inside."

"Our instructions are not to open it," said Luis.

"Well, those aren't my instructions," said Jane, waving the Uzi around injudiciously. "Open the fucking suitcase, Bill."

"Hey? You wouldn't shoot your old pal and fuck mate?" I said, my hands raised. The Burroughs suitcase clonked to the floor.

"That we were shag buddies back in Miami and even in Boca del Diablo doesn't mean shit out here in the jungle. Here it's a fucking cockfight day and night with no quarter. Everything has a beginning, a middle and an end, if you get my drift."

Who wasn't surprised? Sooner or later every woman in my life, including my mother, fucked me over. Besides I didn't give a hoot any more about the suitcase, now that we'd stumbled on the bonanza of cash. Then a sinking feeling overcame me. Maybe Jane had no intention of sharing this unexpected bounty.

Next moment she fired off a burst from the Uzi that put everyone horizontal, kissing the floor tiles. Was Jane capable of cold-blooded murder? Anything was possible.

The deafening pitch of rotor blades slicing the ether intruded.

Another attack chopper came in low and fast from the gray horizon. Its heavy machineguns raked the landscape around the pool. No more surface-to-air missiles soared aloft to bring down this new nine-hundred-pound gorilla. Only the screams of the mortally wounded. Aunt Ida's mercenaries were shit out of Stingers and shit out of luck.

"Okay, Bill, put your pistol on the floor where I can see it and open the suitcase," said Jane. She waved the Uzi in the direction of Luis and Georgina. "You two freeze. If you move, I'll kill you."

I followed her instructions to the letter, using a obsidian knife from Aunt Ida's desk to pry open the suitcase's locks.

The Apache roared away to wreak havoc elsewhere, replaced by a Blackhawk transport model that hovered over the pool area just to the side of the chateau. Anything in Aunt Ida's office that was lightweight and not tacked down was caught up in a swirling maelstrom created by the churning helicopter props. The Blackhawk settled to within fifteen feet of the pool deck. Heavy ropes tumbled from the open doorways on either side of the bird, down which commandoes from some elite Mexican anti-cartel unit repelled in rapid succession. The ground clean-up crew.

With a pinging sound, one lock of the suitcase snapped open. Then the other.

Jane leaned in close. Her hot breath tickled the hairs on the back of my neck. Slowly I lifted the lid.

First up, a stack of old white shirts, yellowed with age, dusted with black, poppy seed-like insect dropping. I threw the shirts aside. Beneath was more clothing, a pair of shit-brown pants with a large stain in the crotch and a man's navy blue bathing trunks similar to those worn by Burt Lancaster in From Here to Eternity. Out they went.

At the very bottom of the suitcase lay a stack of typewriter-sized pages tied together with a black ribbon. The sheets were a sickly bile color, pulpy with age. Their corners chipped and flaking. As I pushed the ribbon aside to read what was typed on the first sheet, the ribbon snapped. The first page read:

Kiss the Devil Good Night
by William Lee

Lee Kiev, the fount of all useless knowledge, had once told

me Burroughs used the pen name William Lee when he published his first book, Junkie.

"What is it?" said Jane.

"It's a manuscript. Some kind of book. Probably written by Burroughs. And if I were a betting man, I'd say it's a book that no one knows exists. A rare find indeed."

"But is it worth anything?"

"If Lee was willing to pay fifty thousand dollars to get his hands on it, it must be worth a shitload."

Alas, life never quite works out the way you hope it will. From the moment sperm impregnates egg in the aftermath of a ribald romp, you, the sorry-assed offspring, are at the mercy of chance, luck and the whims of the gods.

Caught somewhere between hell and high water, Jane and I stared at the pile of pages, considering its potential value and weighing on the opposite side of the scale all the trouble and hardship that seeking it out had brought. It was at that moment that the Blackhawk chose to ascend skyward. Climbing just above the former roofline of the chateau, it hung suspended, its rotors thrashing.

In the fury of the resulting updraft, the impossible, the unthinkable, the unspeakable, the inevitable happened. Before our eyes the brittle pulp paper manuscript, caught in the cyclone, crumbled. Turned to dust and blew the fuck away.

"Holy moley! I never expected that to happen," I said. "We almost made literary history and poof." I snapped my fingers.

"One less thing to worry about," said Jane.

The helicopter moved off. Mouth agape I gawked at the pulpy remains of the manuscript settling to the floor like half-baked memories at a funeral.

At that moment Luis decided it was time to reassert his control. Out of the corner of my eye I saw him bend down and jerk the Saturday Night Special from his sock, where it clung like a bur. How he had reacquired it, I had no idea. The pistol was small caliber but at close range still deadly.

He raised his arm, drawing down on the unsuspecting Jane, who was bent over tying closed one of the bags of cash. On Special Forces autopilot I flipped backwards, distracting Luis, landing on one hand. My other hand scooping up the .45 from the floor. My momentum carrying me forward into a shoulder roll. I fired coming out of the roll. The bullet entered Luis' left cheek and exited through the top of his skull, taking most of the back of his head off with it. Blood and brains splattered hither and yon.

Okay, sure, Jane had run over her husband with their rental car. Killed him deader than a squirrel that had made the fatal decision to cross the road in front of a speeding automobile. But the annihilation of Niles was a spur of the moment thing, born out of years of grinding rage and pent-up anger. In the normal course, Jane was no killer.

Luckily, I was.

Luis fell over, a dead weight.

Jane looked from the deceased Luis to me and back again.

"I owe you," she said, casting me one of those half smiles that can mean just about anything.

"Let's just scram outa here."

Jane nodded toward Georgina, who was looking strung out and somewhat the worse for wear.

"What are we going to do with your new fuck buddy?"

"How do you know about that?" I asked.

Jane said, "It's for you to decide whether she lives or dies." With that, she put the Uzi strap around her neck, picked up two of the bags of cash and started down the hall toward the stairs.

I looked after her.

She had a great walk-away ass sway. You could put it on a video loop and watch for hours. Not perfect, mind you. But in the scheme of things, close enough for government work. I should know. I'd had plenty of experience working for the government. In I-rack. Up in Decatur on the big waste disposal trucks. On the license plate press over at Oopawalla.

I looked at Georgina. Her teeth chattered. She was scared shitless.

No one is ready to die.

"Lie down," I said. "On your stomach."

I tied her up six ways to Sunday. Picked up the other two bags of cash and made like the roadrunner.

Standing on the front steps of the chateau, we could hear gunfire in the distance, but not close at hand. All the action seemed to have moved to another part of the estancia. The pool deck was littered with the dead, mostly cartel soldiers. Jane was for scooting around the pool and down various garden paths to our old friend the VW Bug.

I argued for an exit out the back, Jack, through the vegetable and flower gardens, past the chicken house, the rabbit hutches and the stables.

We went for the VW.

Amid other burnt-out vehicles, the Bug sat miraculously unscathed. Inside we discovered Aunt Ida, sprawled in the backseat in a pool of blood. She'd been gut shot. She was passed out, but came around as we fumbled around trying to stash the bags of cash in the car. With her in the back, there was no room for the money.

I looked at the wound. Her small intestines bulged from it like a segment of bloody garden hose. A shitload of blood had soaked the backseat. There was no doubt in my mind. Aunt Ida was toast.

"Everything you touch turns to shit," she said, looking at me with a jaundiced eye. Her eyes rolled around for a while. She gasped a few times. Spit up some blood.

"This has nothing to do with me," I said.

"It's that rightwing ideologue, Burke. He's after my soul. I met him five years ago when I first arrived in Mexico City. He wanted me to do a lap dance for him and his friends. I told him to take a hike. He's been on my ass ever since."

"You'd have been good at it," I said. "Lap dancing I mean."

"You think so?" She smiled wanly.

"We need the VW," I said. "We can't take you."

"Why would you take me anywhere? You hate my guts."

"You did do a number on me."

With a groan Aunt Ida reached behind her. Held out to me a .38 revolver.

"Do me a favor," she said.

There were two bullets left in the cylinder.

"Where's Edie?" I asked.

"There's an island near Cancún. The Island of Women. It has some beautiful beaches. Check it out. Get a room, take your socks off, get your rocks off, figure out what you're going to do with the rest of your pathetic life."

Aunt Ida laughed with a lot of pain. There was more pain as we lugged her out of the car.

"You never did get into my chinchilla, boyo," she said.

"Look the other way," I said.

She did.

The sound of the shot was deafening.

18

Needless to say, Rodolfo was less than overjoyed to see us come sailing through the front door of the Colonial Hotel, sweaty, disheveled, covered in grime and blood. He handed me the room key with his usual pomposity. It was good to be back.

"Nice to see you," I said. "How was your weekend?"

If he'd stuck out his tongue, I would have grabbed it and hauled his ass over the front desk into the lobby and kicked the crap out of him. But he turned away and started shuffling through a stack of old, unclaimed mail.

Upstairs Jane shed her clothes and got in the shower.

While she lathered up, I stood at the sink examining my teeth. They looked okay. I turned and watched her. There was no shower curtain. I never got tired of watching her.

The VW keys bounced up and down in my hand.

"We can't turn the car in with all the blood in the back seat. I'd better take it out into the country and torch it," I said. "I'll jog back. A good run will settle my nerves."

I drove into a fallow field five miles outside Boca del Diablo, doused the Bug with gasoline and threw a lit match. WWWWHOOOOOF!

With nary a backward glance, I turned and jogged in the direction of town. This time I didn't run into any armed peasants. They were all over at Hacienda de Sade raising Cain.

When I got back, Jane and her clothes were gone.

So was the money, except for a Hotel Colonial envelope containing a stack of Benjamin Franklins fat enough to add up to ten grand. The same amount Lee had promised to pay me for delivering the Burroughs suitcase.

I'd been expecting something like this since Jane took her little bus trip up to Mérida to "clear her head." Whatever we'd had had run its course. Had lost its forward momentum. If we'd stayed together, we would always have been trying to retrieve those heady, hopeless days back in Miami when we first hung out together at Compass House. Coming into all that money and coming so close to her own death must have decided Jane. The icing on the adios cake.

There was no note.

I found an overlooked peach-colored thong in the top drawer of the dresser. It was a frilly thing of no great substance. Drawing it to my nose, I sniffed luxuriantly, as if it were the first pour of a three-hundred dollar bottle of old Bordeaux. Something my father would have bought to impress himself. I stuffed the unwashed thong into my pocket.

Such is the stuff that dreams are made of.

The next day I checked out and caught the bus to Cancún. I asked the bus driver about The Island of Women.

"A quiet place," he said. "Not so spoiled by the all the tourists from New York and Chicago." He told me where to catch the ferry.

When I got to Isla Mujeres, as the bus driver called it, I took a room at the Hotel Luna located on a back street of the main town. There was no pool, but the weekly rate was bargain basement and the owner was friendly. He and his wife both spoke a little gringo. And the white sand and turquoise water of Playa Norte was just a few blocks' walk.

The Hotel Luna was a two-story, seven-room operation overlooking a small courtyard. The owner's place was in the front. An old fridge, where you could keep your Tecate cold, stood in one corner of the courtyard. My room and three others were on the second floor. The only other guests were a French couple, there for sex in the sun. Bukowski would have stayed at the Hotel Luna.

By day two I was into a routine. I usually went to the beach early in the morning before the distraction of all the topless European chicks sunbathing to beat the band. At eight o'clock they were still snoozing after a night of booze, pot, ecstasy and sex. After my swim I devoured huevos rancheros, refried beans and a cerveza at my favorite dive bar and meandered the narrow streets in the hope of spotting Edie. When it got too hot, I went back to the hotel for a cool Tecate and a snooze. Sometimes the soft, lyrical, afternoon love making of the French couple, who rented the room next to mine, lulled me to sleep. If that didn't work, reading a few pages of Crime and Punishment (which I'd found in a junk shop for ten pesos) always did the trick.

I wondered if the skinny French woman faked her orgasms.

I'd been on Isla Mujeres for a week when I was drawn to the profile of a big-boned, blond gringa woman at the supermarket. She was pushing a cart full of groceries. A baby sat in the child seat. I had a feeling I'd met the woman somewhere before. Maybe in an airport bar?

Then I realized it was Edie. She looked transformed. No longer nervous and high strung. No longer dreaming of some other life. She looked like she belonged there in that grocery store with that kid.

At the cash register she joked in Spanish with the checkout woman. Two older children, who had been playing outside, came at Edie's call to help carry the plastic sacks of groceries. I watched from a distance as they entered through the wrought-iron gate leading to the rear of a backstreet house. The front portion of the house was a dental clinic.

I staked out the house. Stalked Edie's movements, looking for the right opportunity.

One day she went by herself to a farmacia. Afterward she stopped in a café for a Coke. I walked up to her table.

"Mind if I sit down," I said.

"I figured you'd show up some day," she said.

I sat down and ordered a Coke. We looked at each other, wondering who we had become.

"Aunt Ida took all the money," said Edie. "Left me at the side of the road."

"Sounds familiar," I said.

"So, how are you, Bill?"

"Aunt Ida's dead," I said.

Edie shrugged. Finished her Coke. Sucked air at the bottom of the glass.

"I'm married with children," she said.

"To a dentist?"

"His wife died. Left him with two young children. Now we have a third. He knows nothing about my other lives."

I was getting bored. It was all so suburban.

"What about Mary Beth and Ben?" I said.

"What about them?" said Edie.

It was a good question.

I got up and went to the cash register and paid for the two Cokes.

When I came back to get my newspaper, Edie said, "Why did you come here, Bill?"

"I just wanted to see how you were," I said.

"I'm fine," she said.

The next day after breakfast I took a long walk south of town along the harbor. At its southern end the harbor was protected from the open sea by several small barrier islands and a spit of land. Here along the main road, a series of marinas had set up shop, catering to gringos and Europeans dreaming of warm Caribbean beaches and el cheapo on-board living. Someone had told me about a good Cuban-style restaurant that was out that way and might be open for lunch.

As I strolled along, a taxi pulled to the curb in front of me. A woman got out. She was much too old and filled in for the crotch-chomping terrycloth shorts she sported along with a gauzy see-through shirt, no doubt made in Sri Lanka or one of those places. On the other hand, overall she looked pretty damn good. Smallish, natural-appearing boobs. Friendly smile.

When she bent over to retrieve the plastic sacks of groceries in the back seat of the taxi, I read the words Key West writ large across the terrycloth covering her sterling buns.

"Hey," I said. "Let me give you a hand with those."

THE END

About The Author

Jonathan Woods writes award-winning noir with a satiric literary twist. He is the author of:

- *Bad Juju & Other Tales of Madness and Mayhem* (New Pulp Press, 2010), which won a Spingtingler Award for best crime story collection and was a featured book at the 2011 Texas Book Festival. New York Magazine called it: "Hallucinatory, hilarious, imaginative noir."
- *A Death in Mexico* (New Pulp Press, 2012), about which Booklist said: "This uncompromising look at racial tensions in a small Mexican town perfectly reflects the mood of border noir...the novel takes us deep into a world of darkness, capturing that same blend of bleakness and all-consuming corruption that drives Orson Welles' classic film *Touch of Evil.*" *A Death in Mexico* has been translated into German.
- *Phone Call from Hell and Other Tales of the Damned* (New Pulp Press, 2014), anointed by ForeWord Reviews as "a masterpiece of noir fiction— organized insanity at its best...wickedly humorous."
- *Kiss the Devil Good Night* (280 Steps, November-2016), about which Booklist quipped:"Pulpy, pervy noir."
- *Hog Heaven*, a satiric crime novel-in-progress about feral hog hunting in Texas.

Jonathan holds degrees from McGill University, New England School of Law and New York University School of Law and practiced law for a multi-national high tech company before turning to writing full time. He studied writing at Southern Methodist University night school and at Bread Loaf, Sewanee, Zoetrope: All-Story and Sirenland Writers' Conferences. He currently lives in San Marcos,

Texas with his artist spouse, Dahlia Woods, a 9-pound golden shih tzu named Pinky (named after the gangster in Graham Greene's *Brighten Rock*) and a 9-pound shih tzu/terrier mix named Ruffy. In San Marcos Jonathan and Dahlia operate an art gallery (Dahlia Woods Gallery), bookstore (Bad Boy Books) and wine bar (Pinky's Wine Bar) located in the historic downtown half a block off the courthouse square.

In addition to his crime fiction, in 2014 Jonathan wrote and produced a 25-minute neo-noir film (dir. by Quincy Perkins) entitled *Swingers Anonymous*, based on his short story of the same title that was first published in the crime story anthology *Dallas Noir* (Akashic Books). *Swingers Anonymous*, the movie, premiered to acclaim at the 2014 Key West Film Festival and in 2015/16 has screened at NewFilmmakers New York Winterfest, the Vancouver Badass Short Film Festival, FilmGate Miami (audience award for best film and best actor award), the Cannes Film Festival (screening at the American Pavilion) and the 21st annual San Antonio Film Festival, the West of Cannes Film Festival, and HollyShorts Film Festival Monthly Screening. The Key West Citizen called the film: "A modern day 'Tell-Tale Heart,' as if Edgar Allan Poe was a post-modern gonzo noir crime storyteller."

Acknowledgements

Thanks to: the members of the Casa Marina writers group (now disbanded): Mike Dennis, Jessica Argyle, Mike Haskins and Sara Goodwin, for getting me from here to there; and to my publisher Chris McVeigh and the entire crew at Fahrenheit Press.

If you enjoyed this book we're sure you'll love these other titles from Fahrenheit Press.

Sparkle Shot by Lina Chern

Jukebox by Saira Viola

All Things Violent by Nikki Dolson

Hidden Depths by Ally Rose

In The Still by Jacqueline Chadwick

Made in the USA
San Bernardino, CA
22 September 2017